From out the Vasty Deep

by

Marie Belloc Lowndes

From out the Vasty Deep
by Marie Belloc Lowndes

Copyright © 2024

All Rights reserved.

No part of this publication may be reproduced, stored in a retrieval system, or transmitted in any form or by any means, electronic, mechanical, photocopying or Otherwise, without the written permission of the publisher.
The author/editor asserts the moral right to be identified as the author/editor of this work.

ISBN: 978-93-63055-22-3

Published by

DOUBLE 9 BOOKS

2/13-B, Ansari Road
Daryaganj, New Delhi – 110002
info@double9books.com
www.double9books.com
Tel. 011-40042856

This book is under public domain

ABOUT THE AUTHOR

Marie Adelaide Elizabeth Rayner Lowndes (5 August 1868 – 14 November 1947), who wrote as Marie Belloc Lowndes, was an English author who wrote a lot of books. She was the sister of the author Hilaire Belloc. She was active from 1898 until her death, and her writing was known for mixing exciting events with psychological ones. Four of her books were made into movies: The Chink in the Armour (1912; adapted in 1922), The Lodger (1913; adapted several times), Letty Lynton (1931; adapted in 1932), and The Story of Ivy (1927; adapted in 1947). The Lodger was also turned into a radio play in 1940 and an opera in 1960. Belloc was born in London's Marylebone on George Street and grew up in La Celle-Saint-Cloud, France. She was the only child of French lawyer Louis Belloc and English feminist Bessie Parkes. Hilaire Belloc was her younger brother. In her last book, The Young Hilaire Belloc, which came out after she died in 1956, she wrote about him. The French painter Jean-Hilaire Belloc was Belloc's grandfather, and the philosopher and priest Joseph Priestley was her great-great-grandfather. It was 53 years after her father died that her mother passed away in 1925.

CONTENTS

CHAPTER I 7
CHAPTER II 14
CHAPTER III 22
CHAPTER IV 30
CHAPTER V 42
CHAPTER VI 50
CHAPTER VII 59
CHAPTER VIII 63
CHAPTER IX 74
CHAPTER X 82
CHAPTER XI 90
CHAPTER XII 95
CHAPTER XIII 103
CHAPTER XIV 108
CHAPTER XV 117
CHAPTER XVI 126
CHAPTER XVII 138
CHAPTER XVIII 148
CHAPTER XIX 154
CHAPTER XX 161
CHAPTER XXI 169

CHAPTER XXII 177
CHAPTER XXIII 185
CHAPTER XXIV 190

CHAPTER I

"I always thought that you, Pegler, were such a very sensible woman."

The words were said in a good-natured, though slightly vexed tone; and a curious kind of smile flitted over the rather grim face of the person to whom they were addressed.

"I've never troubled you before in this exact way, have I, ma'am?"

"No, Pegler. That you certainly have not."

Miss Farrow looked up from the very comfortable armchair where she was sitting—leaning back, with her neatly shod, beautifully shaped feet stretched out to the log fire. Her maid was standing a little to the right, her spare figure and sallow face lit up by the flickering, shooting flames, for the reading-lamp at Miss Farrow's elbow was heavily shaded.

"D'you really mean that you won't sleep next door to-night, Pegler?"

"I wouldn't be fit to do my work to-morrow if I did, ma'am." And Miss Farrow quite understood that that was Pegler's polite way of saying that she most definitely did refuse to sleep in the room next door.

"I wish the ghost had come in here, instead of worrying you!" As the maid made no answer to this observation, her mistress went on, turning round so that she could look up into the woman's face: "What was it exactly you *did* see, Pegler?" And as the other still remained silent, Miss Farrow added: "I really do want to know! You see, Pegler—well, I need hardly tell you that I have a very great opinion of you."

And then, to the speaker's extreme surprise, there came a sudden change over Pegler's face. Her pale countenance flushed, it became discomposed, and she turned her head away to hide the springing tears.

Miss Farrow was touched; as much touched as her rather hard nature would allow her to be. This woman had been her good and faithful friend, as well as servant, for over twelve years.

She sprang up from her deep chair with the lightness of a girl, though she was over forty; and went and took the other's hand. "Pegler!" she exclaimed. "What's the matter, you dear old thing?"

But Pegler wrenched away her hand, rather ungraciously. "After two such nights as I've had," she muttered, "it's no wonder I'm a bit upset."

Excellent maid though she was—Miss Farrow had never known anyone who could do hair as Pegler could—the woman was in some ways very unconventional, very unlike an ordinary lady's maid.

"Now do tell me exactly what happened?" Miss Farrow spoke with a mixture of coaxing and kindly authority. "What do you think you saw? I need hardly tell you that *I* don't believe in ghosts." As the maid well knew, the speaker might have finished the sentence with "or in anything else." But that fact, Pegler being the manner of woman she was, did not detract from the affection and esteem in which she held her lady. You can't have everything—such was her simple philosophy—and religious people do not always act up to their profession. Miss Farrow, at any rate in her dealings with Pegler, was always better than her word. She was a kind, a considerate, and an intelligent mistress.

So it was that, reluctantly, Pegler made up her mind to speak. "I'd like to say, ma'am," she began, "that no one said nothing to me about that room being haunted. You was the first that mentioned it to me, after I'd spoken to you yesterday. As you know, ma'am, the servants here are a job lot; they don't know nothing about the house. 'Twasn't till to-day that one of the village people, the woman at the general shop and post office, let on that Wyndfell Hall was well known to be a ghosty place."

There was a pause, and then Pegler added: "Still, as you and I well know, ma'am, tales don't lose nothing in the telling."

"Indeed they don't! Never mind what the people in the village say. This kind of strange, lonely, beautiful old house is sure to be said to be haunted. What *I* want to know is what *you* think you saw, Pegler—" The speaker looked sharply into the woman's face.

"I don't like to see you standing, ma'am," said Pegler inconsequently. "If you'll sit down in your chair again I'll tell you what happened to me."

Miss Farrow sank gracefully down into her deep, comfortable chair. Again she put out her feet to the fire, for it was very cold on this 23rd of December, and she knew she had a tiring, probably a boring, evening before her. Some strangers of whom she knew nothing, and cared less, excepting that they were the friends of her friend and host, Lionel Varick, were to arrive at Wyndfell Hall in time for dinner. It was now six o'clock.

"Well," she said patiently, "begin at the beginning, Pegler. I wish you'd sit down too—somehow it worries me to see you standing there. You'll be tempted to cut your story short."

Pegler smiled a thin little smile. In the last twelve years Miss Farrow had several times invited her to sit down, but of course she had always refused, being one that knew her place. She had only sat in Miss Farrow's presence during the days and nights when she had nursed her mistress through a serious illness—then, of course, everything had been different, and she had had to sit down sometimes.

"The day before yesterday—that is the evening Miss Bubbles arrived, ma'am—after I'd dressed you and you'd gone downstairs, and I'd unpacked for Miss Bubbles, I went into my room and thought how pleasant it looked. The curtains was drawn, and there was a nice fire, as you know, ma'am, which Mr. Varick so kindly ordered for me, and which I've had the whole week. Also, I will say for Annie that even if she is a temporary, she is a good housemaid, making the girls under her do their work properly."

Pegler drew a long breath. Then she went on again: "I sat down just for a minute or two, and I turned over queer—so queer, ma'am, that I went and drew the curtains of one of the windows. Of course it's a much bigger room than I'm generally accustomed to occupy, as you know, ma'am. And I just threw up the window—it's what they call a guillotine window—and there I saw the water, you know, ma'am, in what they call the moat—"

"Yes," said Miss Farrow languidly. "Yes, Pegler, go on."

"As I looked down, ma'am, I had an awful turn. There seemed to me to be something floating about in the water, a little narrow thing like a child's body—and—and all on a sudden a small white face seemed to look up into mine! Oh, it was 'orrible!" Pegler did not often drop an aitch, but when she did so forget herself, she did it thoroughly.

"As I went on looking, fascinated-like"—she was speaking very slowly now—"whatever was down there seemed to melt away. I didn't say nothing that evening of what had happened to me, but I couldn't keep myself from thinking of it. Well, then, ma'am, as you know, I came and undressed you, and I asked you if you'd like the door kept open between our two rooms. But you said no, ma'am, you'd rather it was shut. So then I went to bed."

"And you say—you admit, Pegler—that nothing *did* happen the night before last?"

Pegler hesitated. "Nothing happened exactly," she said. "But I had the most awful feeling, ma'am. And yes—well, something did happen! I heard a kind of rustling in the room. It would leave off for a time, and, then begin again. I tried to put it down to a mouse or a rat—or something of that sort."

"That," said Miss Farrow quietly, "was probably what it was, Pegler."

As if she had not heard her lady's remark, the maid went on: "I'd go off to sleep, and then suddenly, I'd awake and hear this peculiar rustle, ma'am, like a dress swishing along—an old-fashioned, rich, soft silk, such as ladies wore in the old days, when I was a child. But that dress, the dress I heard rustling, ma'am, was a bit older than that."

"What *do* you mean, Pegler?"

The maid remained silent, her eyes were fixed; it was as if she had forgotten where she was.

"And what exactly happened last night?"

"Last night," said Pegler, drawing a long breath, "last night, ma'am—I know you won't believe me—but I saw the spirit!"

Miss Farrow looked up into the woman's face with an anxious, searching glance.

She felt disturbed and worried. A great deal of her material comfort—almost, she might have truly said, much of her happiness in life—depended on Jane Pegler. In a sense Blanche Farrow had but two close friends in the world—her host, Lionel Varick, the new owner of Wyndfell Hall; and the plain, spare, elderly woman standing now before her. She realized with a sharp pang of concern what Pegler's mental defection would mean to her. It would be dreadful, *dreadful*, if Pegler began seeing ghosts, and turning hysterical.

"What was the spirit like?" she asked quietly.

And then, all at once, she had to suppress a violent inclination to burst out laughing. For Pegler answered with a kind of cry, "A 'orrible happarition, ma'am!"

Miss Farrow could not help observing a trifle satirically: "That certainly sounds most unpleasant."

But Pegler went on, speaking with a touch of excitement very unusual with her: "It was a woman—a woman with a dreadful, wicked, spiteful face! Once she came up close to my bed, and I wanted to scream out, but I couldn't—my throat seemed shut up."

"D'you mean you actually saw what you took to be a ghost?"

"I did see a ghost, ma'am; not a doubt of it! She walked up and down that room in there, wringing her hands all the time—I'd heard the expression, ma'am, but I'd never seen anyone do it."

"Did anything else happen?"

"At last she went over to the window, and—and I'm afraid you won't believe me, ma'am—but there seemed no curtains there any more, nothing but just an opening into the darkness. I saw her bend over—" An expression of terror came over the woman's face.

"But how could you *see* her," asked Miss Farrow quickly, "if there was no light in the room?"

"In a sort of way," said Pegler somberly, "the spirit was supplying the light, as it were. I could see her in the darkness, as if she was a lamp moving about."

"Oh, Pegler, Pegler!" exclaimed Miss Farrow deprecatingly.

"It's true, ma'am! It's true as I'm standing here." Pegler would have liked to add the words "So help me God!" but somehow she felt that these words would not carry any added conviction to her mistress. And, indeed, they would not have done so, for Miss Farrow, though she was much too polite and too well-bred ever to have said so, even to herself, did not believe in a Supreme Being. She was a complete materialist.

"And then, ma'am, after a bit, there it would begin, constant-like, all over again."

"I don't understand...."

"I'd go to sleep, and tell myself maybe that it was all a dream—argue with myself, ma'am, for I'm a sensible woman. And then all at once I'd hear that rustle again! I'd try not to open my eyes, but somehow I felt I must see what was happening. So I'd look at last—and there she'd be! Walking up and down, walking up and down, her face—oh, ma'am, her face staring-like most 'orrible—and wringing her hands. Then she'd go over to the window, lean out, and disappear, down into the black water!"

In a calmer tone Pegler added: "The moat used to be much bigger and deeper than it is now, ma'am—so they all say."

"All?" said Miss Farrow sharply. "Who do you mean by 'all'?"

"The people about the place, ma'am."

"I can't help wishing, Pegler, that you hadn't told this strange story to the servants. You see it makes it so awkward for Mr. Varick."

Pegler flushed uncomfortably. "I was that scared," she murmured, "that I felt I must tell somebody, and if you tell one, as I did, you tell all. I'm sorry I did it, ma'am, for I'm afraid I've inconvenienced you."

"It can't be helped," said Miss Farrow good-naturedly. "I know you wouldn't have done it if you could have helped it, Pegler. But of course in a way it's unlucky."

"I've pointed out to them all that there never is but one room haunted in a house as a rule," said the maid eagerly, "and I think they all quite sees that, ma'am. Besides, they're very pleased with Mr. Varick. You know what he did to-day, ma'am?"

"No," said Miss Farrow, looking up and smiling, "what did he do?"

"He called them all together, without distinction of class, so to speak, ma'am, and he told them that if he was pleased with the way in which his Christmas party went off, he'd give them each a five-pound note at the end of the month. It made them forget the haunted room, I can tell you, ma'am!" She added grudgingly, "He *is* a kind gentleman, and no mistake."

"Indeed he is! I'm glad that you see that now, Pegler." Miss Farrow spoke with a touch of meaning in her voice. "I did a very good turn for myself when I got him out of that queer scrape years ago."

"Why yes, ma'am, I suppose you did." But Pegler's tone was not as hearty as that of her lady.

There was a pause. "Then what have you settled to do about to-night?"

"If you don't mind, ma'am—I'm arranging to sleep in what they call the second maid's room. There is a bell through, ma'am, but you'll have to go into the next room to ring it, for you know, ma'am, that it's the next room that ought to have been your room by rights."

"I wish now that I'd taken it and put you in here," said Miss Farrow ruefully.

"They're going to keep up a good fire there. So when you go in you won't get a chill."

"That does seem luxurious," said Miss Farrow, smiling. She loved luxury, and it was pleasant to think that there should be a fire kept up in an empty room just so that she shouldn't feel a chill when she went in for a moment to ring for her maid!

"By the way, I hope there's a fireplace in your room, Pegler"—the words were uttered solicitously.

"No, there isn't, ma'am. But I don't mind that. I don't much care about a fire."

"There's no accounting for taste!"

Miss Farrow took up her book again, and Pegler, as was her way, slid noiselessly from the room—not through the door leading into the haunted chamber, but out on to the beautiful panelled landing, now gay with bowls of hothouse flowers which had come down from London that morning by passenger train, and been brought by car all the way from Newmarket.

CHAPTER II

The book Miss Farrow held in her hand was an amusing book, the latest volume of some rather lively French memoirs, but she put it down after a very few moments, and, leaning forward, held out her hands to the fire. They were not pretty hands: though small and well-shaped, there was something just a little claw-like about them; but they were very white, and her almond-shaped nails, admirably manicured, gleamed in the soft red light.

Yes, in spite of this stupid little *contretemps* about Pegler, she was glad indeed that circumstances over which she had had rather more control than she liked to think had made it impossible for her to go out to Monte Carlo this winter. She had been sharply vexed, beside herself with annoyance, almost tempted to do what she had never yet done—that is, to ask Lionel Varick, now so delightfully prosperous, to lend her a couple of hundred pounds. But she had resisted the impulse, and she was now glad of it.

After all, there's no place like dear old England at Christmas time. How much nicer, too, is a bachelor host than a hostess! A bachelor host? No, not exactly a bachelor host, for Lionel Varick was a widower. Twice a widower, if the truth were known. But the truth, fortunately, is not always known, and Blanche Farrow doubted if any other member of the circle of friends and acquaintances he had picked up in his adventurous, curious life knew of that first—now evidently by him almost forgotten—marriage. It had taken place years ago, when Varick was still a very young man, and to a woman not of his own class. They had separated, and then, rather oddly, come together again. Even so, her premature death had been for him a fortunate circumstance.

It was not Varick who had told Blanche Farrow of that painful episode of his past life. The story had come to her knowledge in a curious, accidental fashion, and she had thought it only fair to tell him what she had learned—and then, half reluctantly, he had revealed something of what he had suffered through that early act of folly. But they had only spoken of it once.

Varick's second marriage, Miss Farrow was almost tempted to call it his real marriage, the news of which he had conveyed to his good friend in a laconic note, had surprised her very much.

The news had found her far away, in Portugal, where, as just a few English people know, there is more than one Casino where mild gambling can be pursued under pleasant conditions. Blanche Farrow would have been hurt if someone had told her that in far-away Portugal Lionel Varick and his affairs had not meant quite so much to her as they would have done if she had been nearer home. Still, she had felt a pang. A man-friend married is often a man-friend marred. But she had been very glad to gather, reading between the lines of his note, that the lady in question was well off. Varick was one of those men to whom the possession of money is as essential to life as the air they breathe is to most human beings. Till this unexpected second marriage of his he had often been obliged to live on, and by, his wits.

Then, some months later—for she and Varick were not given to writing to one another when apart, their friendship had never been of that texture—she had received a sad letter from him saying that his wife was seriously ill. The letter had implied, too, that he ought to have been told, before the marriage had taken place, that his wife's family had been one riddled with consumption. Blanche had written back at once—by that time she was a good deal nearer home than Portugal, though still abroad—asking if she could "do anything?" And he had answered that no, there was nothing to be done. "Poor Milly" had a horror of sanatoriums, so he was going to take her to some quiet place on the south coast. He had ended his note with the words: "I do not think it can last long now, and I rather hope it won't. It is very painful for her, as well as for me." And it had not lasted very long. Seven weeks later Miss Farrow had read in the first column of the *Times* the announcement: "Millicent, only daughter of the late George Fauncey, of Wyndfell Hall, Suffolk, and the beloved wife of Lionel Varick."

She had been surprised at the addition of the word "beloved." Somehow it was not like the man she thought she knew so well to put that word in.

That was just over a year ago. But when she had met Varick again she had seen with real relief that he was quite unchanged—those brief months of wedded life had not apparently altered him at all. There was, however, one great difference—he was quite at ease about money. That was all—but that was a great deal! Blanche Farrow and Lionel Varick had at any rate one thing in common—they both felt a horror of poverty, and all that poverty implies.

Gradually Miss Farrow had discovered a few particulars about her friend's dead wife. Millicent Fauncey had been the only child of a rather eccentric Suffolk squire, a man of great taste, known in the art world of London as a collector of fine Jacobean furniture, long before Jacobean furniture had become the rage. After her father's death his daughter, having let Wyndfell Hall, had wandered about the world with a companion till she had drifted across her future husband's path at an hotel in Florence.

"What attracted me," Lionel Varick had explained rather awkwardly on the only occasion when he had really talked of his late wife to Blanche Farrow, "was her helplessness, and, yes, a kind of simplicity."

Blanche had looked at him a little sharply. She had never known Lionel attracted by weakness or simplicity before. All women seemed attracted by him—but he was by no means attracted by all women.

"Poor Milly didn't care for Wyndfell Hall," he had gone on, "for she spent a very lonely, dull girlhood there. But it's a delightful place, and I hope to live there as soon as I can get the people out to whom it is now let. 'Twon't be an easy job, for they're devoted to it."

Of course he had got them out very soon, for, as Blanche Farrow now reminded herself, Lionel Varick had an extraordinary power of getting his own way, in little and big things alike.

It was uncommonly nice of Lionel to have asked her to be informal hostess of his first house party! Unluckily it was an oddly composed party, not so happily chosen as it might have been, and she wondered uneasily whether it would be a success. She had never met three of the people who were coming to-night—a Mr. and Miss Burnaby, an old-fashioned and, she gathered, well-to-do brother and sister, and their niece, Helen Brabazon. Miss Brabazon had been an intimate friend, Miss Farrow understood the only really intimate friend, of Lionel Varick's late wife. He had spoken of this girl, Helen Brabazon, with great regard and liking—with rather more regard and liking than he generally spoke of any woman.

"She was most awfully kind to me during that dreadful time at Redsands," he had said only yesterday. And Blanche had understood the "dreadful time" referred to the last weeks of his wife's life. "I've been to the Burnabys' house a few times, and I've dined there twice—an infamously bad cook, but very good wine—you know the sort of thing?"

Remembering that remark, Blanche now asked herself why Lionel had included these tiresome, old-fashioned people in his party. Then she told herself that it was doubtless because the niece, who lived with them, couldn't leave them to a solitary Christmas.

Another guest who was not likely to add much in the way of entertainment to the party was an enormously rich man called James Tapster. Tapster was a cynical, rather unpleasant person, yet on one occasion he had helped Varick out of a disagreeable scrape.

If the host had had his way there would also have been in the party a certain Dr. Panton. But at the last moment he had had to "chuck." There was a hope, however, that he might be able to come after Christmas. Dr. Panton was also associated with the late Mrs. Varick. He had attended her during the last long weeks of her life.

Blanche Farrow's face unconsciously brightened as she remembered Sir Lyon Dilsford. He was an intelligent, impecunious, pleasant kind of man, still, like his host, on the sunny side of forty. Sir Lyon was "in the City," as are now so many men of his class and kind. He took his work seriously, and spent many hours of each day east of Temple Bar. By way of relaxation he helped to run an Oxford College East-End Settlement. "A good chap,"—that was how Blanche summed him up to herself.

Lionel had asked her if she could think of any young people to ask, and she had suggested, with some hesitation, her own niece, Bubbles Dunster, and Bubbles' favourite dancing partner, a young man called Bill Donnington. Bubbles had arrived at Wyndfell Hall two days ago. Donnington had not been able to leave London till to-day.

Bubbles? Blanche Farrow's brows knit themselves as she thought of her niece, namesake, and godchild.

Bubbles was a strange girl, but then so many girls are strange nowadays! Though an only child, and the apple of her widowed father's eyes, she had deliberately left her home two years ago, and set up for herself in London, nominally to study art. At once she had become a great success—the kind of success that counts nowadays. Bubbles' photograph was always appearing in the *Sketch* and in the *Daily Mirror*. She was constantly roped in to help in any smart charity affair, and she could dance, act, and sell, with the best. She was as popular with women as with men, for there was something disarming, attaching, almost elfish, in Bubbles Dunster's charm. For one thing, she was so good-natured, so kindly, so always eager to do someone a good turn— and last, not least, she had inherited her aunt's cleverness about clothes! She dressed in a way which Blanche Farrow thought ridiculously *outré* and queer, but still, somehow, she always looked well-dressed. And though she had never been taught dressmaking, she could make her own clothes when put to it, and was always willing to help other people with theirs.

Hugh Dunster, Bubbles' father, did not often favour his sister-in-law with a letter, but she had had a letter from him three days ago, of which the most important passage ran: "I understand that Bubbles is going to spend Christmas with you. I wish you'd say a word to her about all this spiritualistic rot. She seems to be getting deeper and deeper into it. It's impairing her looks, making her nervous and almost hysterical—in a word, quite unlike herself. I spoke to her some time ago, and desired her most earnestly to desist from it. But a father has no power nowadays! I have talked the matter over with young Donnington (of whom I sometimes suspect she is fonder than she knows), and he quite agrees with me. After all, she's a child still, and doesn't realize what *vieux jeu* all that sort of thing is. I insisted on reading to her 'Sludge, the Medium,' but it made no impression on her! In a sense I've only myself to thank, for I used to amuse myself in testing her amazing thought-reading powers when she was a little girl."

Bubbles had now been at Wyndfell Hall two whole days, and so far her aunt had said nothing to her. Somehow she felt a certain shyness of approaching the subject. In so far as she had ever thought about it—and she had never really thought about it at all—Miss Farrow regarded all that she knew of spiritualism as a gigantic fraud. It annoyed her fastidiousness to think that her own niece should be in any way associated with that kind of thing. She realized the temptation it must offer to a clever girl who, as her father truly said, had had as a child an uncanny power of thought-reading, and of "willing" people to do what she liked.

Blanche Farrow smiled and sighed as she stared into the fire. How the world had changed! She could not imagine her own father, though he had been far less conventional than was Hugh Dunster, talking her over with a young man.

Poor Bill Donnington! Of course he was devoted to Bubbles—her slave, in fact. Blanche had only seen him once; she had thought him sensible, undistinguished, commonplace. She knew that he was the third or fourth son of a worthy North-country parson—in other words, he "hadn't a bob." He was, of course, the last man Bubbles would ever think of marrying. Bubbles, like most of her set, was keenly alive to the value of money. Bubbles, as likely as not, would make a set, half in fun, half in earnest, at James Tapster!

To tell the truth, Miss Farrow had not forgotten Bubbles when she had assented to Lionel Varick's suggestion that rich, if dull-witted, James Tapster should be included in the party.

In what was called the moat garden of Wyndfell Hall, twilight was deepening into night. But Lionel Varick, who was now pacing up and down the broad path which followed the course of the moat, could still see, sharply outlined against the pale winter sky, the vision of tranquil beauty and the storehouse of archaeological and antiquarian interest which was now his home.

By his special orders the windows had been left uncurtained. There were lights in a great number of the rooms—indeed, the lower part of the house was brilliantly illuminated. But as the windows in the beautiful linen-panelled hall were diamond-paned, the brilliance was softened, and there was something deliriously welcoming, almost fairy-like, in the picture the old house presented to its new owner's eager gaze.

After a while he stayed his steps near the narrow brick bridge which spanned the moat where a carriage road connected the domain of Wyndfell Hall with the outside world, and, as he stood there in the gathering twilight, he looked a romantic figure. Tall and well-built, he took, perhaps, an almost excessive care over his dress. Yet there was nothing effeminate or foppish about his appearance.

A follower of that now forgotten science, phrenology, would have been impressed by Lionel Varick's head. It was large and well-shaped, with a great deal of almost golden hair, now showing a white thread or two, which did not, however, detract from his look of youth. He had a fine broad forehead; deep, well-set grey eyes; and a beautiful, sensitive mouth, which he took care not to conceal with a moustache. Thus in almost any company he would have looked striking and distinguished—the sort of man of whom people ask, "Who is that standing over there?"

Varick was a man of moods—subject, that is, to fits of exultation and of depression—and yet with an amazing power of self-control, and of entirely hiding what he felt from those about him.

To-night his mood was one of exultation. He almost felt what Scots call "fey." Something seemed to tell him that he was within reach of the fruition of desires which, even in his most confident moments, had appeared till now wildly out of any possibility of attainment. He came, on both his father's and his mother's side, of people who had lived for centuries the secure, pleasant life of the English county gentry. But instead of taking advantage of their opportunities, the Varicks had gone not upwards, but steadily downwards—the final crash having been owing to the folly, indeed the far more than folly, as Lionel Varick had come to know when still a child, of his own father.

Lionel's father had not lived long after his disgraceful bankruptcy. But he had had time to imbue his boy with an intense pride in the past glories of the Varick family. So it was that the shabby, ugly little villa where his boyhood had been spent on the outskirts of a town famous for its grammar-school, and where his mother settled for her boy's sake after her husband's death, had been peopled to young Varick with visions of just such a country home as was this wonderful old house now before him.

No wonder he felt "fey" to-night. Everything was falling out as he had hoped it would do. He had staked very high—staked, indeed, all that a man can stake in our complex civilization, and he had won! In the whole wide world there was only one human being who wished him ill. This was an elderly woman, named Julia Pigchalke, who had been his late wife's one-time governess and companion. She had been his enemy from the first day they had met, and she had done her utmost to prevent his marriage to her employer. Even now, in spite of what poor Milly's own solicitor called his "thoughtful generosity" to Miss Pigchalke, the woman was pursuing Varick with an almost insane hatred. About six months ago she had called on Dr. Panton, the clever young medical man who had attended poor Mrs. Varick during her last illness. She had formulated vague accusations against Varick—accusations of cruelty and neglect of so absurd a nature that they refuted themselves. Miss Pigchalke's behaviour was the more monstrous that she had already received the first fifty pounds of the hundred-pound pension her friend's widower had arranged to give her.

In a will made before her marriage, the late Mrs. Varick had left her companion two thousand pounds, and though the legacy had been omitted from her final will, Varick had of his own accord suggested that he should allow Miss Pigchalke a hundred a year. She had begun by sending back the first half-yearly cheque; but she had finally accepted it! To-night he reminded himself with satisfaction that the second fifty pounds had already been sent her, and that this time she would evidently make no bones about keeping the money.

Making a determined effort, he chased her sinister image from his thoughts, and turned his mind to the still attractive woman who was about to act as hostess to his Christmas party.

His keen face softened as he thought of Blanche Farrow. Poor, proud, well-bred and pleasant, poor only in a relative sense, for she was the only unmarried daughter of an Irish peer whose title had passed away to a distant cousin. Miss Farrow could have lived in comfort and in dignity on what income she had, but for one inexplicable failing—the more old-fashioned and severe of her friends and relatives called it a vice.

Soon after she had come into the enjoyment of her few hundreds a year, some rich, idle acquaintance had taken Blanche to Monte Carlo, and there, like a duck to water, she had taken to play! Henceforth gambling—any kind of gambling—had become her absorbing interest in life. It was well indeed that what fortune she had was strictly settled on her sisters' children, her two brothers-in-law being her trustees. With one of them, who was really wealthy, she had long ago quarrelled. With the other, now a widower, with only a life interest in his estate, she was on coldly cordial terms, and sometimes, as was the case now, acted as chaperon to his only child, her niece and namesake, Bubbles Dunster.

Blanche Farrow never begged or borrowed. When more hard hit than usual, she retired, alone with her faithful maid, to some cheap corner of the Continent; and as she kept her money worries to herself, she was well liked and popular with a considerable circle.

Such was the human being who in a sense was Lionel Varick's only close friend. They had met in a strange way, some ten years ago, in what Miss Farrow's sterner brother-in-law had called a gambling hell. And, just as we know that sometimes Satan will be found rebuking sin, so Blanche Farrow had set herself to stop the then young Lionel Varick on the brink. He had been in love with her at that time, and on the most unpleasant evening when a cosy flat in Jermyn Street had been raided by the police, he had given Blanche Farrow his word that he would never play again; and he had kept his word. He alone knew how grateful he had cause to be to the woman who had saved him from joining the doomed throng who only live for play.

And now there was still to their friendship just that delightful little touch of sentiment which adds salt and savour to almost every relation between a man and a woman. Though Blanche was some years older than Lionel, she looked, if anything, younger than he did, for she had the slim, upright figure, the pretty soft brown hair, and the delicate, finely modelled features which keep so many an Englishwoman of her type and class young—young, if not in years, yet young in everything else that counts. Even what she sometimes playfully called her *petit vice* had not made her haggard or worn, and she had never lost interest in becoming, well-made clothes.

Blanche Farrow thought she knew everything there was to know about Lionel Varick, and, as a matter of fact, she did know a great deal no one else knew, though not quite as much as she believed. She knew him to be a hedonist, a materialist, a man who had very few scruples. But not even to herself would she have allowed him to be called by the ugly name of adventurer. Perhaps it would be truer to say—for she was a very clever woman—that even if, deep in her heart, she must have admitted that such a name would have once suited him, she could now gladly tell herself that "all that" lay far behind him. As we have seen, he owed this change in his circumstances to a happy draw in the lottery of marriage, a draw which has so often turned an adventurer of sorts into a man of substance and integrity.

CHAPTER III

There is generally something a little dull and formal during the first evening of a country house party; and if this is true when most of the people know each other, how far more so is it the case with such a party as that which was now gathered together at Wyndfell Hall!

Lionel Varick sat at one end of the long oak refectory table, Blanche Farrow at the other. But though the table was far wider than are most refectory tables (it was believed to be, because of its width, a unique specimen), yet Blanche, very soon after they had sat down, told herself that there was something to be said, after all, for the old-fashioned, Victorian mahogany. Such a party as was this party would have sorted themselves out, and really enjoyed themselves much more, sitting in couples round an ordinary dining-table, than at this narrow, erstwhile monastic board. Here they were just a little bit too near together—too much *vis-à-vis*, so Blanche put it to herself with a dissatisfied feeling.

But soon things began going a little better. It had been her suggestion that champagne should be offered with the soup, and already it was having an effect. She was relieved to see that the oddly assorted men and women about her were brisking up, and beginning to talk, even to laugh, with one another.

On the host's right sat Miss Burnaby. She was at once quaint and commonplace looking, the most noticeable thing about her being the fact that she wore a cap. It was made of fine Mechlin lace threaded with pale-blue ribbon, and, to the woman now looking at her, suggested an interesting survival of the Victorian age. Quite old ladies had worn such caps when she, Blanche Farrow, was a child!

The rest of Miss Burnaby's costume consisted of a high black silk dress, trimmed with splendid point lace.

Miss Burnaby was evidently enjoying herself. She had taken a glass of sherry, was showing no fear of her champagne, and had just helped herself substantially to the delicious sole which was one of the special triumphs of the French *chef* who had come down for a month to Wyndfell Hall. He and

Miss Farrow had discussed to-night's menu together that morning, and he had spoken with modest enthusiasm of this *Sole à la Cardinal*....

On the other side of the host sat Helen Brabazon.

Blanche looked at the late Mrs. Varick's one intimate friend with critical interest. Yes, Miss Brabazon looked Somebody, though a somewhat old-fashioned Somebody, considering that she was still quite a young woman. She had good hair, a good complexion, and clear, honest-looking hazel eyes; but not her kindest friends would have called her pretty. What charm she had depended on her look of perfect health, and her alert, intelligent expression of face. Miss Farrow, who was well read, and, indeed, had a fine taste in literature, told herself suddenly that Miss Brabazon was rather her idea of Jane Austen's Emma! Her dark-blue velvet dress, though it set off her pretty skin, and the complexion which was one of her best points, yet was absurdly old, for a girl. Doubtless Miss Brabazon's gown had been designed by the same dressmaker who had made her mother's presentation dress some thirty years before. Such dressmakers are a quaint survival of the Victorian age, and to them old-fashioned people keep on going from a sense of loyalty, or perhaps because they are honestly ignorant of what strides in beauty and elegance other dressmakers have made in the last quarter of a century.

The hostess's eye travelled slowly round the table. How ludicrous the contrast between Helen Brabazon and Bubbles Dunster! Yet they were probably very much of an age. Bubbles, who looked such a child, must now be—yes, not far from two-and-twenty.

Miss Farrow checked a sigh. She had been twenty-one herself—but what a charming, distinguished, delightful twenty-one—when she had formed one of a little group round the font of St. Peter's, Eaton Square. She remembered what an ugly baby she had thought Bubbles, and how she had been anything but pleased when someone present facetiously observed that god-mother and godchild had very much the same type of nose and ears and mouth!

To-night Bubbles was wearing an eccentric, and yet very becoming garment. To the uninitiated it might have appeared fashioned out of an old-fashioned chintz curtain. As a matter of fact, the intricate flower pattern with which it was covered had been copied on a Lyons loom from one of those eighteenth century embroidered waistcoats which are rightly prized by connoisseurs. The dress was cut daringly low, back and front, especially back, and the girl wore no jewels. But through her "bobbed" hair was tucked a brilliant little silk flag, which carried out and emphasized the colouring of the flowers scattered over the pale pink silk of which its wearer's gown was made.

Bubbles, in that staid and decorous company, looked as if she had wandered in from some gay Venetian masquerade.

She was now sitting between the millionaire, James Tapster, and her own friend, Bill Donnington. When she had heard that she had been placed next Donnington, Bubbles had pouted. "I'd rather have had Sir Lyon," she exclaimed, "or even the old 'un!"—for so she irreverently designated Helen Brabazon's uncle, Mr. Burnaby.

But Blanche Farrow had been firm. Sir Lyon must of course be on her own right hand, Mr. Burnaby on her left. It is always difficult to arrange a party of four ladies and five men. She had suggested more than one other pleasant woman to make up the party to ten, but Varick had had some objection to each—the objection usually taking the line that the person proposed would not "get on" with the Burnabys.

Blanche again wondered why their host had been so determined to have Helen Brabazon at his first house-party, if her coming meant the inclusion of her tiresome uncle and aunt? And then she felt a little ashamed of herself. One of the best points about Lionel Varick was his sense of gratitude to anyone who had done him a good turn. Gratitude had been the foundation of their own now many-year-long friendship.

The food was so very good, there was so much of it, and doubtless those who had journeyed down to Wyndfell Hall to-night were all so hungry, that there was rather less talk going on round the table than might have been expected. But now and again the hostess caught a fleeting interchange of words. She heard, for instance, old Miss Burnaby informing young Donnington that she had been a good deal on the Continent as a young woman, and had actually spent a year in Austria a matter of forty years ago.

As the meal went on, Miss Farrow gradually became aware that Bubbles provided what life and soul there was in the dull party. But for Bubbles, but for her infectious high spirits and vitality, how very heavy and stupid the meal they were now ending would have been! She asked herself, for perhaps the twentieth time in the last three-quarters of an hour, why her friend had brought together such a curious and ill-assorted set of people.

At last she looked across at Miss Burnaby, and gradually everyone got up.

Varick was at the door in a moment, holding it open, and, as they filed by him, managing to say a word to each of the four ladies. "Bravo, Bubbles!"

Blanche heard him whisper. "You're earning your Christmas present right royally!" and the girl's eyes flashed up into her host's with a mischievous, not over-friendly glance. Miss Farrow was aware that Bubbles did not much care for Lionel Varick. She rather wondered why. But she was far too shrewd not to know that there's no accounting either for likings or dislikings where a man and a woman are concerned.

As she shepherded her little party across the staircase lobby, she managed to mutter into her niece's ear: "I want you to take on Miss Burnaby for me, Bubbles—I'm anxious to make friends with Helen Brabazon."

There are times when what one must call for want of a better term the social rites of existence interfere most unwarrantably with the elemental happenings of life. But on this first evening at Wyndfell Hall the coming of coffee and of liqueurs proved a welcome diversion. Miss Burnaby smiled a pleased smile as she sipped the Benedictine which a footman had poured into a tall green-and-gold Bohemian liqueur-glass for her. She, at any rate, was enjoying her visit. And so, Blanche Farrow decided, was the old lady's niece, for "How beautiful and perfect everything is!" exclaimed the girl; and indeed the room in which they now found themselves was singularly charming.

But somehow Miss Farrow felt that the speaker was not alluding so much to the room, as to the way everything was being done, and her heart warmed to the girl, for she was really anxious that Lionel's first party should be a success.

When they had settled themselves in the lovely, delicately austere-looking white parlour, as it was called, which again suggested to Blanche Farrow the atmosphere of Jane Austen's "Emma," Bubbles dutifully sat herself down by Miss Burnaby. Soon she was talking to that lady in a way which at once fascinated and rather frightened her listener. Bubbles had a very pretty manner to old people. It was caressing, deferential, half-humorously protecting. She liked to shock and soothe them by turns; and they generally yielded themselves gladly, after a little struggle, both to the shocking and to the soothing.

Miss Farrow and Helen Brabazon sat down at the further end of the delightful, gladsome-looking room. It was hung with a delicate, faded Chinese paper; and against the walls stood a few pieces of fine white lacquer furniture. The chairs were painted—some French, some Heppelwhite.

Over the low mantelpiece was framed a long, narrow piece of exquisite embroidery.

"I suppose you have often stayed here?" began Miss Farrow civilly.

Helen Brabazon looked at her, surprised. "I've never been here before!" she exclaimed. "How could I have been? I've only known Mr. Varick for, let me see,"—she hesitated—"a very little over a year."

"But you were a great friend of his wife's—at least so I understood?"

Blanche concealed, successfully, her very real astonishment. She had certainly been told by Lionel that Miss Brabazon and "poor Milly" had been intimate friends; that this fact was, indeed, the only link between Miss Brabazon and her host.

The girl now sitting opposite to her flushed deeply, and suddenly Blanche Farrow realized that there was a good deal of character and feeling in the open, ingenuous face.

"Yes, that's true. We became great friends"—a note of emotion broke into the steady, well-modulated voice—"but our friendship was not an old friendship, Miss Farrow. I only knew Milly—well, I suppose I knew her about ten weeks in all."

"Ten weeks in all?" This time Blanche Farrow could not keep the surprise she felt out of her voice. "What an extraordinary mistake for me to have made! I thought you had been life-long friends."

Helen shook her head. "What happened was this. A friend of mine—I mean a really old friend—had a bad illness, and I took her down to Redsands—you may know it, a delightful little village not far from Walmer. I took a house there, and Mr. and Mrs. Varick had the house next door. We made friends, I mean Mr. Varick and myself, over the garden wall, and he asked me if I would mind coming in some day and seeing his wife. I had a great deal of idle time on my hands, so very soon I spent even more time with the Varicks than I did with my friend, and she—I mean poor Milly— became very, very fond of me."

There was a pause. And then the younger woman went on: "And if we knew each other for such a short time, as one measures time, I on my side soon got very fond of Milly. Though she was a good deal over thirty"—again the listener felt a thrill of unreasoning surprise—"there was something very simple and young about poor Milly."

The speaker stopped, and Blanche, leaning forward, exclaimed: "I am deeply interested in what you tell me, Miss Brabazon! I have never liked to say much to Lionel about his wife; but I have always so wondered what she was really like?"

"She simply adored Mr. Varick," Helen answered eagerly. "She worshipped him! She was always making plans as to what she and 'Lionel' would do when she got better. I myself thought it very wrong that all of them, including Dr. Panton, entered into a kind of conspiracy not to let her know how ill she was."

"I think that was right," said Blanche Farrow shortly. "Why disturb her happiness—if indeed she was happy?"

"She was indeed!--very, very happy!" cried Helen. "She had had a miserable life as a girl, and even after she was grown up. When she met Mr. Varick, and they fell in love at first sight, she'd hardly ever seen a man to speak to, excepting some of her father's tiresome old cronies—"

"Was she pretty?" asked Blanche abruptly.

"Oh, no,"—the other shook her head decidedly. "Not at all pretty—in fact I suppose most people would have called her *very* plain. Poor Milly was sallow, and, when I knew her, very thin; but I believe she'd never been really strong, never really healthy." She hesitated, and then said in a low voice: "That made Mr. Varick's wonderful devotion to her all the more touching."

Blanche Farrow hardly knew what to say. "Yes, indeed," she murmured mechanically.

Lionel devoted to a plain, unhealthy woman? Somehow she found it quite impossible to believe that he could ever have been that. And yet there was no doubting the sincerity of the girl's accents.

"Both Dr. Panton and I used to agree," Helen went on, "that he didn't give himself enough air and exercise. I hired a car for part of the time, and used to take him out for a good blow, now and again."

"And what did Mrs. Varick really die of?" asked Blanche Farrow.

"Pernicious anaemia," answered Helen promptly. "It's a curious, little-known disease, from what I can make out. The doctor told me he thought she had had it for a long time—or, at any rate, that she had had it for some years before she married Mr. Varick."

There was a pause.

"I wonder why they didn't come and live here?" said Miss Farrow thoughtfully.

"Oh, but she hated Wyndfell Hall! You see, her father's whole mind had been set on nothing but this house, and making it as perfect as possible. It was in a dreadful state when he inherited it from an old cousin; yet he was offered, even so, an enormous sum for some of the wonderful oak ceilings. But he refused the offer—indignantly, and he set himself to make it what it must have been hundreds of years ago."

"He hardly succeeded in doing that," observed Blanche Farrow dryly. "Our ancestors lived less comfortably than we do now, Miss Brabazon. Instead of beautiful old Persian carpets, there must have been rushes on all the floors. And as for the furniture of those days—it was probably all made of plain, hard, unpolished wood."

"Well, at any rate,"—the girl spoke with a touch of impatience—"Milly hated this place. She told me once she had never known a day's real happiness till her marriage. That's what made it seem so infinitely sad that it lasted such a short time."

"I suppose," said the other slowly, "that they were married altogether about seven months?"

"I fancy rather longer than that. She was quite well, or so she thought, when she married. They travelled about for a while on the Continent, and she told me once she enjoyed every minute of it! And then her health began to give way, and they took this house at Redsands. They chose it because Mr. Varick knew something of the doctor there—he didn't know him very well, but they became very great friends, in fact such friends that poor Milly left him a legacy—I think it was five hundred pounds. Dr. Panton was most awfully good to her, but of course he hadn't the slightest idea that she was leaving him anything. I never saw a man more surprised than he was when I told him about it the day of her death. Mr. Varick asked me to do so, and he was quite overcome."

She smiled. Five hundred pounds evidently did not seem very much to Miss Brabazon.

"I suppose she had a good deal of money?"

The late Mrs. Varick's friend hesitated a moment, then answered at last, "I think she had about twenty thousand pounds—at least I know that that sum was mentioned in the *Times* list of wills."

The other was startled—disagreeably startled. She had understood, from something Lionel had said to her, that he now had five thousand a year. "This place must be worth a good deal," she observed. She told herself that perhaps the late Mrs. Varick had left twenty thousand pounds in money, and that the bulk of her income had come from land.

"Yes, but unfortunately poor Milly couldn't leave Wyndfell Hall to Mr. Varick. He only has a life interest in it."

Helen Brabazon spoke in a curiously decided way, as if she were used to business.

Blanche was again very much surprised. She had certainly understood that this wonderful old house and its very valuable contents belonged to Lionel Varick absolutely. "Are you sure of that?" she began—and then she stopped speaking, for her quick ears had detected the sound of an opening and shutting door.

CHAPTER IV

After a few moments the five men sorted themselves among the ladies. Old Mr. Burnaby and young Donnington went and sat by Bubbles, the gloomy-looking James Tapster also finally sidling uncertainly towards her. Sir Lyon civilly devoted himself to Miss Burnaby; and Lionel Varick came over to where Blanche Farrow was sitting, and said something to her in a low voice.

Thus was Helen Brabazon for the moment left out in the cold. She turned, and opening a prettily bound book which was on a table close to her elbow, began to read it.

Varick looked dubiously at his silent guest. Leaning again towards Miss Farrow he whispered: "I don't know what one does on such occasions, Blanche. Ought not we to have a round game or something?"

She smiled into his keen, good-looking face. "You *are* a baby! Or are you only pretending, Lionel? Everyone's quite happy; why should we do anything?"

"As a matter of fact, both Mr. Burnaby and Miss Burnaby spoke before dinner as if they expected to be entertained in some way."

"I'll think something out," she said a little wearily. "Now go and do your duty—talk to Miss Brabazon!"

She got up and moved slowly towards the fireplace, telling herself the while, with a certain irritation, that Lionel was not showing his usual alert intelligence. It was all very well to invite this young woman who had been so kind to poor Milly; and the fact that she and her tiresome old uncle and aunt were, if Lionel was right, very wealthy, was not without a certain interest. But still—!

Blanche, with a certain grim, inward smile, remembered a story she had thought at the time rather funny. That of a lady who had said to her husband, "Oh, do come and see them, they are so very rich." And he had answered, "My dear, I would if it were catching!"

Unfortunately, Blanche Farrow had only too much reason to know that wealth is not catching. Also, to one with her brilliant, acute mind, there was something peculiarly irritating in the sight of very rich people who didn't know how to use their wealth, either to give themselves, or others, pleasure. Such people, she felt sure, were Mr. and Miss Burnaby—and doubtless, also, their heiress, Helen Brabazon.

"Bubbles!" she exclaimed imperiously, under her breath. "Come here for a minute." And Bubbles, with a touch of reluctance, got up and left the three men to whom she was talking.

As she came towards her, her aunt was struck by the girl's look of ill-health and unease.

"I wish you could think of something that would stir us all up," she said in a low voice. And then, in a lower voice still, for her niece was now close to her, "The Burnabys look the sort of people who would enjoy a parlour game," she said rather crossly.

And then, all of a sudden, Bubbles gave a queer little leap into the air. "I've got it!" she exclaimed. "Let's hold a séance!"

"A séance?" repeated Blanche Farrow in a dubious tone. "I don't think Miss Burnaby would enjoy that at all."

"Oh, but she would!"—Bubbles spoke confidently. "Didn't you hear her at dinner? She was telling Sir Lyon about some friend of hers who's become tremendously keen about that sort of thing. To tell you the truth, Blanche" (these two had never been on very formal terms together, and in a way Bubbles was much fonder of her aunt than her aunt was of her)—"To tell you the truth, Blanche," she repeated, "ever since I arrived here I've told myself that it would be rather amusing to try something of the kind. It's a strange old house; there's a funny kind of atmosphere about it; I felt it the moment I arrived."

The other looked at her sharply. "I've always avoided that sort of thing, and I don't see it doing you much good, Bubbles! You know how your father feels about it?"

Miss Farrow did not often interfere in other people's affairs, but she had suddenly remembered certain phrases in her brother-in-law's letter.

"Daddy has been put up to making a fuss by a goody-goody widow who's making up to him just now." Bubbles spoke lightly, but she looked vexed.

Blanche Farrow felt sorry she had said anything. Bubbles was behaving very nicely just now. It was the greatest comfort to have her here. So she said, smiling, "Oh, well, I shan't regret your trying something of the kind if you can galvanize these dull folk into life."

"I'll do more than that," said Bubbles easily. "I'll give them creeps! But, Blanche? I want you to back me up if I say I'm tired, or don't want to go on with it."

Blanche Farrow felt surprised. "I don't quite understand," she exclaimed. "Aren't we going to do table-turning?"

"No," said the girl deliberately. "We're going to have a séance—a sitting. And I'm going to be the medium."

"Oh, Bubbles! Is that wise?" She looked uncomfortably into the girl's now eager, flushed face. "D'you think you know enough about these people to be a success at it this very first evening?"

Bubbles' gift of thought reading would of course come in; also the girl was a clever actress; still, that surely wouldn't take her very far with a set of people of whom she knew *nothing*.

"The only one I'm afraid of," said Bubbles thoughtfully, "is Mr. Burnaby. He's such a proper old thing! He might really object—object on the same ground as Daddy's tiresome widow does. However, I can but try."

She pirouetted round, and quickly drew with her foot a gilt footstool from under an Empire settee. She stood upon it and clapped her hands. "Ladies and gentlemen!" she cried. "This is a time of year when ghosts are said to walk. Why shouldn't we hold a séance, here and now, and call up spirits from the vasty deep?"

"But will they come?" quoted Sir Lyon, smiling up into her eager, sensitive little face.

Sir Lyon was quite enjoying Lionel Varick's Christmas house-party. For one thing, he was interested in his host's personality. In a small way he had long made a study of Lionel Varick, and it amused him to see Varick in a new rôle—that of a prosperous country gentleman.

Suddenly Bubbles found an ally in a most unexpected quarter. Helen Brabazon called out: "I've always longed to attend a séance! I did once go to a fortune-teller, and it was thrilling—."

Bubbles stepped down off her footstool. She had the gift—which her aunt also possessed—of allowing another to take the field.

"If it was so exciting," said Lionel Varick dryly, "I wonder that you only went once, Miss Brabazon."

Helen's face grew grave. "I'll tell you about it some day," she said in a low voice; "as a matter of fact, it was just before you and I first met."

"Yes," said Varick lightly. "And what happened? Do tell me!"

Helen turned to him, and her voice dropped to a whisper. "She described Milly—I mean the fortune-teller described Milly, almost exactly. She told me that Milly was going to play a great part in my life."

And then she felt sharply sorry she had said as much or as little as she had said, for her host's face altered; it became, from a healthy pallor, a deep red.

"Forgive me!" she exclaimed. "Forgive me! I oughtn't to have told you—"

"Don't say that. You can tell *me* anything!"

Blanche Farrow, who had now moved forward to the fireplace, would again have been very much surprised had she heard the intense, intimate tone in which Lionel Varick uttered those few words to his late wife's friend.

Helen blushed—a deep, sudden blush—and Sir Lyon, looking at her across the room, told himself that she was a remarkable-looking girl, and that he would like to make friends with her. He liked the earnest, old-fashioned type of girl—but fate rarely threw him into the company of such a one.

"It is quite unnecessary for any of you to move," observed Bubbles in a business-like tone; "but we are likely to obtain much better results if we blow out the candles. The firelight will be quite enough."

And then, to everyone's surprise, Miss Burnaby spoke. Her voice was gentle and fretful. "I thought that there always had to be a medium at a séance," she observed; "when I went with a friend of mine to what she called a Circle, there was a medium there, and we each paid her half-a-crown."

"Of course there must be a medium," said Bubbles quickly. "And *I* am going to be the medium this time, Miss Burnaby; but it will be all free and for nothing—I always do it for love!"

Varick looked at his young guest with a good deal of gratitude. He had never numbered himself among the girl's admirers. To him Bubbles was like a caricature of her aunt. But now he told himself that there was something to say, after all, for this queer younger generation who dare everything! He supposed that Bubbles was going to entertain them with a clever exhibition of brilliant acting. Lionel Varick was no mean actor himself, and it was as connoisseur, as well as expert, that he admired the gift when it was practised by others.

Spiritualism, table-turning, and fortune-telling—he bracketed them all together in his own mind—had never interested him in the least. But he realized dimly what a wonderful chance this new fashionable craze—for so he regarded it—gives to the charlatan. He had always felt an attraction to that extraordinary eighteenth century adventurer, Cagliostro, and to-night he suddenly remembered a certain passage in Casanova's memoirs.... He felt rather sorry that they hadn't planned out this—this séance, before the rest of the party had arrived. He could have given Bubbles a few "tips" which would have made her task easy, and the coming séance much more thrilling.

The company ranged themselves four on each side.

Miss Burnaby sat on one side of the fireplace, her brother on the other. Next to the old lady was Sir Lyon; then Helen Brabazon; last their host.

On the opposite side, next to Mr. Burnaby, sat the fat-visaged James Tapster; by him was Blanche Farrow, looking on the proceedings with a certain cynical amusement and interest, and next to Blanche, and nearest to where Bubbles had now established herself on one of those low chairs which in England is called a nursery chair, and in France a *prie-dieu*, was young Donnington. He, alone of the people there, looked uncomfortable and disapproving.

After they had all been seated, waiting they hardly knew for what, for a few moments, Bubbles leapt from her low chair and blew out all the candles, a somewhat lengthy task, and one which plunged the room into almost darkness. But she threw a big log of wood on the fire, and the flames shot up, filling the room with shafts of rosy, fitful light.

There was a pause. Varick said something in a rather cheerful, matter-of-fact voice to Miss Brabazon, and Bubbles turned round sharply: "I'm afraid we ought to have complete silence—even silence of thought," she said solemnly.

Blanche Farrow looked at the girl. What queer jargon was this? In the wavering light thrown by the fire Bubbles' face looked tense and rather strained.

Was it possible, Blanche asked herself with a touch of uneasiness, that the child was taking this seriously—that she *believed* in it at all? Her father thought so, but then Hugh Dunster was such an old fool!

The moments ran by. One or two of the chairs creaked. James Tapster yawned, and he put up his hand rather unwillingly to hide his yawn. He thought all this sort of thing very stupid, and so absolutely unnecessary. He had enjoyed listening to Miss Bubbles' cheerful, inconsequent chatter. It irritated him that she should have been dragged away from him—for so he put it to himself—by that unpleasant, supercilious woman, Blanche Farrow. It was a pity that a nice girl like Miss Bubbles had such an aunt. Only the other day he had heard a queer story about Miss Farrow. The story ran that she had once been caught in a gambling raid, and her name kept out of the papers by the influence of a man in the Home Office who had been in love with her at the time.

And then he looked up, startled for once—for strange, untoward sounds were issuing from the lips of Bubbles Dunster. The girl was leaning forward, her elbows on her knees, crouched upon the low chair, her slight, sinuous little figure bathed in red light. She was groaning, rocking herself backwards and forwards convulsively. To most of those present it was a strange, painful exhibition—painful, yet certainly thrilling!

Suddenly she began to speak, and the words poured from her lips with a kind of breathless quickness. But the strange, uncanny, startling thing about it was that the voice which uttered these staccato sentences was not Bubbles' well modulated, drawling voice. It was the high, peevish voice of a *child*—a child speaking queer, broken English. Everyone present, even including Varick and Blanche Farrow, who both believed it to be a clever and impudent piece of impersonation, was startled and taken aback by the extraordinary phenomena the girl now presented. Her eyes were closed, and yet her head was thrust forward as if she was staring at the big, now roaring, wood fire before her.

Rushing out through her scarcely open lips, came the sing-song words: "Why bring Laughing Water here? Laughing Water frightened. Laughing Water want to go away. Laughing Water hates this house. Please, Miss Bubbles, let Laughing Water go away!" And Bubbles—if it was Bubbles—twisted and turned and groaned, as if in agony.

And then, to the amazement of all those who were there, young Donnington, his face set in grim lines, suddenly addressed Bubbles, or the little pleading creature that appeared to possess the girl: "Don't be frightened," he said soothingly. "No one's going to hurt Laughing Water. Everyone in this room is good and kind."

In answer, there broke from Bubbles' lips a loud cry: "No, no, no! Bad people—cruel people—here! Bad spirits, too. Bad chair. Laughing Water sitting on torture chair! Miss Bubbles change chair. Then Laughing Water feel better."

Bubbles got up as an automaton might have got up, and Donnington, pushing forward one of the painted chairs, drew the low, tapestry covered *prie-dieu* from under her.

She gave a deep, deep sigh as she sat down again. Then she turned herself and the chair round till she was exactly facing Varick. In a voice which had suddenly become much more her own voice she addressed him, speaking slowly, earnestly: "I see a lady standing behind you. She is very stern-looking. She has a pale, worn face, and dark blue eyes. They are very like your eyes. Her hair is parted in the middle; it is slightly grey. She must have passed over about fifteen to twenty years ago. I think it is your mother. She wants to, she wants to—" Bubbles hesitated, and then, speaking now entirely in her own voice, she exclaimed with a kind of gasp—"to warn you of danger."

Varick opened his lips, and then he closed them. He felt shaken with an over-mastering emotion, as well as intense surprise, and, yes, of fierce anger with the girl for daring to do this—to him.

But Bubbles began again, staring as if at something beyond and behind him. "Now there's another figure, standing to your left. She is still near the earth plane. I cannot place her at all. She is short and stout; her grey hair is brushed back from her forehead. I do not feel as if you had known her very long."

Her voice died away, then suddenly became stronger, more confident: "Your mother—if it is your mother—is trying to shield you from her."

She remained silent for a while. She seemed to be listening. Then she spoke again: "I get a word—what is it?—not *Ardour? Aboard?* No, I think it's *Arbour!*"

She gazed anxiously into Varick's pale, set face. "She says, 'Remember the *Arbour*.' D'you follow me?"

She asked the question with a certain urgency, and Bubbles' host nodded, imperceptibly.

Then she left him, dragging her chair along till she was just opposite Helen Brabazon.

"I see a man standing behind you," she began; "he is dressed in rather curious, old-fashioned cricketing clothes."

A look of amazement and understanding passed over Helen's face.

Bubbles went on, confidently: "He is a tall, well-set-up man. He has light brown hair and grey eyes. He is smiling. I think it is your father. Now he looks grave. He is uneasy about you. He is sorry you came here, to Wyndfell Hall. Do you follow me?"

But Helen shook her head. She felt bewildered and oppressed. "I wonder," she said falteringly, "if he could give me a sign? I do so long to know if it is *really* my dear, dear father."

Blanche Farrow turned a little hot. It was too bad of Bubbles to do the thing in this way!

"He says—he says—I hear him say a word—" Bubbles stopped and knit her brows. "'Girl, girl'—no, it isn't 'girl'—"

"Girlie?" murmured Helen under her breath.

"Yes, that's it! 'Girlie'—he says *'girlie.'*"

Helen Brabazon covered her face with her hands. She was deeply moved. What wonderful thing was this? She told herself that never, never would she allow herself to speak lightly or slightingly of spiritualism again! As far as she knew, no one in that room, not even her uncle or aunt, was aware that "girlie" had been her long dead father's pet name for his only child.

And then, quite suddenly, Bubbles' voice broke into a kind of cry. "Take care!" she said. "Take care! I see another form. It has taken the place of your father. I think it is the form of a woman who has passed over, and who loved you once, but whose heart is now full of hatred. D'you follow me? Quick! quick! She's fading away!"

Helen shook her head. "No," she said in a dull voice, "I don't follow you at all."

She felt acutely, unreasonably disappointed. There was no one in the world who had first loved and then hated her, or who *could* hate her. She cast her mind back to some of her schoolfellows; but no, as far as she knew they were all still alive, and there was not one of them to whom these exaggerated terms of love and hatred could be applied.

Bubbles dragged her chair on till she was just opposite Sir Lyon Dilsford.

He put up his hand: "Will you kindly pass me by, Laughing Water?" he said, in his full, pleasant voice. "I'm an adept, and I don't care for open Circles. If you don't mind, will you pass on?"

And Bubbles dragged on her chair again over the Aubusson carpet.

She was now opposite Miss Burnaby, and the old lady was looking at her with an air of fear and curiosity which strangely altered her round, usually placid face.

"I see a tall young man standing behind you," began Bubbles in a monotonous voice. "He has such a funny-looking long coat on; a queer-shaped cap, too. Why, he's dripping with water!"

And then, almost as if in spite of herself, Miss Burnaby muttered: "Our brother John, who was drowned."

"He wants me to tell you that he's very happy, and that he sends you your father's and mother's love."

Bubbles waited for what seemed quite a long time, then she went on again: "I see another man. He is a very good-looking man. He has a high forehead, blue eyes, and a golden mustache. He is in uniform. Is it an English uniform?"

Miss Burnaby shook her head.

"I think it's an Austrian uniform," said Bubbles hesitatingly; then she continued, in that voice which was hers and yet not hers, for it seemed instinct with another mind: "He says, 'My love! My love, why did you lack courage?'"

The old lady covered her face with her hands. "Stop! Please stop," she said pitifully.

Bubbles dragged her chair across the front of the fire till she was exactly opposite Mr. Burnaby.

For a few moments nothing happened. The fire had died down. There was only a flicker of light in the room. Then all at once the girl gave a convulsive shudder. "I can't help it," she muttered in a frightened tone. "Someone's coming through!"

All the colour went out of the healthy old man's face. "Eh, what?" he exclaimed uneasily.

Like Mr. Tapster, he had thought all this tomfoolery, but while Bubbles had been speaking to, or at, his sister, he had felt amazed, as well as acutely uncomfortable.

And then there burst from Bubbles' lips words uttered in a broken, lamenting voice—a young, uncultivated woman's voice: "I did forgive you—for sure. But oh, how I've longed to come through to you all these years! You was cruel, cruel to me, Ted—and I was kind to you."

Then followed a very odd, untoward thing. Mr. Burnaby jumped up from his chair, and he bolted—literally bolted—from the room, slamming the door behind him.

Bubbles gave a long, long sigh, and then she said feebly: "I'm tired. I can't go on any longer now." She spoke in her natural voice, but all the lilt and confidence were as if drained out of it.

Someone—perhaps it was Donnington, who had got up—began relighting the candles.

No one spoke for what seemed a long time. And then, to the infinite relief of Varick and Miss Farrow, the door opened, and the butler appeared, followed by the footmen. They were bringing in various kinds of drinks.

The host poured out and mixed a rather stiff brandy and soda, and took it over to Miss Burnaby. "Do drink this," he said solicitously. "And forgive me, Miss Burnaby—I'm afraid I was wrong to allow this—this—" he did not know quite what to say, so he ended lamely, "this séance to take place."

Then he poured out another stiff brandy and plain water and drank it himself.

Donnington turned to Miss Farrow. "I have never known Bubbles so—so wonderful!" he exclaimed in a low voice. "There must be something in the atmosphere of this place which made it easier than usual."

Blanche Farrow looked at him searchingly. "Surely you don't believe in it?" she whispered incredulously. "Of course it was a mixture of thought-reading and Bubbles' usual quickness!"

"I don't agree with you—I wish I could." The young man looked very pale in the now bright light. "I thoroughly disapprove of it all, Miss Farrow. I wish to God I could stop Bubbles going in for it!"

"I agree with you that it's very bad for her."

The girl had gone away, right out of the circle. She was sitting on a chair in the far corner of the room; her head, bent over a table, rested on her arms.

"She'll be worn out—good for nothing to-morrow," went on Donnington crossly. "She'll have an awful night too. I might have thought she'd be up to something of the sort! One of the servants told her to-night that this house is haunted. She'll be trying all sorts of experiments if we can't manage to stop her. It's the only thing Bubbles really lives for now, Miss Farrow."

"I'm afraid it is"—Blanche felt really concerned. What had just taken place was utterly unlike anything she had ever imagined. And yet—and yet it didn't amount to very much, after all! The most extraordinary thing which had happened, to her mind, was what had been told to old Miss Burnaby.

And then all at once she remembered—and smiled an inward, derisive little smile. Why, of course! She had overheard Miss Burnaby tell her neighbour at dinner that as a girl she had stayed a winter in Austria. How quick, how clever Bubbles had been—how daring, too! Still, deep in her heart, she was glad that her niece had not had time to come round to where she, herself, had been sitting. Bubbles knew a good deal about her Aunt Blanche, and it certainly would not have been very pleasant had the child made use of her knowledge—even to a slight degree.... Miss Farrow went up to the table on which now stood a large lacquer tray, and poured herself out a glass of cold water. She was an abstemious woman.

"I think some of us ought to go up to bed now" she said, turning round. "It isn't late yet, but I'm sure we're all tired. And we've had rather an exciting evening."

There was a good deal of hand-shaking, and a little talk of plans for the morrow. Bubbles had come over, and joined the others, but she was still curiously abstracted.

"Where's Mr. Burnaby?" she asked suddenly. "Wasn't he at the séance?"

"He's gone to bed," said his sister shortly.

Her host was handing the old lady a bedroom candle, and she was looking up at him with a kind of appeal in her now troubled and bewildered face.

"I feel I owe you an apology," he said in a low voice. "Bubbles Dunster has always possessed extraordinary powers of thought-reading. I remember hearing that years ago, when she was a child. But of course I had no idea she had developed the gift to the extent she now has—or I should have forbidden her to exercise it to-night."

After the three other women had all gone upstairs, Blanche Farrow lingered a moment at the bottom of the staircase; and Varick, having shepherded Sir Lyon, young Donnington, and James Tapster into the hall, joined her for a few moments.

"Bubbles is an extraordinary young creature," he said thoughtfully. "I shouldn't have thought it within the power of any human being to impress me as she impressed me to-night. What a singular gift the girl has!"

Somehow Blanche felt irritated. "She has a remarkable memory," she said dryly. "And also the devil's own impudence, Lionel." And then she told him of the few words she had overheard at dinner of the winter Miss Burnaby had spent in Austria a matter of forty years ago.

"Yes, that's all very well! But it doesn't account for her absolutely correct description of my mother, or—or—"

"Yes?" said his companion sharply.

"Well—of her mention of the word 'arbour.' The last time I saw my mother alive was in the arbour of our horrible little garden at Bedford."

"That," said Blanche thoughtfully, "was, I admit, pure thought-reading. Good-night, Lionel."

Varick remained standing at the foot of the staircase for quite a long while.

Yes, it had been thought-reading, of course. But very remarkable, even so. It was years since he had thought of that last painful talk with his mother. She had warned him very seriously of certain—well, peculiarities of his character. The long-forgotten words she had used suddenly leapt into his mind as if written in letters of fire: "Your father's unscrupulousness, matched with my courage, make a dangerous combination, my boy."

As he lit a cigarette, his hand shook a little, but the more he thought of it, the more he told himself that for all that had occurred with relation to himself to-night there was an absolutely natural explanation.

Take the second figure Bubbles had described? It was obviously that of the woman on whom he had allowed his mind to dwell uneasily, intensely, this afternoon. She was his only enemy—if you could call the crazy creature who had been poor Milly's companion an enemy.

The odious personality of the absurdly named Julia Pigchalke was still very present to him as he turned and joined his men guests in the beautiful camber-roofed and linen-panelled room known as the hall. She was the one fly, albeit a very small fly, in the ointment of his deep content.

CHAPTER V

It was a good deal more than an hour later—in fact nearer twelve than eleven o'clock—when young Donnington got up from the comfortable chair where he had been ensconced, and put down the book which he had been reading.

All the other men of the party, with the exception of old Mr. Burnaby—who had gone to bed for good after his dramatic bolt from the drawing-room—had disappeared some time ago. But Donnington had stayed on downstairs, absorbed in a curious, privately printed book containing the history of Wyndfell Hall.

Suddenly his eyes fell on the following passage:

> "Every piece of the furniture in 'the White Parlour,' as it is still called, is of historic value and interest. To take but one example. A low, high-backed chair, covered with *petit point* embroidery, is believed to have been the *prie-dieu* on which the Princesse de Lamballe knelt during the whole of the night preceding her terrible death. In a document which was sold with the chair in 1830, her servant—who, it appears, had smuggled the chair into the prison—recounts the curious fact that the poor Princess had a prevision that she was to be *torn in pieces*. She spent the last night praying for strength to bear the awful ordeal she knew lay before her."

Donnington shut the book. "That's strange!" he muttered to himself as he got up.

After putting the book back in the bookcase where he had found it, he stood and looked round the splendid apartment with a mixture of interest and delighted attention.

Yes, this wonderful old "post and panel" dwelling was the most beautiful of the many beautiful old country houses with which he had made acquaintance in the last two or three years; and it was awfully good of Bubbles to have got him asked here! Even if she hadn't actually suggested he should come, he knew that of course he owed his being here to her.

The queer, enigmatic, clever girl had the whole of Donnington's steadfast heart. Since he had first met Bubbles—only some eighteen months ago, but it now seemed an eternity—all life had been different.

At first she had at once repelled, attracted, and shocked him. He had been much taken aback when she had first proposed coming to see him, unchaperoned, in the modest rooms he occupied in Gray's Inn. Then, after she had twice invited herself to tea, her constant comings seemed quite natural. Sometimes she would be accompanied by a friend, either another girl or a man, and they would form a merry, happy little party of three or four. But of course he was far, far happiest when she came alone. Almost from the first moment there had been a kind of instinctive intimacy between them, and very soon she had learnt to rely on him—even to take his advice about little things—and to come to him with all her troubles.

Bubbles Dunster had already been what Donnington in his own mind called "deeply bitten" with spiritualism before they had met; yet he had known her for some considerable time before she had allowed him to know it. Even now she tried, ineffectually, to keep him outside all that concerned that part of her life. But, as he once had told her with more emotion than he generally betrayed, he would have followed her down to hell itself.

There came a cloud over his honest face as he thought of what had happened this very evening. And yet, and yet he had to admit that even now he could never make up his mind—he never knew, that is, how far what took place was due to a supernatural agency, or how much to Bubbles' uncanny quickness and cleverness.

What was more strange, considering how well he knew her, Donnington did not really know how much she herself believed in it all. As a rule—probably because she knew how anxious and troubled he felt about the matter—Bubbles would very seldom discuss with him any of the strange happenings in which she was so absorbed. And yet, now and again, almost as if in spite of herself, she would ask him if he would care to come to a séance, or invite him to witness an exceptionally remarkable manifestation at some psychic friend's house.

It had early become impossible for him, apart from everything else, to accept the easy "all rot" theory, for Bubbles' occult gifts were really very remarkable and striking. They had become known to the now large circle of intelligent people who make a study of psychic phenomena, and among them, just because she was an "amateur," she was much in request.

But it had never occurred to him, from what he had been told of the party now gathered together, that there would be the slightest attempt at the sort of thing which had happened to-night. He felt sharply irritated with

Miss Farrow, whom he had never liked, and also with Lionel Varick. He knew that Bubbles' father had written to her aunt; he had himself advised it, knowing, with that shrewd, rather pathetic instinct which love gives to some natures, that Bubbles thought a great deal of her aunt—far more, indeed, than her aunt did of her. He told himself that he would speak to Miss Farrow to-morrow—have it out with her.

Rather slowly and deliberately, for he was a rather slow and deliberate young man, he put out the lights of the three seven-branched candlesticks which illumined the beautiful old room; and, as he moved about, he suddenly became aware that nearly opposite the door giving into the staircase lobby was a finely-carved, oak, confessional-box. What an odd, incongruous ornament to have in a living-room!

The last bedroom candlestick had gone, and temporarily blinded by the sudden darkness, he groped his way up the broad, shallow stairs to the corridor which he knew ultimately led to his room.

He was setting his feet cautiously one before the other on the landing, his eyes by now accustomed to the grey dimness of a winter night, for the great window above the staircase was uncurtained, when *Something* suddenly loomed up before him, and he felt his right arm gripped.

He gave a stifled cry. And then, all at once, he knew that it was Bubbles—only Bubbles! He felt her dear nearness rushing, as it were, all over him. It was all he could do to prevent himself from taking her in his arms.

"Bill? That *is* you, isn't it?" she asked in a low whisper. "I'm so frightened—so frightened! I should have come down long ago—but I thought some of the others were still there. Oh! I wish I'd come down! I've been waiting up here so long—and oh, Bill, I'm very cold!" She was pressing up close to him, and he put his arm round her—in a protecting, impersonal way.

"I wish we could go and sit down somewhere," she went on plaintively. "It's horrible talking out here, on the landing. I suppose it wouldn't do, Bill, for you to come into my room?"

"No, that wouldn't do at all," he said simply. "But look here, Bubbles—would you like to go downstairs again, into the hall? It's quite warm there,"—he felt that she was really shivering.

"I'm cold—I'm cold!"

"Put on something warmer," he said—or rather ordered. "Put on your fur coat. Is it downstairs? Shall I go and fetch it?"

She whispered, "It's in my room—I know where it is. I know exactly where Pegler put it."

She left him standing in the corridor, and went back into her room. The door was wide open, and he could see that she was wearing a white wrapper covered with large red flowers—some kind of Eastern, wadded dressing-gown. He heard a cupboard door creak, and then she came out of the room dragging her big fur coat over her dressing-gown; but he saw that her feet were bare—she had not troubled to put on slippers.

"Go back," he said imperiously, "and put some shoes on, Bubbles—you'll catch your death of cold."

How amazing, how incredible, this adventure would have appeared to him even a year ago! But it seemed quite natural now—simply wilful Bubbles' way. There was nothing Bubbles could do which would surprise Donnington *now*.

"Don't shut your door," he muttered. "It might wake someone up. Just blow out the candles, and leave the door open."

She obeyed him; and then he took her arm—again blinded by the sudden obscurity in which they were now plunged.

"I hate going downstairs," she said fretfully. "Somehow I feel as if downstairs were full of Them!"

"Full of *them*?" he repeated. "What on earth do you mean, Bubbles?"

And Bubbles murmured fearfully: "You know perfectly well what I mean. And it's all my fault—all my fault!"

He whispered rather sternly back: "Yes, Bubbles, it *is* your fault. Why couldn't you leave the thing alone just for a little while—just through the Christmas holidays?"

"I felt so tempted," she muttered. "I forget who it was who said 'Temptation is so pleasing because it need never be resisted.'"

He uttered an impatient exclamation under his breath.

"Let's sit down on the staircase," she pleaded, "I'm warmer now. I think this would be a nice place to sit down."

She sank down on one of the broad, low steps just below the landing, and pulled him down, nestling up close to him. "Oh, Bill," she whispered, "it *is* a comfort to be with you—a real comfort. You don't know what I've gone through since I came up to bed. I felt all the time as if Something was trying to get at me—something cruel, revengeful, miserable!"

"You ate too much at dinner," he said shortly. "You oughtn't to have taken that brandy-cherries ice."

They had very soon got past the stage during which Donnington had tried to say pretty things to Bubbles.

"Perhaps I did"—he felt the gurgle of amusement in her voice. "I was very hungry, and the food here is very good. It must be costing a lot of money—all this sort of thing. How nice to be rich! Oh, Bill, how *very* nice to be rich!"

"I don't agree," he said sharply. "Varick doesn't look particularly happy, that I can see."

"I wonder if Aunt Blanche would marry him *now*?"

"I don't suppose he'd give her the chance—now."

It wasn't a very chivalrous thing to say, or hear said, and Bubbles pinched him so viciously that he nearly cried out.

"You're not to talk like that of my Aunt Blanche. Quite lately—not three months ago—someone asked her to marry him for the thousandth time! But of course she said no—as I shall do to you, a thousand times too, if we live long enough."

She waited a moment, then said slowly: "Her man's rather like you. He's very much what you will be, Bill, in about thirty years from now—a plain, good, priggish old fellow. Of course you know who it is? Mark Gifford, of the Home Office. Aunt Blanche only keeps in with him because he's very useful to her sometimes."

And then she added, with a touch of strange cruelty, "Just as *I* shall always keep in with you, Bill, however tiresome and disagreeable you may be! Just because I find you so useful. You're being useful now; I don't feel frightened any more."

She drew herself from the shelter of his strong, protecting arm, and slid along the polished step till she leant against the banister. He could just see the whiteness of her little face shining out of the big fur collar.

"If you're feeling all right again," he said rather coolly, "I think we'd both better go to bed. Speaking for myself, I feel sleepy!"

But she was sliding towards him again, and again she clutched his arm. "No, no," she whispered. "Let's wait just a little longer, Bill. I—I don't feel quite comfortable in that room. I wonder if they'd give me a new room to-morrow? It's funny, I'm not a bit frightened at what they call the haunted room here—the room that's next to Aunt Blanche's, in the other wing of the house. A woman who killed her little stepson is supposed to haunt that room."

"I know," said Donnington shortly. "I've been reading about it in a book downstairs. *I* shouldn't care to sleep in a room where such a thing had been done—ghost or no ghost!"

And then Bubbles said something which rather startled him. "Bill," she whispered, leaning yet closer to him, "*I* raised that ghost two nights ago."

"What do you mean?" he asked sternly.

"I mean that Aunt Blanche and that tiresome Pegler of hers had already been here a week and nothing had happened. And then—the first night I was in the house the ghost appeared!"

She was shivering now, and, almost unwillingly, he put his arm round her again. "Rot!" he exclaimed. "Don't let yourself think such things, Bubbles—"

"I know you don't believe it, Bill, but I *have* got the power of raising Them."

"I don't know whether I believe it or not," he said slowly. "And I—I sometimes wonder if *you* believe it, Bubbles, or if you're only pretending?"

There was a pause. And then Bubbles said in a strange tone: "'Tisn't a question of believing it now, Bill. I *know* it's true! I wish it wasn't."

"If it's true," he said, "or even if you only believe it's true, what on earth made you do what you did to-night?"

"It was so deadly," she exclaimed, "so deadly dull!" She yawned. "You see, I can't help yawning even at the recollection of it!"

And in the darkness her companion smiled.

"I felt as if I wanted to wake them all up! Also I felt as if I wanted to know something more about them than I did. Also"—she hesitated.

"Yes?" he said questioningly.

"I rather wanted to impress Aunt Blanche." The words came slowly, reluctantly.

"I wonder what made you want to do that?" asked Donnington dryly.

"Somehow—well, you know, Bill, that sort of cool unbelief of hers stings me. She's always thought I make it all up as I go along."

"You do sometimes," he said in a low voice.

"I used to, Bill—but I don't now: it isn't necessary."

He turned rather quickly. "Honest Injun, Bubbles?"

"Yes. Honest Injun!" There was a pause. "What do you think of Varick?" she suddenly whispered.

"I think *Mr.* Varick," answered Donnington coldly, "is a thoroughly nice sort of chap. I like his rather elaborate, old-fashioned manners."

"He's a queer card for all his pretty manners," muttered Bubbles; and somehow Donnington felt that something else was on the tip of her tongue to say, but that she had checked herself, just in time.

"I wish," he said earnestly, "I do wish, Bubbles, that you and I could have a nice, old-fashioned Christmas. They sent up to-night to know if Mr. Varick would allow some of his holly to be cut for decorating the church— why shouldn't we go down to-morrow and help? Do, Bubbles—to please me!"

"I will," she said penitently. "I will, dearest."

Donnington sighed—a short, quick sigh. He could remember the exquisite thrill it had given him when she had first uttered the word—in a crowd of careless people. Now, when Bubbles called him "dearest" it did not thrill him at all, for he knew she said it to a great many people—and yet it always gave him pleasure to hear her utter the dear, intimate little word to him.

"Get up and go to bed, you naughty girl!" he said good-humouredly, but there was a great deal of tenderness in his low, level tone.

She rose quickly to her feet. All her movements were quick and lightsome and free. There was a touch of Ariel about Bubbles, so Bill Donnington sometimes told himself.

They walked up the few shallow steps together, she still very close to him. And then, when they were opposite her door, she exclaimed, but in a very low whisper: "Now you must say the prayer with me—for me!"

"The prayer? What *do* you mean, Bubbles?"

"You know," she muttered:

"Matthew, Mark, Luke and John,
Bless the bed that I lie on—

"What's after that?" she asked.

He went on, uttering the quaint words very seriously, very reverently:

"Four corners to my bed,
Four Angels round my head;

>One to watch and one to pray,
>One to keep all fears away" —

"No," she exclaimed fretfully. "'One to keep my soul in bed.' That's what *I* say. I don't want my poor little soul to go wandering about this beautiful, terrible old house when I'm asleep. Good-night, Goody goody!"

She put up her face as a child might have done, and he bent down and kissed her, as he might have kissed a wilful, naughty child who had just told him she was sorry for something she had done.

"God bless you," he said huskily. "God bless and keep you from any real harm, Bubbles my darling."

CHAPTER VI

As regarded Lionel Varick, the second day of his house-party at Wyndfell Hall opened most inauspiciously, for, when approaching the dining-room, he became aware that the door was not really closed, and that Mr. Burnaby and his niece were having what seemed to be an animated and even angry discussion.

"I don't like this place, and I don't care for your fine friend, Mr. Varick—" Such was the very unpleasant observation which the speaker's unlucky host overheard.

There came instant silence when he pushed open the door, and Helen with heightened colour looked up, and exclaimed: "My uncle has to go back to London this morning. Isn't it unfortunate? He's had a letter from an old friend who hasn't been in England for some years, and he feels he must go up and spend Christmas with *him*, instead of staying with us here."

Varick was much taken aback. He didn't believe in the old friend. His mind at once reverted to what had happened the night before. It was the séance which had upset Mr. Burnaby—not a doubt of it! Without being exactly unpleasant, the guest's manner this morning was cold, very cold— and Varick himself was hard put to it to hide his annoyance.

He had taken a great deal of trouble in the last few months to conciliate this queer, disagreeable, rather suspicious old gentleman, and he had thought he had succeeded. The words he had overheard when approaching the dining-room showed how completely he had failed. And now Bubbles Dunster, with her stupid tomfoolery, was actually driving Mr. Burnaby away!

But Mr. Burnaby's host was far too well used to conceal his thoughts, and to command his emotions, to do more than gravely assent, with an expression of regret. Nay more, as some of the others gradually lounged in, and as the meal became a trifle more animated, he told himself that after all Mr. Burnaby might have turned out a spoil-sport, especially with regard to a secret, all-important matter which he, the convener of this curiously assorted Christmas party, had very much at heart.

Even so, for the first time in their long friendship, he felt at odds with Blanche Farrow. She ought to have stopped the séance the moment she saw whither it was tending! His own experience of Bubbles' peculiar gift had been very far from agreeable, and had given him a thoroughly bad night. That strange, sinister evocation of his long-dead mother had stirred embers Varick had believed to be long dead—embers he had done his best, as it were, to stamp out from his memory.

Another thing which added to his ill-humour was the fact that Bubbles, alone of the party, had not come down to breakfast. In such matters she was an absolute law unto herself; but whereas during the first two days of the girl's stay at Wyndfell Hall her host had been rather glad to miss her at breakfast—it had been a cosy little meal shared by him and Blanche—he now resented her absence. He told himself angrily that she ought to have been there to help to entertain everybody, and to cheer up sulky James Tapster. The latter had asked: "Where's Miss Bubbles?" with an injured air—as if he thought she ought to be forming part of the excellent breakfast.

Mr. Burnaby was determined to get away from Wyndfell Hall as soon as possible, and by eleven o'clock the whole party, excepting Bubbles, was in the hall, bidding him good-bye. And then it was that Varick suddenly realized with satisfaction that both Miss Burnaby and Helen regarded the departure of their kinsman with perfect equanimity. Was it possible that Helen was *glad* her uncle and guardian was leaving her alone—for once? The thought was a very pleasant one to her present entertainer and host.

Even so, after he and Blanche Farrow turned away from the porch where they had been speeding the parting guest, she noticed that Varick looked more annoyed, more thoroughly put out, than she had ever seen him—and she had seen him through some rather bad moments in the long course of their friendship!

"I hope Bubbles won't try on any more of her thought-reading tomfoolery," he said disagreeably. "What happened last night has driven Mr. Burnaby away."

"I think you're wrong," said Blanche quickly. "I'm certain he received the letter of which he spoke."

"I don't agree with you"; and it was with difficulty that Varick restrained himself from telling her what he had overheard the unpleasant old man say to his niece.

"I think we shall get on all the better without him," said Blanche decidedly.

She vaguely resented the way in which Varick spoke of Bubbles. After all, the girl had come to Wyndfell Hall out of the purest good nature—in order to help them through with their party.

"Oh, well, I daresay you're right." (He couldn't afford to quarrel with Blanche.) "And I forgot one thing. I've heard from Panton—"

"You mean your doctor friend?" she said coldly.

"Yes, and he hopes to be here sooner than he thought he could be. He's a good chap, Blanche"—there came a note of real feeling into Varick's voice—"awfully hard-worked! I hope we'll be able to give him a good time."

"He'll have to sleep in the haunted room."

"That won't matter. He wouldn't believe in a ghost, even if he saw one! Be nice to him, for my sake; he was awfully good to me, Blanche."

And Blanche Farrow softened. There was a very good side to her friend Lionel. He was one of those rare human beings who are, in a moral sense, greatly benefited by prosperity. In old days, though his attractive, dominant personality had brought him much kindness, and even friendship, of a useful kind, his hand had always been, as Blanche Farrow knew well, more or less against every man. But now?—now he seemed to look at the world through rose-coloured glasses.

He glanced at the still very attractive woman standing by his side, his good-humour quite restored. "A penny for your thoughts!" he said jokingly.

Blanche shook her head, smiling. Not for very much more than a penny would she have told him the thought that had suddenly come, as such thoughts will do, into her mind. That thought was, how extraordinary had been Varick's transformation from what a censorious world might have called an unscrupulous adventurer into a generous man of position and substance—all owing to the fact that some two years ago he had drifted across an unknown woman in a foreign hotel!

Even to Blanche there was something pathetic in the thought of "poor Milly," whose birthplace and home this beautiful and strangely perfect old house had been. It was Milly—not that sinister figure that Pegler thought she had seen—whose form ought to haunt Wyndfell Hall. But there survived no trace, no trifling memento even, of the dead woman's evidently colourless personality.

And as if Varick had guessed part of what was passing through her mind, "Any news of the ghost, Blanche?" he asked jokingly. "How's my friend Pegler this morning?"

"Pegler's quite all right! I'm the person who ought to have seen the ghost—but of course I neither saw nor heard anything."

As they came through into the hall where the rest of the party were gathered together, Blanche heard Helen Brabazon exclaim: "This is a most wonderful old book, Mr. Varick! It gives such a curious account of a ghost who is supposed to haunt this house—the ghost of a most awfully wicked woman who killed her stepson by throwing him into the moat, and then drowned herself—"

Mr. Tapster, who seldom contributed anything worth hearing to the conversation, suddenly remarked: "The ghost has been seen within the last two days by one of the servants here."

"Who told you that?" asked Varick sharply.

"My valet; I always hear all the news from him."

Helen clapped her hands. "How splendid!" she cried. "That makes everything simply perfect!" She turned her eager, smiling face on Lionel Varick, "I've always longed to stay in a haunted house. I wish the ghost would appear to me!"

"Don't wish that, Miss Brabazon."

It was Sir Lyon's quiet voice which uttered those five words very gravely.

Sir Lyon liked Helen Brabazon. She was the only one of the party, with the exception of Bill Donnington, whom he did like. He was puzzled, however, by her apparent intimacy with their attractive host. How and where could Varick have come across the Burnabys and their niece? They had nothing in common with his usual associates and surroundings. In their several ways they were like beings from different planets.

Sir Lyon knew a great deal about Lionel Varick, though he had seen nothing of him during the few months Varick's married life had lasted.

Like Miss Farrow, Sir Lyon was honestly glad that his present host, after turning some dangerous corners, had drifted, by an amazing series of lucky bumps, into so safe and pleasant a haven. There are certain people, who, when unsatisfied, and baulked of whatever may be their hidden desires, are dangerous to their fellows. Such a man, Sir Lyon was secretly convinced, had been Lionel Varick. Such, evidently, was he no longer.

"Would you like to see the haunted room?" He heard Varick ask the question in that deep, musical voice which many people found so attractive. Helen eagerly assented, and they disappeared together.

Sir Lyon and Bill Donnington went off to the library, and for a few moments Blanche Farrow and Miss Burnaby were alone together in the hall. "Your niece seems to have very remarkable psychic gifts," said the old lady hesitatingly.

And Blanche suddenly remembered—Why, of course! Miss Burnaby had been one of the people most strongly affected by what had happened the night before; she must choose her words carefully. So, "Bubbles has a remarkable gift of thought-reading," she answered quietly. "Personally I am quite convinced that it's not anything more."

"Are you?" There was a curious, questioning look on Miss Burnaby's usually placid face. "D'you think then, that what happened last night was *all* thought-reading?"

"Certainly I think so! But I admit that perhaps I am not a fair judge, for I haven't the slightest belief in what Bubbles would call occultism."

"I know a lady who goes in for all that sort of thing," said Miss Burnaby slowly. "My brother disapproves of my acquaintance with her. She once took me to what is called a Circle, and, of course, I could not help feeling interested. But the medium who was there was not nearly as remarkable as Miss Dunster seems to be; I mean she did not get the same results—at any rate, not in my case."

"I'm afraid what happened last night rather upset you," said Blanche uncomfortably. "I know it would have annoyed me very much if the same thing had happened to me."

"It is true that I was, as a girl, engaged to an Austrian officer. We were very devoted to one another, but my dear father refused his consent. So what occurred last night brought back many painful memories."

Miss Burnaby spoke very simply, but there was a note of deep sadness in her voice, and Blanche told herself that she had been wrong in regarding her as simply a dull, conventional, greedy old woman.

"I'm very sorry now that I allowed Bubbles to do it," she exclaimed. "I'm afraid it upset your brother, too, very much?"

Again there came a curious change over Miss Burnaby's face. She hesitated perceptibly—and then answered: "I would not say so to any of the younger people here, of course. But, as a matter of fact, my brother had a very unpleasant experience as a young man. He fell in love, or thought he fell in love, with a young woman. It was a very unfortunate and tragic affair—for, Miss Farrow, the unhappy young person killed herself! I was very young at the time, and I was not supposed to know anything about it. But of course I did know. Poor Ted had to give evidence at the inquest. It was dreadful, *dreadful*! We have never spoken of it all these many years we have lived together. You realize, Miss Farrow, that the young person was not in our class of life?"—the old lady drew herself up stiffly.

Blanche felt much relieved when, at that moment Bubbles appeared. She made a delightful, brilliant, Goya-like picture, in her yellow jumper and long chain of coral beads. But she looked very tired.

"Have all the others gone out?" she asked languidly. And before Blanche could answer, Miss Burnaby, murmuring something about having letters to write, quickly left the room. The sight of the girl affected her painfully; but it also intensified her longing for what she had heard called "a private sitting."

"Lionel is showing Miss Brabazon over the house. She's very much thrilled over Pegler's experience. I can't make that girl out—can you, Bubbles?"

Miss Farrow drew nearer to the fire. "She's such a queer mixture of shrewdness and simplicity," she went on. "She doesn't seem ever to have gone anywhere, or seen anyone, and yet she's so—so mature! I believe she's exactly your age."

"I feel about a hundred to-day," said Bubbles wearily.

Blanche was wondering how she could open on the subject about which she'd promised to speak to the girl. Somehow she always very much disliked speaking to Bubbles of what she called, in her own mind, "all that unhealthy rot and nonsense!" And yet she must say something—she had promised Lionel Varick to do so.

Bubbles' next words gave her no opening.

"I have no use for Helen Brabazon," she said pettishly. "A very little of her would bore me to death. But still, I amused myself at dinner last night thinking what I should do if I had all her money."

"All her money?" repeated Blanche, puzzled.

"Don't you know that she's one of the richest girls in England?"

"Is that really true?"—Blanche felt surprised, and more than surprised, keenly interested. "How d'you know, Bubbles? Lionel never told me—."

Bubbles gave a quick, queer look at her aunt. "Mr. Tapster told me all about her last night," she answered. "I suppose because he's so rich himself he takes a kind of morbid interest in other rich people. He said that she's the owner of one of the biggest metal-broking businesses—whatever that may mean—in the world. But her uncle and aunt have never allowed her to know anyone or to see anyone outside their own tiresome, fuggy old lot. They've a perfect terror of fortune-hunters, it seems. The poor girl's hardly ever spoken to a man—not to what *I* should call a man! I'm surprised they allowed her to come here. I heard her tell Sir Lyon last night at dinner that this was the first time she'd ever paid what she called a country visit. Apparently Harrogate or Brighton is those awful old people's idea of a pleasant change. Up to now Miss Helen's own idea of heaven seems to have been Strathpeffer."

"How very strange!" But Blanche Farrow was not thinking of Helen Brabazon's possible idea of heaven as she uttered the three words.

Bubbles chuckled. "I touched the old gentleman up a bit yesterday, didn't I, Blanche?"

This gave her aunt the opportunity for which she was seeking. "You did! And as a result he made up some cock-and-bull excuse and went back to London this morning. Lionel is very much put out about it."

"I should have thought Lionel would have been glad," said Bubbles, and there came into her voice the touch of slight, almost insolent, contempt with which she generally spoke of Lionel Varick.

"He was very far from glad; he was furious," said Blanche gravely.

"I only did it because he said he wanted his guests entertained," said Bubbles sulkily.

And then, after there had been a rather long silence between them, she asked: "What did *you* think of it, Blanche? You'd never been at a séance before, had you?"

Miss Farrow hesitated. "Of course I was impressed," she acknowledged. "I kept wondering how you did it. I mean that I kept wondering how those people's thoughts were conveyed to your brain."

"Then you didn't believe that I saw anything of the things I said I saw?" said Bubbles slowly. "You thought it was all fudge on my part?"

Her aunt reddened. "I don't quite know what you mean by saying that. Of course I don't believe you saw the—the figures you described so clearly. But I realized that in some queer way you must have got hold of *the memory* of your victims. Lionel admits that you did so in his case."

"Does he indeed?" Bubbles spoke with sharp sarcasm.

There rose before her a vision of her host's pale, startled face. In some ways he had been the most inwardly perturbed of her last night's sitters, and she, the medium, had been well aware of it.

"I wonder," she said suddenly and inconsequently, "if Lionel has some enemy—I mean a woman—in his life, of whom his friends know nothing?"

Blanche looked dubiously at the girl. "That's the sort of thing one can never know about a man," she said slowly.

"The woman I mean"—Bubbles was going on rather quickly and breathlessly now—"is not a young woman. She's about sixty, I should think. She has a plain, powerful face, with a lot of grey hair turned off her forehead."

"Have you ever seen such a person with Lionel?" asked Miss Farrow.

"No, not exactly."

"What *do* you mean, Bubbles?"

"I can't quite explain what I mean. Even before the séance I seemed to *feel* her last night. I suppose *you* would say I saw her in his mind—in what some people would call his inner consciousness."

Blanche stared at the girl uncomfortably. "D'you mean you can always see what people are thinking of?" she exclaimed.

Bubbles burst out laughing. "Of course I can't! You needn't feel nervous." She went up to her aunt, and thrust her hand through the other's arm. "Don't be worried, old thing"—she spoke very affectionately. "I've promised Bill that I'll put everything of the kind he and father disapprove of away—just while I'm here! But still, Blanche—"

Miss Farrow had never seen the girl in this serious, thoughtful mood before. "Yes," she said. "Yes, Bubbles?"

"Oh, well, I only just wanted to quote something to you that's rather hackneyed."

"Hackneyed?" repeated Miss Farrow.

"There are more things in heaven and earth, my dear, than are dreamt of in *your* philosophy."

Blanche Farrow felt a little piqued. "I've never doubted that," she said curtly.

CHAPTER VII

Meanwhile, one of the subjects of their discussion was thoroughly enjoying her tour of Wyndfell Hall; and as she entered each of the curious, stately rooms upstairs and down, Helen Brabazon uttered an exclamation of pleasure and rather naïve admiration. Not a corner or a passage-way but had some fine piece of old furniture, some exquisite needle-picture or panel of tapestry, in keeping with the general character of the ancient dwelling place.

Her cicerone would have enjoyed their progress more had it not been that his companion frequently referred to his late wife. "How strange that Milly did not love this wonderful old house!" she exclaimed. And then, when they had gone a little further on, she suddenly asked: "I wish you'd tell me which was Milly's room? Surely she must have been happy here sometimes!"

But the new master of Wyndfell Hall had never even thought of asking which had been his wife's room. And, on seeing the troubled, embarrassed look which crossed his face while he confessed his ignorance, Helen felt sharply sorry that she had asked the question. To his relief, she spoke no more of Milly, and of Milly's association with the house which so charmed and attracted her.

One of the strangest, most disturbing facts about our complex human nature is how very little we know of what is passing in another's mind. Helen Brabazon would have been amazed indeed had she seen even only a very little way into her present companion's secret thoughts. How surprised she would have been, for instance, to know that the only thing about herself Varick would have liked altered was her association with that part of his life to which he never willingly returned, even in his thoughts. The part of his life, that is, which had been spent by his dying wife and himself at Redsands. It was with nervous horror that he unwillingly recalled any incident, however slight, connected with those tragic weeks. And yet Helen, had she been asked, would have said that he must often dwell on them in loving retrospect. She honestly believed that the link between them, even now, was a survival of what had been their mutual affection for the then dying woman, and the touching dependence that same woman had shown on their joint love and care.

As they wandered on together, apparently on the most happily intimate terms of liking and of friendship, about the delightful old house, there was scarce a thought in Lionel Varick's mind that would not have surprised, disturbed, and puzzled his companion.

For one thing, he was looking at Helen Brabazon far more critically than he had looked at any woman for a very long time, telling himself, rather ruefully the while, that she was not the type of girl that at any time of his life would have naturally attracted him. But he was well aware that this was his misfortune, not his fault; and he did like her—he did respect her.

How strange it was to know that in her well-shaped little hand there lay such immense potential power! Varick fully intended that that little hand should one day, sooner rather than later, lie, confidingly, in his. And when that happened he intended to behave very well. He would "make good," as our American cousins call it; he would go into public life, maybe, and make a big name for himself, and, incidentally, for her. What might he not do, indeed—with Helen Brabazon's vast fortune joined to her impeccable good name! He did not wish to give up his own old family name; but why should they not become the Brabazon-Varicks? So far had he actually travelled in his own mind, as he escorted his young lady guest about the upper rooms and corridors of Wyndfell Hall.

As he glanced, now and again, at the girl walking composedly by his side, he felt he would have given anything—*anything*—to have known what was behind those candid hazel eyes, that broad white brow. Again he was playing for a great stake, and playing, this time, more or less in the dark....

His mind and memory swung back, in spite of himself, to his late wife. Milly Fauncey had liked him almost from the first day they had met. It had been like the attraction—but of course that was the very last simile that would have occurred to Varick himself—of a rabbit for a cobra. He had had but to look at the self-absorbed, shy, diffident human being, to fascinate and draw her to himself. The task would have been almost too easy, but for the dominant personality of poor Milly's companion, Julia Pigchalke. She had fought against him, tooth and claw; but, cunning old Dame Nature had been on his side in the fight, and, of course, Nature had won.

Miss Pigchalke had always made the fatal mistake of keeping her ex-pupil too much to herself. And during a certain fatal three days when the companion had been confined to her hotel bedroom by a bad cold, the friendship of shy, nervous Milly Fauncey, and of bold, confident Lionel Varick, had fast ripened, fostered by the romantic Italian atmosphere.

During these three days Varick, almost without trying to do so, had learnt all there was to learn of the simple-minded spinster and of her financial circumstances. But he was not the man to take any risk, and he had actually paid a flying visit to London—a visit of which he had later had the grace to feel secretly ashamed—for it had had for object that of making quite sure, at Somerset House, that Miss Fauncey's account of herself was absolutely correct.

Yes, the wooing of Milly Fauncey had been almost too easy, and he knew that he was not likely to be so fortunate this time. But now the prize to be won was such an infinitely greater prize!

He told himself that he mustn't be impatient. This, after all, was only the second day of Helen Brabazon's stay at Wyndfell Hall. Perhaps it was a good thing that her cantankerous old uncle had betaken himself off. Misfortune had a way of turning itself into good fortune where Lionel Varick was concerned; for he was bold and brave, as well as always ready to seize opportunity at the flood.

When, at last, they had almost finished their tour of the house, and he was showing her into the haunted room, she clapped her hands delightedly. "This is exactly the sort of room in which one would expect to meet a ghost!" she exclaimed.

The room into which she had just been ushered had, in very truth, a strange, unused, haunted look. Very different from that into which Helen had just peeped. For Miss Farrow's present bed-chamber, with its tapestried and panelled walls, its red brocaded curtains, and carved oak furniture, the whole lit up by a bright, cheerful fire, was very cosy. But here, in the haunted room next door, the fire was only lit at night, and now one of the windows over the moat was open, and it was very cold.

Helen went over to the open window. She leant over and stared down into the dark, sullen-looking water.

"How beautiful this place must be in summer!" she exclaimed.

"I hope you will come and see it, this next summer."

Varick spoke in measured tones, but deep in his heart he not only hoped, but he was determined on something very different—namely, that the girl now turning her bright, guileless, eager face to his would then be installed at Wyndfell Hall as his wife, and therefore as mistress of the wonderful old house. And this hope, this imperious determination, turned his mind suddenly to a less agreeable subject of thought—that is, to Bubbles Dunster.

Had he known what he now knew about Bubbles' curious gift, he would not have included her in his Christmas party. He felt that she might become a disturbing element in the pleasant gathering. Also he was beginning to suspect that she did not like him, and it was a disagreeable, unnerving suspicion in his present mood.

"What do you think of Bubbles Dunster?" he asked.

"Oh, I like her!" cried Helen. "I think she's a wonderful girl!" And then her voice took on a graver tinge: "I couldn't help being very much impressed last night, Mr. Varick. You see, my father, who died when I was only eight years old, always called me 'Girlie.' Somehow that made me feel as if *he was really there*."

"And yet," said Varick slowly, "Bubbles told you nothing that you didn't know? To my mind what happened last night was simply a clever exhibition of thought-reading. She's always had the gift."

"The odd thing was," said Helen, after a moment's hesitation, "that she said my father didn't like my being here. *That* wasn't thought-reading—"

"There's something a little queer—a little tricky and malicious sometimes—about Bubbles," he said meaningly.

Helen looked at him, startled. "Is there really? How—how horrid!" she exclaimed.

"Yes, you mustn't take everything Bubbles says as gospel truth," he observed, lighting a cigarette. "Still, she's a very good sort in her way."

As he looked at her now puzzled, bewildered face, he realized that he had produced on Helen's mind exactly the impression he had meant to do. If Bubbles said anything about him which—well, which he would rather was left unsaid—Helen would take no notice of it.

CHAPTER VIII

The party spent the rest of the morning in making friends with one another. Mr. Tapster had already singled out Bubbles Dunster at dinner the night before. He was one of those men—there are many such—who, while professing to despise women, yet devote a great deal of not very profitable thought to them, and to their singular, unexpected, and often untoward behaviour!

As for Sir Lyon Dilsford, he was amused and touched to discover that, as is so often the case with a young and generous-hearted human being, Helen Brabazon had a sincere, if somewhat vague, desire to use her money for the good of humanity. He was also touched and amused to find how ignorant she was of life, and how really child-like, under her staid and sensible appearance. Of what she called "society" she cherished an utter contempt, convinced that it consisted of frivolous women and idle men—in a word, of heartless coquettes and of fortune-hunters. To Helen Brabazon the world of men and women was still all white and all black. Sir Lyon, who, like most intelligent men, enjoyed few things more than playing schoolmaster to an attractive young woman, found the hour that he and Miss Brabazon spent together in the library of Wyndfell Hall speed by all too quickly. They were both sorry when the gong summoned them to luncheon.

After a while Varick had persuaded Miss Burnaby to put on a hat and jacket, and go for a little walk alone with him, while Blanche Farrow went off for a talk with young Donnington. Bubbles was the subject of their conversation, and different as were the ingenuous young man and his somewhat cynical and worldly companion, they found that they were cordially agreed as to the desirability of Bubbles abandoning the practices which had led to Mr. Burnaby's abrupt departure that morning.

"Of course, I think them simply an extension of the extraordinary thought-reading gifts she had as a small child," observed Blanche.

"I wish I could think it was only that—I'm afraid it's a good deal more than mere thought-reading," Donnington said reluctantly.

Luncheon was a pleasant, lively meal; and after they had all had coffee and cigarettes, Bubbles managed to press almost the whole party into the business of decorating the church. Their host entered into the scheme with seeming heartiness; but at the last moment he and Blanche Farrow elected to stay at home with Miss Burnaby.

The younger folk started off, a cheerful party—James Tapster, who, as the others realized by something he said, hadn't been into a church for years (he said he hated weddings, and, on principle, never attended funerals); Sir Lyon, who was always at anyone's disposal when a bit of work had to be done; Helen Brabazon, who declared joyfully that she had always longed to decorate a country church; Bubbles herself, who drove the donkey-cart piled high with holly and with mistletoe; and Donnington, who pulled the donkey along.

Suffolk is a county of noble village churches; but of the lively group of young people who approached it on this particular Christmas Eve, only Donnington understood what a rare and perfect ecclesiastical building stood before them. He had inherited from a scholarly father a keen interest in church architecture, and he had read an account of Darnaston church the night before in the book which dealt with Wyndfell Hall and its surroundings.

They were met in the porch by the bachelor rector. "This is really kind!" he exclaimed. "And it will be of the greatest help, for I've been sent for to a neighbouring parish unexpectedly, and I'm afraid that I can't stop and help you."

As the little party passed through into the church, more than one of them was impressed by its lofty beauty. Indeed, the word which rose to both Sir Lyon's and Donnington's lips was the word "impressive." Neither of them had ever seen so impressive a country church.

When lifted from the donkey-cart the little heap of holly and other greenery looked pitifully small lying on the stone floor of the central aisle; and though everyone worked with a will, there wasn't very much to show for it when Mr. Tapster declared, in a cross tone, that it must be getting near tea-time.

"It's much more nearly finished than any of you realize," said Bubbles good-humouredly. "I've done this sort of thing every year since I was quite a kid. Bill and I will come down after tea and finish it up. We shan't want *you*."

"I shouldn't mind coming back," exclaimed Helen Brabazon. "I've enjoyed every minute of the time here!"

But Bubbles declared that she didn't want any of them but Bill. All she would ask the other men to do would be to cut down some trails of ivy.

She explained that she always avoided the use of ivy unless, as in this case, quantity rather than quality was required.

So they all tramped cheerfully back to Wyndfell Hall.

Tea was served in the library, and the host looked on with benign satisfaction at the lively scene, though Blanche Farrow saw his face change and stiffen, when his penetrating eyes rested in turn for a long moment on Bubbles' now laughing little face. Perhaps because of that frowning look, she drew the girl after her into the hall. "Come in here for a moment, Bubbles—I want to speak to you. I've just heard Helen Brabazon say something about raising the ghost. No more séances while I'm in command here—is that understood?"

And Bubbles looked up with an injured, innocent expression. "Of course it's understood! Though, as a matter of fact, Miss Burnaby has already asked me to give her a private sitting."

"You must promise me to refuse, Bubbles—" Miss Farrow spoke very decidedly. "I don't know how you do what you did last night, and, to tell you the truth, I don't care—for it's none of my business. But there was one moment this morning when I feared that horrid Mr. Burnaby was going to take his sister and his niece away—and that really would have been serious!"

"Serious?" queried Bubbles. "Why serious, Blanche? We should have got on very well without them."

Her aunt looked round. They were quite alone, standing, for the moment, in a far corner of the great room, near the finely carved confessional box, which seemed, even to Blanche Farrow, an incongruous addition to the furniture.

"You're very much mistaken, Bubbles! Lionel would have never forgiven you—or me. He attaches great importance to these people; Helen Brabazon was a great friend of his poor wife's." She hesitated, and then said rather awkwardly: "I sometimes wish you liked him better; he's a good friend, Bubbles."

"I should think more a bad enemy than a good friend," muttered the girl, in so low a voice that her aunt hardly caught the ungracious words.

That was all—but that was enough. Blanche told herself that she had now amply fulfilled the promise she had made to Lionel Varick when the two had stood speeding their parting guest this morning from Wyndfell Hall. Even quite at the end Mr. Burnaby had been barely civil. He seemed to think that there had been some kind of conspiracy against him the night before; and as they watched the car go over the moat bridge, Varick had muttered: "I wouldn't have had this happen for a thousand pounds!" But he had recovered his good temper, and even apologized to Blanche for having felt so much put out by the action of a cantankerous old man.

The others were now all streaming into the hall, and Bubbles would hardly allow the good-natured Sir Lyon and Bill Donnington to finish their cigarettes before she shooed them out to cut down some ivy. Varick looked annoyed when he heard that the decorations in the church were not yet finished. "Can't we bribe some of the servants to go down and do them?" he asked. "It seems a shame that you and Donnington should have to go off there again in the cold and darkness."

But in her own way Bubbles had almost as strong a will as had her host. She always knew what she wanted to do, and generally managed to do it. "I would much rather finish the work myself, and I think Bill would rather come too," she said coolly.

So once more the little donkey-cart was loaded up with holly and trails of ivy, and the two set off amid the good-natured comments and chaff of the rest of the party. James Tapster alone looked sulky and annoyed. He wondered how a bright, amusing girl like Bubbles Dunster could stand the company of such a commonplace young man as was Bill Donnington.

As they reached the short stretch of open road which separated Wyndfell Hall from the church, Bubbles felt suddenly how cold it was.

"I think we shall have snow to-morrow," said Donnington, looking round at his companion. He could only just see her little face in the twilight, and when they finally passed through the porch in the glorious old church, it seemed, for the first few moments, pitch-dark.

"I'll tell you what I like best about this church," said the girl suddenly.

"For my part," said Donnington simply, "I like everything about it."

He struck a match, and after a few minutes of hard work, managed to light several of the hanging oil lamps.

"What I like best," went on Bubbles, "are the animals up there."

She pointed to where, just under the cambered oak roof, there ran a dado, on which, carved in white bas-relief, lions, hares, stags, dogs, cats, crocodiles, and birds, formed a singular procession, which was continued round the nave and choir.

"Yes, I like them too," assented Donnington slowly. "Though somehow I did feel this afternoon that they were out of place in a church."

"Oh, how can you say that?" cried the girl. "I love to think of them here! I'm sure that at night they leap joyfully down, and skip about the church, praising the Lord."

"Bubbles!" he exclaimed reprovingly.

"Almost any animal," she said, with a touch of seriousness, "is nicer, taking it all in all, than almost any human being." And then she quoted in the deep throaty voice which was one of her greatest charms:

"A robin redbreast in a cage
Puts all Heaven in a rage."

"The one *I* should like to see put over every manger is:

"A horse misus'd upon the road
Calls to Heaven for human blood,"

said Donnington.

"Oh!" she cried, "and Bill, surely the best of all is:

"A skylark wounded on the wing,
A cherubim doth cease to sing."

Donnington smiled. "I suppose I'm more practical than you are," he said. "If I were a schoolmaster, I'd have inscribed on the walls of every classroom:

"Kill not the moth or butterfly,
For the Last Judgment draweth nigh."

They worked very hard during the half-hour that followed, though only the finishing touches remained to be done. Still, it meant moving a ladder about, and stretching one's arms a good deal, and Bubbles insisted on doing her full share of everything.

"Let's rest a few minutes," she said at last, and leading the way up the central aisle, she sat down wearily in one of the carved choir stalls.

Then she lifted her arms, and putting her hands behind her neck, she tipped her head back.

The young man came and sat down in the next stall. Bubbles was leaning back more comfortably now, her red cap almost off her head. There was a great look of restfulness on her pale, sensitive face.

She put out her hand and felt for his; after a moment of hesitation he slid down and knelt close to her.

"Bubbles," he whispered, "my darling—darling Bubbles. I wish that here and now you would make up your mind to give up everything—" He stopped speaking, and bending, kissed her hand.

"Yes," she said dreamily. "Give up everything, Bill? Perhaps I will. But what do you mean by everything?"

There was a self-pitying note in her low, vibrant voice. "You know it is given to people, sometimes, to choose between good and evil. I'm afraid"— she leant forward, and passed her right hand, with a touch of tenderness most unusual with her, over his upturned face and curly hair—"I'm afraid, Bill, that, almost without knowing it, I chose evil, 'Evil, be thou my good.' Isn't that what the wicked old Satanists used to say?"

"Don't you say it too!" he exclaimed, sharply distressed.

"I know I acted stupidly—in fact, as we're in a church I don't mind saying I acted very wrongly last night."

Bubbles spoke in a serious tone—more seriously, indeed, than she had ever yet spoken to her faithful, long-suffering friend. "But a great deal of what happens to me and round me, Bill, I can't help—I wish I could," she said slowly.

"I don't quite understand." There was a painful choking feeling in his throat. "Try and tell me what you mean, Bubbles."

"What I mean is clear enough"—she now spoke with a touch of impatience. "I mean that wherever I am, *They* come too, and gather about me. It wasn't my fault that that horrible Thing appeared to Pegler as soon as I entered the house."

"But why should you think the ghost Pegler saw—if she did see it— had anything to do with you? Wyndfell Hall has been haunted for over a hundred years—so the village people say."

"Pegler saw nothing till I came. And though I struggle against the belief, and though I very seldom admit it, even to myself, I know quite well, Bill, that I'm never really alone—never free of Them unless—unless, Bill, I'm in a holy place, when they don't dare to come."

There was a tone of fear, of awful dread, in her voice. In spite of himself he felt impressed.

"But why should they come specially round *you*?" he asked uneasily.

"You know as well as I do that I'm a strong medium. But I'll tell you, Bill, something which I've never told you before."

"Yes," he said, with a strange sinking of the heart. "What's that, Bubbles?"

"You know that Persian magician, or Wise Man, whom certain people in London went cracked over last spring?"

"The man you *would* go and see?"

"Yes, of course I mean that man. Well, when he saw me he made his interpreter tell me that he had a special message for me—"

Bubbles was leaning forward now, her hands resting on Bill's shoulders. "I wonder if I ought to tell you all he said," she whispered. "Perhaps I ought to keep it secret."

"Of course you ought to tell me! What was the message?"

"He said that I had rent the veil, wilfully, and that I was often surrounded by the evil demons who had come rushing through; that only by fasting and praying could I hope to drive them back, and close the rent which I had made."

"I shouldn't allow myself to think too much of what he said," said Bill hoarsely. "And yet—and yet, Bubbles? There may have been something in it—."

He spoke very earnestly, poor boy.

"Of course there was a great deal in it. But they're not always demons," she said slowly. "Now, for instance, as I sit here, where good, simple people have been praying together for hundreds of years, the atmosphere is kind and holy, not wicked and malignant, as it was last night."

She waited a moment, then began again, "I remember going into a cottage not long ago, where an old man holds a prayer meeting every Wednesday evening—he's a Dissenter—you know the sort of man I mean? Well, I felt extraordinarily comforted, and *left alone*."

Her voice sank to a low whisper. "I suppose"—there came a little catch in her voice—"I suppose, Bill, that I am what people used to call 'possessed.' In old days I should have been burnt as a witch. Sometimes I feel as if a battle were going on round me and for me—a battle between good and evil spirits. That was what I was feeling last night, before you came up. I couldn't rest—I couldn't stay in bed. I felt as if I must move about to avoid—"

"To avoid what?" he asked.

"—Their clutchings."

Her voice dropped. "I've been in old houses where I seemed to know everything about every ghost!"—she tried to smile. "People don't change when they what we call die. If they're dull and stupid, they remain dull and stupid. But here in Wyndfell Hall, I'm frightened. I'm frightened of Varick—I feel as if there were something secret, secret and sinister, about him. I seem to hear the words, 'Beware—beware,' when he is standing by me. What do *you* think about him, Bill? There are a lot of lying spirits about."

"I haven't thought much about Varick one way or the other," said Donnington reluctantly. "But I should have thought he was a good chap. See how fond Miss Farrow is of him?"

"That doesn't mean much," she said dreamily. "Blanche doesn't know anything about human nature—she only thinks she does. She's no spiritual vision left at all."

"I'm sorry you have that feeling about Varick," said Bill uncomfortably.

"Varick is never alone," said Bubbles slowly. "When I first arrived, and he came out to the porch to meet me, there was Something standing by him, which looked so real, Bill, that I thought it really was a woman of flesh and blood. I nearly said to him, 'Who's that? Introduce me.'"

"D'you mean you think you actually see spirits, even when you're not setting out to do so, Bubbles?" asked. Bill.

She had never said that to him before. But then this was the first time she had ever talked to him as freely and as frankly as she was talking now.

"Yes, that's exactly what I do mean," she said. "It's a sort of power that grows—and oh, Bill, I'd do anything in the world to get rid of it! But this woman whom I saw standing by Lionel Varick in the porch was not a spirit. She was an astral body; that is, she was alive somewhere else: it was her thoughts—her vengeful, malicious thoughts—which brought her here."

"I can't believe that!" he exclaimed.

"It's true, Bill. Though I never saw an astral body before, I knew that Thing to be one—as soon as I realized it wasn't a real woman standing there."

"What was she like?" he asked, impressed against his will.

"An ugly, commonplace-looking woman. But she had a powerful, determined sort of face, and she was staring up at him with a horrible expression: I could see that she hated him, and wished him ill—"

"Have you ever seen the—the Thing again?"

Yes, of course I have. The same astral body was there last night. It was from her that his mother was trying to shield him."

"But you've never seen this astral body—as you call it—excepting on those two occasions?"

Bubbles hesitated. "I've only seen her clearly twice. But during the week that I've been here, I've often felt that she was close to Lionel Varick."

"And what's your theory about her? Why does she hate him, I mean?"

"My theory—?" the girl hesitated again. "I should think it's someone he was fond of when he was a young man, and whom he treated badly. She's ugly enough now—but then women do change so."

"Bubbles," he uttered her name very seriously.

"Yes, Bill?"

"Surely you can stop yourself seeing these kind of strange, dreadful, unnatural things?"

Bubbles did not answer all at once. And then she said: "Yes—and no, Bill! It sometimes happens that I see what you would call a ghost without wishing to see it; yet I confess that sometimes I *could* stop myself. But it excites and stimulates me! I feel a sort of longing to be in touch with what no one else is in touch with. But I'll tell you one thing"—she was pressing up closer to him now, and his heart was beating.... If only this enchanted hour could go on—if only Bubbles would continue in this gentle, sincere, confiding mood—

"Yes," he said hoarsely, "what will you tell me?"

"I never see anything bad when I'm with you. I think I saw your Guardian Angel the other day, Bill."

He tried to laugh.

"Indeed I did! Though you are so tiresome and priggish," she whispered, "though often, as you know, I should like to shake you, still, I know that you've chosen the good way; that's why our ways lie so apart, dearest—"

As she uttered the strange words, she had slid down, and was now lying in his arms, her face turned up to his in the dim light....

Their ways apart? Ah, no! He caught her fiercely to his heart, and for the first time their lips met in a long, clinging kiss.

Then, all at once, he got up and pulled Bubbles on to her feet. "We must be going back to the house," he said, speaking with a touch of hardness and decision which was rare in his dealings with the girl.

"Watch with me, and pray for me," she muttered—and then: "You don't know what a comfort you are to me, Bill."

A wild wish suddenly possessed him to turn and implore her, now that she was in this strange, gentle, yielding mood, to marry him at once—to become his wife in secret, under any conditions that seemed good to her! But he checked the impulse, drove it back. He felt that he would be taking a mean advantage if he did that now. She had once said to him: "I *must* marry a rich man, Bill. I should make any poor man miserable."

He had never forgotten that, nor forgiven her for saying it—though he had never believed that it was true.

Almost as if she was reading into his mind, Bubbles said wistfully: "You won't leave off caring for me, Bill? Not even if I marry somebody else? Not even—?" She laughed nervously, and her laugh, to Donnington a horrible laugh, echoed through the dimly lit church. "Not even," she repeated, "if I bring myself to marry Mr. Tapster?"

He seized her roughly by the arm. "What d'you mean, Bubbles?" he asked sternly.

"Don't do that! You hurt me—I was only joking," she said, shrinking back. "But you are really *too* simple, Bill. Didn't it occur to you that Mr. Tapster had been asked here for me?"

"For you?" He uttered the words mechanically. He understood now why men sometimes murder their sweet-hearts—for no apparent motive.

"He's not a bad sort. It isn't his fault that he's so repulsive. It wouldn't be fair if he was as rich as that, and good-looking, and amiable, and agreeable, as well—would it?"

They were walking down the church, and perhaps Bubbles caught a glimpse into his heart: "I'm a beast," she exclaimed. "A beast to have spoiled our time together in this dear old church by saying that to you about Mr. Tapster. Try and forget it, Bill!"

He made no answer. His brain was in a whirlwind of wrath, of suspicion, of anger, of sick jealousy. This was the real danger—not all the nonsense that Bubbles talked about her power of raising ghosts, and of being haunted by unquiet spirits. The real danger the girl was in now was that of being persuaded into marrying that loathsome Tapster—for his money.

He left her near the door while he went back to put out the lights. Then he groped his way to where she was standing, waiting for him. In the darkness he looked for, found, and lifted, the heavy latch. Together they began pacing down the path between the graves in the churchyard, and then all of a sudden he put his hand on her arm: "What's that? Hark!" he whispered.

He seemed to hear issuing from the grand old church a confused, musical medley of sounds—a bleating, a neighing, a lowing, even a faint trumpeting, all mingling together and forming a strange, not unmelodious harmony.

"D'you hear anything, Bubbles?" he asked, his heart beating, his face, in the darkness, all aglow.

"No, nothing," she answered back, surprised. "We must hurry, Bill. We're late as it is."

CHAPTER IX

It had been Bubbles' happy idea that the children of the tiny hamlet which lay half-a-mile from Wyndfell Hall, should have a Christmas tree. Hers, also, that the treat for the children was to be combined with the distribution of a certain amount of coal and of other creature comforts to the older folk.

All the arrangements with regard to this double function had been made before the party at Wyndfell Hall had been gathered together. But still, there were all sorts of last things to be thought of, and Lionel Varick and Bubbles became quite chummy over the affair.

Blanche Farrow was secretly amused to note with what zest her friend threw himself into the rôle of country squire. She thought it a trifle absurd, the more so that, as a matter of fact, the people of Wyndfell Green were not his tenants, for he had only a life interest in the house itself. But Varick was determined to have a good, old-fashioned country Christmas; and he was seconded in his desire not only by Bubbles, but by Helen Brabazon, who entered into everything with an almost childish eagerness. Indeed, the doings on Christmas Day brought her and Bubbles together, too. They began calling each other by their Christian names, and soon the simple-minded heiress became as if bewitched by the other girl.

"She's a wonderful creature," she confided to that same wonderful girl's aunt. "I've never known anyone in the least like Bubbles! At first I confess I thought her very odd—she almost repelled me. But now I can see what a kind, good heart she has, and I do hope she'll let me be her friend."

"I think you would be a very good friend for Bubbles," answered Blanche pleasantly. "You're quite right as to one thing, Miss Brabazon—she has a very kind, warm heart. She loves to give people pleasure. She's quite delightful with children."

The speaker felt that it would indeed be a good thing if Bubbles could attach herself to such a simple yet sensible friend as was this enormously rich girl. "And if you really like Bubbles," went on Blanche Farrow deliberately, "then I should like just to tell you one or two things about her."

Helen became all eager, pleased attention. "Yes?" she exclaimed. "I wish you would! Bubbles interests me more than anyone I ever met."

"I want to tell you that I and Bubbles' father very much regret her going in for all that—that occultism, I believe it's called."

"But you and Mr. Varick both think it's only thought-reading," said Helen quickly.

Blanche felt rather surprised. It was acute and clever of the girl to have said that. But no doubt Miss Burnaby had repeated their conversation.

"Yes; I personally think it's only thought-reading. Still, it's thought-reading carried very far. The kind of power Bubbles showed the night before last seems to me partly hypnotic, and that's why I disapprove of it so strongly."

"I agree," said Helen thoughtfully. "It was much more than ordinary thought-reading. And I suppose that it's true that she thought she saw the—the spirits she described so wonderfully?"

"I doubt if even she thought she actually saw them. I think she only perceived each image in the mind of the person to whom she was speaking."

"I suppose," asked Helen hesitatingly, "that you haven't the slightest belief in ghosts, Miss Farrow?"

"No, I haven't the slightest belief in ghosts," Blanche smiled. "But I do believe that if a person thinks sufficiently hard about it, he or she can almost evolve the figure of a ghost. I think that's what happened to my maid the other night. Pegler's a most sensible person, yet she's quite convinced that she saw the ghost of the woman who is believed to have killed her little stepson in the room next to that in which I am now sleeping."

And then as she saw a rather peculiar look flit over her companion's face, she added quickly: "D'you think that you have seen anything since you've been here, Miss Brabazon?"

Helen hesitated. "No," she said. "I haven't exactly seen anything. But—well, the truth is, Miss Farrow, that I do feel sometimes as if Wyndfell Hall was haunted by the spirit of my poor friend Milly, Mr. Varick's wife. Perhaps I feel as I do because, of course, I know that this strange and beautiful old house was once her home. It's pathetic, isn't it, to see how very little remains of her here? One might, indeed, say that nothing remains of her at all! I haven't even been able to find out which was her room; and I've often wondered in the last two days whether she generally sat in the hall or in that lovely little drawing-room."

"I can tell you one thing," said Blanche rather shortly, "that is that there is a room in this house called 'the schoolroom.' It's between the dining-room and the servants' offices. I believe it was there that Miss Fauncey, as the people about here still call her, used to do her lessons, with a rather disagreeable woman rejoicing in the extraordinary name of Pigchalke, who lived on with her till she married."

"That horrible, horrible woman!" exclaimed Helen. "Of course I know about *her*. She adored poor Milly. But she was an awful tyrant to her all the same. She actually wrote to me some time ago. It was such an odd letter—quite a mad letter, in fact. It struck me as so queer that before answering it I sent it on to Mr. Varick. She wanted to see me, to talk to me about poor Milly's last illness. She has a kind of crazy hatred of Mr. Varick. Of course I got out of seeing her. Luckily we were just starting for Strathpeffer. I put her off—I didn't actually refuse. I said I couldn't see her then, but that I would write to her later."

"Lionel mentioned her to me the other day. He allows her a hundred a year," said Blanche indifferently.

"How very good of him!" in a very different tone of voice she said musingly: "I have sometimes wondered if the room I'm sleeping in now was that in which Milly slept as a girl. Sometimes I feel as if she was close to me, trying to speak to me—it's a most queer, uncanny, horrid kind of feeling!"

Blanche and Bubbles knew from experience that Christmas Day in the country is not invariably a pleasant day; but they had thought out every arrangement to make it "go" as well as was possible. They were all to have a sort of early tea, and then those who felt like it would proceed to the village schoolroom, and help with the Christmas Treat.

An important feature of the proceedings was to be a short speech by Lionel Varick. Blanche had found, to her surprise and amusement, that he had set his heart on making it. He wanted to get into touch with his poorer neighbours—not only in a material sense, by distributing gifts of beef and blankets; that he had already arranged to do—but in a closer, more human sense. No one she had ever known desired more ardently to be liked than did the new owner of Wyndfell Hall.

The programme was carried out to the letter. They all drank a cup of tea standing in the hall when dressed ready for their expedition. Everyone was happy, everyone was in a good humour—excepting, perhaps, Bill Donnington. The few words Bubbles had said concerning Mr. Tapster had frightened, as well as angered him. He watched the unattractive millionaire with jealous eyes. It was only too clear that Bubbles had fascinated James

Tapster, as she generally did all dull and unimaginative people. But Donnington, perforce, had to keep his jealous feelings to himself; and after they had all reached the school-room of the pretty, picturesque little village, he found he had far too much to do in helping to serve the hungry children and their parents with the feast provided for them, to have time for private feelings of fear, jealousy and pain.

A small platform had been erected across one end of the room. But the programme of the proceedings which were to take place thereon only contained two items. The first of these took most of the Wyndfell Hall house-party completely by surprise; for Bubbles and her aunt had kept their secret well.

Tables had been pushed aside, benches put end to end; the whole audience, with Lionel Varick's guests in front, were seated, when suddenly there leapt on to the platform the strangest and most fantastic-looking little figure imaginable!

For a moment no one, except Bill Donnington, guessed who or what the figure was. There came a great clapping of hands and stamping of feet—for, of course, it was Bubbles! Bubbles dressed up as a witch—red cloak, high peaked hat, short multi-coloured skirt, high boots and broom-stick—all complete!

When the applause had died down, she recited a quaint little poem of her own composition, wishing all there present the best of luck in the coming year. And then she executed a kind of fantastic *pas seul*, skimming hither and thither across the tiny stage.

Everyone watched her breathlessly: Donnington with mingled admiration, love, and jealous disapproval; James Tapster with a feeling that perhaps the time had come for him to allow himself to be "caught" at last; Helen Brabazon with wide-eyed, kindly envy of the other girl's cleverness; Varick with a queer feeling of growing suspicion and dislike.

Finally, Bubbles waved her broom-stick, and more than one of those present imagined that they saw the light, airy-looking little figure flying across the hall, and so out of a window—.

The whole performance did not last five minutes, and yet few of those who were present ever forgot it. It was so strange, so uncanny, so vivid. Bill Donnington heard one of the village women behind him say: "There now! Did you ever see the like? She was the sort they burnt in the old days, and I don't wonder, either."

After this exciting performance the appearance of "the squire," as some of the village people were already beginning to call him, did not produce, perhaps, quite the sensation it might have done had he been the first instead of the second item on the programme. But as he stood there, a fine figure of a man, his keen, good-looking face lit up with a very agreeable expression of kindliness and of good-will, a wave of appreciation seemed to surge towards him from the body of the hall.

Poor Milly's father had been the sort of landowner—to the honour of England be it said the species has ever been comparatively rare—who regarded his tenants as of less interest than the livestock on his home farm. What he had done for them he had done grudgingly; but it was even now clear to them all that in the new squire they had a very different kind of gentleman.

Varick was moved and touched—far more so than any of those present realized. The scene before him—this humble little school-room, and the simple people standing there—meant to him the fulfilment of a life-long dream. And that was not all. As he was hesitating for his first word, his eyes rested on the front bench of his audience, and he saw Helen Brabazon's eager, guileless face, upturned to his, full of interest and sympathy.

He also felt himself in touch with the others there. Blanche, looking her own intelligent, dignified, pleasant self, was a goodly sight. Sir Lyon Dilsford, too, was in the picture; but Varick felt a sudden pang of sympathy for the landless baronet. Sir Lyon would have made such a good, conscientious squire; he was the kind of man who would have helped the boys to get on in the world—the girls, if need be, to make happy marriages. James Tapster looked rather out of it all; he looked his apathetic, sulky self—a man whom nothing would ever galvanize into real good-fellowship. How could so intelligent a woman as Blanche think that any money could compensate a clever, high-spirited girl like Bubbles for marrying a James Tapster? Varick was glad Bubbles was not "in front." She was probably divesting herself of that extraordinary witch costume of hers behind the little curtained aperture to his left.

And then, all at once, he realized that Bubbles was among his audience after all! She was sitting by herself, on a little stool just below the platform. He suddenly saw her head, with its shock of dark-brown hair, and there came over him a slight feeling of discomfort. Bubbles had worked like a Trojan. All this could not have happened but for her; and yet—and yet Varick again told himself that he could very well have dispensed with Bubbles from his Christmas house party. There was growing up, in his dark, secretive heart, an unreasoning, violent dislike to the girl.

All these disconnected thoughts flashed through his mind in something under half-a-minute, and then Varick made his pleasant little speech, welcoming the people there, and saying he hoped there would ensue a long and pleasant connection between them.

There was a great deal more stamping of feet and handclapping, and then gradually the company, gentle and simple, dispersed.

Miss Farrow still had long and luxuriant hair, and perhaps the pleasantest half-hour in each day had come to be that half-hour just before she dressed for dinner, when Pegler, with gentle, skilful fingers, brushed and combed her mistress's beautiful tresses, and finally dressed them to the best advantage.

On Christmas night this daily ceremony had been put off till Miss Farrow's bed-time, when, after a quiet, short evening, the party had broken up on the happiest terms with one another.

As Blanche sat down, and her maid began taking the hairpins out of her hair, she told herself with a feeling of gratification that this had been one of the pleasantest Christmas days she had ever spent. Everything had gone off so well, and she could see that Varick had enjoyed every moment of it, from his surprise distribution of little gifts to his guests at breakfast, to the last warm, grateful hand-shake on the landing outside her door.

"Were you in the school-room, Pegler?" she asked kindly. "It was really rather charming, wasn't it? Everyone happy—the children and the old people especially. And they all *so* enjoyed Miss Bubbles' dressing up as a witch!"

"Why, yes," said Pegler grudgingly. "It was all very nice, ma'am, in a way, and, as you say, it all went off very well. But there's a queer rumour got about already, ma'am."

"A queer rumour? What d'you mean, Pegler?"

"Quite a number of the village folk say that Mr. Varick's late lady, the one who used to live here—" Pegler stopped speaking suddenly, and went on brushing her mistress's hair more vigorously.

"Yes, Pegler?"—Miss Farrow spoke with a touch of impatience. "What about Mrs. Lionel Varick?"

"Well, ma'am, I don't suppose you'll credit it, but quite a number of them do say that her sperrit was there during this afternoon. One woman I spoke to, who was school-room maid here a matter of twenty years back, said she saw her as clear as clear, up on the platform, wearing the sort of grey dress she used to wear when she was a girl, ma'am, when her father was still alive. None of the men seem to have seen her—but quite a number of the women did. The post-mistress says she could have sworn to her anywhere."

"What absolute nonsense!"

Blanche felt shocked as well as vexed.

"It was when Mr. Varick was making that speech of his," said Pegler slowly. "If you'll pardon me, ma'am, for saying so, it don't seem nonsense to me. After what I've seen myself, I can believe anything. Seeing is believing, ma'am."

"People's eyes very often betray them, Pegler. Haven't you sometimes looked at a thing and thought it something quite different from what it really was?"

"Yes, I have," acknowledged Pegler reluctantly. "And of course, the lighting was very bad. Some of the people hope that Mr. Varick's going to bring electric light into the village—d'you think he'll do that, ma'am?"

"No," said Miss Farrow decidedly. "I shouldn't think there's a hope of it. The village doesn't really belong to him, Pegler. It was wonderfully kind of him to give what he did give to-day, to a lot of people with whom he has really nothing to do at all."

And then, after her maid had gone, Blanche lay in bed, and stared into the still bright fire. Her brain seemed abnormally active, and she found it impossible to go to sleep. What a curious, uncanny, uncomfortable story— that of "poor Milly's" ghost appearing on the little platform of the village school-room! There seems no measure, even in these enlightened days, to what people will say and believe.

And then there flashed across her a recollection of the fact that Bubbles had been there, sitting just below Lionel Varick. Strange, half-forgotten stories of Indian magic—of a man hung up in chains padlocked by British officers, and then, a moment later, that same man, freed, standing in their midst, the chains rattling together, empty—floated through Blanche Farrow's mind. Was it possible that Bubbles possessed uncanny powers— powers which had something to do with the immemorial magic of the immemorial East?

Blanche had once heard the phenomenon of the vanishing rope trick discussed at some length between a number of clever people. She had paid very little attention to what had been said at the time, but she now strained her memory to recapture the sense of the words which had been uttered. One of the men present, a distinguished scientist, had actually seen the trick done. He had seen an Indian swarm up the rope and disappear—into thin air! What had he called it? Collective hypnotism? Yes, that was the expression he had used. Some such power Bubbles certainly possessed, and perhaps to-day she had chosen to exercise it by recalling to the minds of those simple village folk the half-forgotten figure of the one-time mistress of Wyndfell Hall. If she had really done this, Bubbles had played an ungrateful, cruel trick on Lionel Varick.

Blanche at last dropped off to sleep, but Pegler's ridiculous yet sinister story had spoilt the pleasant memories of her day, and even her night, for she slept badly, and awoke unrefreshed.

∴

CHAPTER X

There are few places in a civilized country more desolate than a big, empty country railway station: such a station as that at Newmarket—an amusing, bustling sight on a race day; strangely still and deserted, even on a fine summer day, when there's nothing doing in the famous little town; and, in the depth of winter, extraordinarily forlorn. The solitariness and the desolation were very marked on the early afternoon of New Year's Eve which saw Varick striding up and down the deserted platform waiting for Dr. Panton, and Dr. Panton's inseparable companion, a big, ugly, intelligent spaniel called Span.

Varick had more than one reason to be grateful to the young medical man with whom Fate had once thrown him into such close contact; and so this last spring, when Panton had had to be in London for a few days, Varick had taken a deal of trouble to ensure that the country doctor should have a good time. But his own pleasure in his friend's company had been somewhat spoilt by something Panton had then thought it right to tell him. This something was that his late wife's one-time companion, Miss Pigchalke, had gone to Redsands, and, seeking out the doctor, had tried to force him to say that poor Mrs. Varick had been ill-treated—or if not exactly ill-treated, then neglected—by her husband, during her last illness.

"I wouldn't have told you, but that I think you ought to know that the woman has an inexplicable grudge against you," he had said.

"Not inexplicable," Varick had answered quietly. "For Julia Pigchalke first came as governess to Wyndfell Hall when my wife was ten years old, and she stayed on with her ultimately as companion—in fact as more friend than companion. Of course I queered her pitch!"

And then, rather hesitatingly, he had gone on to tell Dr. Panton that he was now paying his enemy an annuity of a hundred a year. This had been left to Miss Pigchalke in an early will made by his poor wife, but it had not been repeated in the testatrix's final will, as Mrs. Varick had fiercely resented Miss Pigchalke's violent disapproval of her marriage.

Panton had been amazed to hear of Varick's quite uncalled-for generosity, and he had exclaimed, "Well, that does take the cake! I wish I'd known this before. Still, I don't think Miss Pigchalke will forget in a hurry what I said to her. I warned her that some of the things she said, or half-said, were libellous, and that it might end very badly for her if she said them again. She took the line that I, being a doctor, was privileged—but I assured her that I was nothing of the kind! Still, she's a venomous old woman, and if I were you I'd write her a solicitor's letter."

That little conversation, which had taken place more than six months ago, came back, word for word, to Varick's mind, as he walked sharply up and down the platform, trying to get warm. It was strange how Miss Pigchalke and her vigorous, unpleasant personality haunted him. But he had found in his passbook only this morning that she had already cashed his last cheque for fifty pounds. Surely she couldn't, in decency, go on with this half-insane kind of persecution if she accepted what was, after all, his free and generous gift every six months?

The train came steaming in, and only three passengers got out. But among them was the man for whom Varick was waiting. And, at the sight of the lithe, alert figure of Dr. Panton, and of the one-time familiar form of good old Span, Varick's troubled, uncomfortable thoughts took wings to themselves and flew away.

The two men's hands met in a firm, friendly grasp. "This *is* jolly," said the younger of the two, as they walked out to the big car. "And I'm ever so much obliged to you for letting me bring Span!"

And Panton did think it very jolly of Varick to have left his guests, and come all this way through the cold to meet him. It was good of him, too, to have let him bring his dog.

As they drove slowly through the picturesque High Street of the famous town, Varick's friend looked about him with keen interest and enjoyment. He had an eager, intelligent, alert mind, and he had never been to Newmarket before.

Once they got clear of the town, and were speeding through the pleasant, typically English country lanes which give Suffolk a peculiarly soothing charm Span (who was a rather large liver-and-white spaniel), lying stretched out sedately at their feet, Varick suddenly asked carelessly: "No more news of my enemy, Miss Pigchalke, I suppose?"

Panton turned to him quickly in the rushing wind: "Yes, something *has* happened. But I didn't think it worth writing to you about. An extraordinary advertisement appeared about a month ago in one of the popular Sunday papers, and Mrs. Bilton—you remember the woman—?"

Varick shook his head. He looked exceedingly disturbed and annoyed, and the man now sitting by his side suddenly regretted that he had said anything about that absurd advertisement.

"Mrs. Bilton was the woman whom I recommended to you as a charwoman, soon after you were settled down at Redsands."

"Yes, I remember the name now. What of her?"

"She came up to see me one evening about a month ago, and she brought the paper—the *News of the World* I think it was—with her."

"Yes," said Varick shortly. "Yes—go on, Panton. What was in the advertisement?"

"The advertisement simply asked for information about you and your doings, past and present, and offered a reward for any information of importance. It was very oddly worded. What I should call an amateur advertisement. Mrs. Bilton came up to consult me as to whether she should write in answer to it. Of course I strongly advised her to do nothing of the kind. As a matter of fact"—Dr. Panton chuckled—"I have reason to believe she *did* write, but I need hardly say that, as far as she was concerned, nothing came of it!"

"I wish you could remember exactly how the advertisement was worded?" said Varick. It was clear that he felt very much disturbed.

"I'm sorry I didn't keep a copy of it; all I can tell you is that it asked for information concerning the past life and career of Lionel Varick, *sometime of Redsands and Chichester.*"

"Chichester?" repeated Varick mechanically.

The name of the Sussex cathedral town held for him many painful, sordid memories. His first wife, the woman whose very existence he believed unknown to everyone who now knew him, with the exception of Blanche Farrow, had been a Chichester woman. It was there that they had lived in poverty and angry misery during the last few weeks of her life.

"Yes, that's all I remember—but I've put it more clearly than the advertisement did."

"What an extraordinary thing!" muttered Varick.

"I don't know that it's so very extraordinary. It was that woman Pigchalke's doing, obviously. As I told you the last time we met, I felt that she would stick at nothing to annoy you. She's quite convinced that you're an out-and-out villain."

Dr. Panton laughed. He really couldn't help it. Varick was such a thoroughly good fellow!

"I wonder," said Varick hesitatingly, "if I could get a copy of that Sunday paper? I feel that it's the sort of thing that ought to be stopped—don't you, Panton?"

"I'm quite sure it didn't appear again in the same paper, or I should have heard of it again. That one particular copy did end by going the whole round of Redsands. I went on hearing about it for, I should think,—well, right up to when I left home."

A rush of blind, unreasoning rage was shaking Varick. Curse the woman! What a brute she must be, to take his money, and go on annoying him in this way. "I wish you'd written and told me about it when it happened," he said sombrely.

The doctor looked at him, distressed. "I'm sorry I didn't, if you feel like that about it!" he exclaimed. "But you were so put out when I told you of the woman's having come to see me, and it was so obvious that the advertisement came from her, that I thought I'd say nothing about it. I wouldn't have told you now, only that you mentioned her."

Varick saw that his friend was very much disturbed. He made a determined effort over himself. "Never mind," he said, trying to smile. "After all, it's of no real consequence."

"I don't know if you'll find it any consolation to be told that that sort of thing is by no means uncommon," said Panton reflectively. "People, especially women, whose minds for any reason have become just a little unhinged, often take that sort of strange dislike to another human being. Sometimes for no reason at all. Every medical man would tell you of half-a-dozen such cases within his own knowledge. Fortunately, such half-insane people generally choose a noted man—the Prime Minister, for instance, or whoever happens to be very much in the public eye. If the persecution becomes quite intolerable there's a police-court case—or the individual is quite properly certified as insane."

And then something peculiar and untoward happened to Lionel Varick. The words rose to his lips: "That horrible woman haunts me—haunts me! I can never get rid of her—she seems always there—"

Had he uttered those words aloud, or had he not? He glanced sharply round, and then, with relief, he made up his mind that he had *not* uttered them, for the man sitting by his side was looking straight before him, with a pleased, interested expression on his plain, intelligent face.

Varick pulled himself together. This would never do! He asked himself, with a touch of acute anxiety, whether it were possible that he was losing his nerve? He had always possessed the valuable human gift of being able to control, absolutely, his secret feelings and his emotions.

"Did I tell you that Miss Brabazon is here?" he asked carelessly.

And the other exclaimed: "I'm glad of that. I formed a tremendously high opinion of that girl last year. By the way, I was surprised to hear, quite by accident, the other day, that she's a lot of money. I don't quite know why, but I formed the impression that it was her friend who was well-to-do—didn't you?"

"I never thought about it," said Varick indifferently. "By the way, Miss Brabazon's old aunt, a certain Miss Burnaby, is here too. It's rather a quiet party, Panton; I hope you won't be bored."

"I'm never bored. Who else have you got staying with you?"

Varick ran over the list of his guests, only leaving out one, and, after a scarcely perceptible pause, he remedied the omission.

"Then there's Miss Farrow's niece; she was called after her aunt, so her real name is Blanche—"

"'Known to her friends as Bubbles,'" quoted Dr. Panton, with a cynical inflection in his voice.

"How do you know that?" exclaimed Varick.

"Because there was a portrait of the young lady in the *Sketch* last week. She seems to be a kind of feminine edition of the Admirable Crichton. She can act, dance, cook—and she's famed as a medium in the psychic world—whatever that may mean!"

"I see you know all about her," observed Varick, smiling.

But though he was smiling at his friend, his inner thoughts were grim thoughts. He was secretly repeating to himself: "Chichester, Chichester? How can she have got hold of *Chichester*?"

Dr. Panton went on: "I'm glad I'm going to meet this Miss Bubbles—I've never met that particular type of young lady before. Though, of course, it's not, as some people believe, a new type. There have always been girls of that sort in the civilized world."

"It's quite true that the most curious thing about Bubbles," said Varick thoughtfully, "is a kind of thought-reading gift. I fancy she must have inherited it from an Indian ancestress, for her great-great-grandfather rescued a begum on her way to be burnt on her husband's funeral pyre. He ultimately married her, and though she never came to England. Bubbles' father, a fool called Hugh Dunster, who's lost what little money he ever had, is one of her descendants. There's something just a little Oriental and strange in Bubbles' appearance."

"This is 'curiouser and curiouser,' as Alice in Wonderland used to say!" exclaimed Panton. "Do you think I could persuade Miss Bubbles to give an exhibition of her psychic gifts?"

The speaker uttered the word "psychic" with a very satiric inflection in his pleasant voice.

Varick smiled rather wryly. "You're quite likely to have an exhibition of them without asking for it! The first evening that my guests were here she held what I believe they call a séance, and as a result Miss Brabazon's uncle, old Burnaby, not only bolted from the room, but left Wyndfell Hall the next morning."

"What an extraordinary thing!"

"Yes," said Varick, "it *was* an extraordinary thing. I confess I can't explain Bubbles' gift at all. At this séance of hers she described quite accurately long dead men and women—"

"Are you sure of that, Varick?"

"Of course I am, for she described my own mother."

There was a pause.

"Being a very intelligent, quick girl, she naturally helps herself out as best she can," went on Varick reflectively.

"Then you're inclined to think her thought-reading is more or less a fraud?" cried Panton triumphantly.

"Less, rather than more, for she's convinced me that she sees into the minds of her subjects and builds up a kind of—of—"

"Description?" suggested the doctor.

"More than that—I was going to say figure. She described, as if she saw them standing there before her, people of whom she'd never even heard—and the descriptions were absolutely exact. But if you don't mind, Panton—"

He hesitated, and the other said, "Yes, Varick?"

"Well, I'd rather you leave all that sort of thing alone, as far as Bubbles Dunster is concerned. Both Miss Farrow and I are very anxious that she shouldn't be up to any more of her tricks while she's here. People don't half like it, you see. Even *I* didn't like it."

Somehow it was a comfort to Varick to talk freely about Bubbles to a stranger—Bubbles had got on his nerves. He would have given a good deal to persuade her to leave Wyndfell Hall; but he didn't know how to set about it. In a sense she was the soul of the party. The others all liked her. Yet he, himself, felt a sort of growing repugnance to her which he would have been hard put to it to explain. Indeed, the only way he could explain it—and he had thought a good deal about it the last few days—was that she undoubtedly possessed an uncanny power of starting into life images which had lain long dormant in his brain.

For one thing—but that, of course, might not be entirely Bubbles' fault—Milly, his poor wife, had become again terribly real to him. It was almost as if he felt her to be alive, say, in the next room—lying, as she had been wont to lie, listening for his footsteps, in the little watering place where they had spent the last few weeks of her life.

He could not but put down that unpleasant, sinister phenomenon to the presence of Bubbles, for he had been at Wyndfell Hall all the summer, and though the place had been Milly's birthplace—where, too, she had spent her melancholy, dull girlhood—no thought of her had ever come to disturb his pleasure in the delightful, perfect house and its enchanting garden. Of course, now and again some neighbour with whom he had made acquaintance would say a word to him indicating what a strange, solitary life the Faunceys, father and daughter, had led in their beautiful home, and how glad the speaker was that "poor Milly" had had a little happiness before she died. To these remarks he, Varick, would of course answer appropriately, with that touch of sad reminiscence which carries with it no real regret or sorrow.

But during the last few days it had been otherwise. He could not get Milly out of his mind, and he had come to feel that if this peculiar sensation continued, he would not be able to bring himself to stay on at Wyndfell Hall after the break-up of his present party.

This feeling of his dead wife's presence had first become intolerably vivid in the village school-room during the children's Christmas Day treat. At one time—so the clergyman had told him—Milly had had a sewing-class for the village girls in that very room; but the class had not been a success, and she had given it up after a few weeks. That was her only association with the ugly little building, and yet—and yet, once he had got well into his speech, he had suddenly *felt her to be there*—and it was not the gentle, fretful, adoring Milly he had known, but a Presence which seemed filled with an awful, clear-eyed knowledge of certain secret facts which his reasoning faculties assured him were only known to his own innermost self.

CHAPTER XI

A turn in the road brought them within sight of Wyndfell Hall, and—"What a singular, wonderful-looking old place!" exclaimed Dr. Panton.

And, indeed, there was something mysteriously alluring in the long, gabled building standing almost, as it were, on an island, among the high trees which formed a screen to the house on the north and east sides. It was something solemn, something appealing—like a melodious, plaintive voice from the long-distant past, out of that Old Country which was the England of six hundred years ago.

"You've no idea how beautiful this place is in summer, Panton—and yet the spring is almost more perfect. You must come again then, and make a really good, long stay."

"Span will enjoy a swim in the moat even now," said the doctor, smiling. They were going slowly over the narrow brick bridge, and so up to the deep-eaved porch.

A butler and footman appeared as if by magic, and the sound of laughing voices floated from behind them. There was a pleasant stir of life and bustle about the delightful old house, or so it seemed to the guest.

He jumped out of the car behind his host, then he turned round. "Span!" he called out. "Span!"

But the dog was still lying on the floor of the car, and he made no movement, still less any attempt to jump down.

"What an extraordinary thing!" exclaimed Span's master. "Come down, Span! Come down at once!"

He waited a moment; then he went forward and tried to drag the dog out. But Span resisted with all his might. He was a big spaniel, and Panton, from where he stood, had no purchase on him. "There's something wrong with him," he said with concern. "Wait a moment, Varick—if you don't mind."

He got up into the car again and patted Span's head. The dog turned his head slowly, and licked his master's hand.

"Now, Span, jump out! There's a good dog!"

But Span never moved.

At last Panton managed to half-shove, half-tumble the dog out. "I've only known him behave like this once before," he muttered, "and that was with a poor mad woman whom I was once compelled to put up in my house for two or three days. He simply wouldn't go near her! He behaved just as he's doing now."

Span was lying on the ground before them, inert, almost as if dead. But his eyes, his troubled, frightened eyes, were very much alive.

Varick went off into the house for a moment. He had never liked dogs; and this ugly brute's behaviour, so he told himself, annoyed him very much.

Span got up and shook himself, almost as if he had been asleep.

Panton bent down. "Span," he said warningly, "be a good dog and behave yourself! Remember what happened to you after the poor lunatic lady went away."

And Span looked up with that peculiar, thoughtful look which dogs sometimes have of understanding everything which is being said to them.

Span had been beaten—a very rare experience for him—after the mad lady had left the doctor's house. But whether he understood or not the exact reference to that odious episode in his happy past life, there was no doubt that Span did understand that his master regarded him as being in disgrace; and it was a very subdued dog that walked sedately into the hall where most of the party were gathered together ready to greet the new-comer.

Miss Farrow was particularly cordial, and so was Helen Brabazon. She and Dr. Panton had become real friends during Mrs. Varick's illness, and they had been at one in their affection for, and admiration of, Lionel Varick during that piteous time. To the doctor (though he would not have admitted it, even to himself, for the world) there had been something very repugnant about the dying woman. Though still young in years, she might have been any age; and she was so fretful and so selfish, hardly allowing her husband out of her sight, while utterly devoted to him, of course, in her queer, egoistic way—and to Miss Brabazon, her kind new friend. The doctor had soon realized that it was the pity which is akin to love which had made Helen become so attached to poor Milly Varick—intense pity for the unhappy soul who was going to lose her new-found happiness. Milly's pathetic cry: "I never had a girl friend before. You can't think how happy it makes me!" had touched Helen to the heart.

Standing there, in that noble old room hung with some beautiful tapestries forming a perfect background to the life and colour which was now filling it, Panton was surprised to find how vividly those memories of last autumn came surging back to him. It must be owing to this meeting with Miss Brabazon—this reunion with the two people with whom he had gone through an experience which, though it so often befalls a kind and sympathetic doctor, yet never loses its poignancy—that he was thinking now so intensely of poor Mrs. Varick.

It was Helen Brabazon who had introduced the new-comer to Miss Farrow, for Varick had disappeared, and soon Dr. Panton was looking round him with interest and curiosity. Most of the people whom he knew to be staying at Wyndfell Hall were present, but not the girl his friend had described—not the girl, that is, whose portrait he had seen in the *Sketch*. Just as he was telling himself this, a door opened, and two people came through together—a tall, fair, smiling young man, and a quaint, slender figure, looking like a child rather than like a woman, whose pale, yet vivid little face was framed in thick, dark brown, bobbed hair, and whose large, bright eyes gleamed mischievously.

Bubbles had chosen to put on this afternoon a long, rose-red knitted jumper over a yellow skirt, and she looked as if she had stepped out from some ancient Spanish religious procession.

"Bubbles," called out her aunt, "this is Dr. Panton. Come and be introduced to him."

Then something very odd happened. Varick joined his new guest at the very same moment that the girl came forward with hand outstretched and a polite word of welcome on her lips; but, before she could speak, Span, who had been behaving with so sedate a dignity that the people present were scarcely conscious of his existence, gave a sudden loud and horrible howl.

His master, disregarding Bubbles' outstretched hand, seized the dog by the collar, rushed with him to the door giving on to the porch, and thrust him out into the cold and darkness.

Span remained quite quiet when on the wrong side of the door. There might have been no dog there.

"I'm so sorry," said Panton apologetically, as he came again towards the tea-table. "I can't think what's the matter with the poor brute. He's almost perfect manners as a rule."

He turned to Miss Brabazon, who laughingly exclaimed: "Yes, indeed! Span's such an old friend of mine that I feel quite hurt. I thought he would be sure to take some notice of me; but I didn't even know he was there till he set up that awful, unearthly howl."

"I think it's very cruel to have turned the dog out into the cold," Bubbles said in her quick, decided way. "There's nothing about dogs I don't know, Doctor—Doctor—"

"—Panton," he said shortly.

"Oh, Panton? May I go out to him, Dr. Panton?" There was a challenge in her tone.

Panton answered stiffly: "By all means. But Span's not always pleasant with complete strangers; and he prefers men, Miss Dunster."

"I think he'll be all right with me."

Bubbles went and opened the door, and a moment later they heard her low, throaty voice talking caressingly to the dog. Span whined, but in a gentle, happy way.

"He's quite good now," she called out triumphantly.

Varick turned to the company: "Will you forgive me for a moment?" he said. "I forgot to say a word to my chauffeur about our plans for to-morrow." And as he went through one door, Bubbles, followed by the now good and repentant Span, appeared through another.

"He's a darling," she cried enthusiastically. "One of the nicest dogs I've ever met!"

She sat down, and endeared herself further to Span by giving him a large piece of cake.

And Dr. Panton, looking at the charming group—for the lithe, dark-haired girl in her brilliant, quaint garment, and the dog over which she was bending, made a delightful group—told himself grudgingly that Miss Bubbles was curiously attractive: far more attractive-looking than he would have thought her to be by the portrait published in the *Sketch*—though even that had been sufficiently arresting to remain in his mind for two or three days. Was there really something Eastern about her appearance? He would never have thought it but for those few words of Varick's. Many English girls have that clear olive complexion, those large, shadowy dark eyes, which yet can light up into daring, fun, and mischief.

But, alas! the story of Span—even this early chapter of the story of his stay at Wyndfell Hall—had not a happy ending. As Varick came forward again among his guests, Span once more set up that sharp, uncanny howl, and this time he cringed and shivered, as well as howled.

Span's master, with an angry exclamation, again dragged the now resisting dog across to the door which led into the outer porch. After he had shut the door, and Span's howls were heard subsiding, he turned to the others apologetically. "I'm really awfully sorry," he exclaimed. "If this sort of thing goes on I'll have to send him home to-morrow."

Poor Panton looked thoroughly put out and annoyed. But Bubbles came to his rescue—Bubbles and the young man whom the doctor now knew to be Bill Donnington.

"Come on, Bill! We'll take him round to the kitchen. You don't mind, do you?"

Span's owner shook his head; devoted though he was to his dog, he felt he could well do without Span for a while.

After Bubbles and Donnington had disappeared together, their eager voices could be heard from the paved court-yard which connected two of the wings of Wyndfell Hall. Span was barking now, barking eagerly, happily, confidently. And when the two young people reappeared they were both laughing.

"He's taken to the cook tremendously," said Bubbles. "And he's even made friends—and that's much more wonderful—with the cat. He went straight up to her and smelt her, and she seemed to be quite pleased with the attention."

She turned to Dr. Panton: "I'll go out presently and see how he's getting on," she added.

He looked at her gratefully. She really was a nice girl! He had thought that she would be one of those disagreeable, forward, self-sufficing, modern young women, who are absorbed only in themselves, and in the effect they produce on other people. But Miss Bubbles was not in the least like that.

Helen Brabazon whispered, smiling: "Isn't Bubbles Dunster a dear, Dr. Panton? She's not like anyone I ever met before—and that makes her all the nicer, doesn't it?"

CHAPTER XII

About an hour after Dr. Panton's arrival, the whole of the party was more or less scattered through the delightful old house, with the exception of Lionel Varick, who had gone off to the village by himself.

But the four ladies finally gathered together in the hall to put in the time between tea and dinner.

Miss Burnaby was soon nodding over a book close to the fire, while Helen Brabazon and Blanche Farrow had brought down their work. This consisted, as far as Helen was concerned, of a complicated baby's garment destined for the Queen's Needlework Guild. Blanche, sitting close to Helen, was bending over a frame containing the intricate commencement of a fruit and bird *petit-point* picture, which, when finished, she intended should form a banner screen for this very room.

Three seven-branched silver candlesticks had now been lighted, and formed pools of soft radiance in the gathering dusk.

After wandering about restlessly for a while, Bubbles ensconced herself far away from the others, in the old carved wood confessional, which had seemed in Donnington's eyes so incongruous and unsuitable an object to form part of the furnishings of a living room.

To Blanche Farrow, the confessional, notwithstanding the beauty of the carving, suggested an irreverent simile—that of a telephone-box. She told herself that only Bubbles would have chosen such an uncomfortable resting-place.

But when stepping up into what had once been the priest's narrow seat, Bubbles called out that it was delightfully nice and quiet in there, as well as dark—for there still hung over the aperture through which she had just passed a curtain of green silk brocade embroidered with pale passion flowers.

There followed a period of absolute silence and quietude in the room. Then the door leading from the outside porch opened, and Varick came in. "I hope I'm not intruding," he exclaimed in his full, resonant voice; and the ladies, with the exception of Bubbles, who remained invisible, looked up and eagerly welcomed him.

During the last few days he had made a real conquest of Miss Burnaby, who, with the one startling exception of the emotion betrayed by her at the séance, secretly struck both him and Blanche Farrow as the most commonplace human being with whom either had ever come in contact.

"I'm quite warm," he said, in answer to the old lady's invitation to come up to the fire. "I had to go down to the village Post Office to see why the London papers hadn't arrived. But I've got them all now."

He came over to where she was sitting and handed her a picture paper. Then he retreated, far from the fire, close to a table which was equidistant from the confessional and the door giving access to the staircase hall. Bringing forward a deep, comfortable chair out of the shadows, he sat down, and opening one of the newspapers he had brought in, began to read it with close attention.

On the table at his elbow, there now stood what looked to Helen's eyes like a bouquet of light. But this only made the soft darkness which filled the further side of the great room seem more intense to those sitting near the fireplace.

They were all pleasantly tired after the doings of the day; and soon Blanche's quick ears caught a faint, regular sound issuing from the far-off confessional. Bubbles, so much was clear, had fallen asleep.

And then, not for the first time in the last few days, the aunt began considering within herself the problem of her niece. Blanche had begun to like Donnington with a cordiality of liking which surprised herself. His selfless love for the girl touched her more than she had thought it possible for anything now to touch her worldly heart. And whereas she would naturally have considered a marriage between the penniless Donnington and brilliant, clever, popular Bubbles as being out of the question, she was beginning to feel that such a marriage might be, nay, almost certainly was, the only thing likely to ensure for Bubbles a reasonably happy and normal life. Blanche Farrow knew enough of human nature to realize that the kind of love Bill Donnington felt for her strange little niece was of a high and rare quality. It was very unlike the usual selfish, acquisitive love of a man for a maid. It was more like the tender, watching, tireless devotion certain mothers have for their children—it was infinitely protecting, infinitely forgiving, infinitely understanding.

Blanche sighed, a long, deep sigh, as she told herself sadly that no one had ever loved *her* like that—not even her old friend Mark Gifford. He had loved her long; in fact he rarely saw her, even now, without asking her to marry him. Also he had been, in his own priggish way, a very, very good and useful friend to her. But still, Blanche knew, deep in her heart, that Mark Gifford disapproved of her, that he often misunderstood her, that he was ashamed of the strength of the attraction which made him still wish to make her his wife, and which had kept him a bachelor. As long as this old friend had known her he had always written her a Christmas letter. The letter had not come this Christmas, and she had missed it. But Mark had no idea of where she was, and—and after all, perhaps his faithful friendship had waned at last from lack of real response.

And then, while thinking these rather melancholy, desultory thoughts, Blanche Farrow suddenly experienced a very peculiar sensation. It was that of finding herself as if impelled to look up from the embroidery-frame over which she was bending.

She did look up; and for a moment her heart—that heart which the way of her life had so atrophied and hardened—seemed to stop beating, for just behind Lionel Varick, whose head was still bent over his newspaper with a complete air of unconcern, interest, and ease—stood, or appeared to stand, two shadowy figures.

She shut her eyes; then opened them again—wide. *The figures were still there*, and they had grown clearer, more definite, especially the countenance of each of the two wraith-like women who stood, like sentinels, one on either side of the seated man.

Blanche gazed at them fixedly for what seemed to her an eternity of time. But even while, in a way, she could not deny the evidence of her senses, she was telling herself that she was really seeing *nothing*—that this extraordinary experience was but another exercise of Bubbles' uncanny power.

And as she, literally not believing the evidence of her senses, stared at the two immobile figures, her eyes became focussed on the face of the woman standing to Varick's right. There was a coarse beauty in the mask-like-looking countenance, but it was a beauty now instinct with a kind of stark ferocity and rage.

At last she slowly concentrated her gaze on the other luminous figure. Though swathed from neck to heel in what Blanche told herself, with a peculiar feeling of horror, were old-fashioned grave-clothes, the second woman yet looked more *real*, more *alive*, than the other. Her face, if deadly pale, was less mask-like, and the small, dark eyes gleamed, while the large, ill-shaped mouth seemed to be quivering.

And then, all at once, the form to Varick's right began to dissolve—to melt, as it were, into the green-grey and blue tapestry which hung across the farther wall of the hall.

But while this curious phenomenon took place, the woman swathed in her grave-clothes remained quite clearly visible....

Suddenly Helen Brabazon started to her feet; she uttered a loud and terrible cry—and at that same moment Blanche saw the more living and sinister of the two apparitions also become disintegrated, and quickly dissolve into nothingness.

Lionel Varick leapt from his chair. His face changed from a placid gravity to one of surprise and distress. "What is it?" he cried, coming forward. "What is it, Miss Brabazon—Helen?"

The girl whom he addressed fell back into her chair. She covered her face with her hands. Twice she opened her lips and tried to speak—in vain. At last she gasped out, "It's all right now. I'll be better in a minute."

"But what happened?" exclaimed Varick. "Did anything happen?"

"I think I must have gone to sleep without knowing it—for I've had a terrible, terrible—nightmare!"

Miss Burnaby got up slowly, deliberately, from her chair near the fire. She also came up to her niece.

"You were working up to the very moment you cried out," she said positively. "I had turned round and I was watching you—when suddenly you jumped up and gave that dreadful cry."

"Do tell us what frightened you," said Varick solicitously.

"Please don't ask me what I saw—or thought I saw; I would rather not tell you," Helen said in a low voice.

"But of course you must tell us!" Miss Burnaby roused herself, and spoke with a good deal of authority. "If you are not well you ought to see a doctor, my dear child."

Helen burst into bitter sobs. "I thought I saw Milly, Mr. Varick—poor, poor Milly! She looked exactly as she looked when I last saw her, in her coffin, excepting that her eyes were open. She was standing just behind you—and oh, I shall never, never forget her look! It was a terrible, terrible look—a look of hatred. Yet I cared for her so much! You know I did all that was possible for one woman to do for another during those few weeks that I knew her?"

Lionel Varick's face turned a curious, greyly pallid tint. It was as if all the natural colour was drained out of it.

"Where's Bubbles?" he asked, in a scarcely audible voice.

For a moment no one answered him, and then Blanche said quietly: "Bubbles is over there, in the confessional, asleep."

He turned and walked quickly over to the carved, box-like confessional, and drew aside the green-embroidered curtain.

Yes, the girl lay there asleep—or was she only pretending? Her breast rose and fell, her eyes were closed.

Varick took hold of her arm with no gentle gesture, and she awoke with a cry of surprise and pain. "What is it? Don't do that!" she said in a hoarse and sleepy tone.

And then, on seeing who it was, she smiled wryly. "Is it forbidden to get in here?" she asked, still speaking in a heavy, dull way. "I didn't know it was,"—and stumblingly she stepped down out of the confessional.

Varick scowled at her, and made no answer to her question. Together they walked over to where the other three were standing—Miss Burnaby still gazing at her niece, with an annoyed, frightened expression on her face.

As Bubbles and Varick came up to her, Helen got up from the chair in which she had sunk back. She held a handkerchief to her face, and was making a great effort to regain her self-control and composure.

"Please forgive me, Mr. Varick. I oughtn't to have told you what I thought I saw—for I'm sure it was only a dream, a horrible, startling dream. But—but you made me tell you, didn't you?"

She looked up into his pale, convulsed face with an anguished expression. "I think I'll go upstairs now, and rest a little before I dress for dinner," and then she walked across the room, and out of the door, with a steady step.

Bubbles stretched out her arms with a weary gesture. "What's all this fuss about?" she asked. "I feel absolutely done—done—done! Not at all as if I'd had a good long sleep. I wonder how long I *was* asleep?"

"You didn't sleep very long," said her aunt dryly—"not half-an-hour in all. I should advise you, Bubbles, to follow Miss Brabazon's example—go up and have a good rest, before getting ready for dinner."

Bubbles turned away. She walked very slowly, with dragging steps, to the door; and a moment later Miss Burnaby also left the room.

Varick walked over towards the fireplace. He held out his hands to the flames—he felt cold, shiveringly cold.

He turned, as he had so often done in the past, for comfort to the woman now standing silent by his side, and who knew at once so much and so little of his real life.

"I wonder what really happened?" he muttered. "It was a most extraordinary thing! I've seldom met anyone so little hysterical or fanciful as—as is Miss Brabazon." And then: "Why, Blanche," he exclaimed, startled, "what's the matter?"

There was a look on her face he had never seen there before—a very troubled, questioning, perplexed look.

"I saw something too, Lionel," she said in a low voice; "I—I saw more than Helen Brabazon admits to having seen."

"*You* saw something?" he echoed incredulously.

"Yes, and were it not that I am an older woman, and have more self-control than your young friend, I should have cried out too."

"What *did* you see?" he asked slowly.

"What I think I saw—for I am quite convinced that I saw nothing at all, and that the extraordinary phenomenon or vision, call it what you will, was only another of Bubbles' tricks—what I saw—" She stopped dead. She found it extraordinarily difficult to go on.

"Yes?" he said sharply. "Please tell me, Blanche. What is it you saw, or thought you saw?"

"I thought I saw *two* women standing just behind your chair," she said deliberately.

Varick made a violent movement—so violent that it knocked over a rather solid little oak stool which always stood before the fire. "I beg your pardon!" he exclaimed; and, stooping, picked the stool up again. Then, "What sort of women?" he asked; and though he tried to speak lightly, he failed, and knew he failed.

"It isn't very easy to describe them," she said reluctantly. "The one was a stout young woman, with a gipsy type of face—that's the best way I can describe it. But the other—"

She waited a full minute, but Varick did not, could not, speak.

She went on:

"The other, Lionel, looked more like—well, like what a ghost is supposed to look like! She was swathed in white from head to foot, and she appeared—I don't quite know how to describe it—as if at once alive and dead. Her face looked dead, but her eyes looked alive."

"Had you ever seen either of these women before—I mean in life?"

He had turned away from her, and was staring into the fire.

"No; I've never seen anyone in the least like either of them."

Varick moved a few steps, and then, as if hardly knowing what he was doing, he began turning over the leaves of the picture paper Miss Burnaby had been reading.

"Do you suppose that Helen Brabazon saw exactly what you saw?" he asked at last.

"No, I'm sure she didn't; for the younger-looking woman had already disappeared, it was as if she faded into nothingness, before Helen Brabazon called out,"—there was a hesitating, dubious tone in Blanche's voice. "But of course we can't tell what exactly she did see. She may have seen something—someone—quite different from what I thought I saw."

Varick began staring into the fire again, and Blanche felt intolerably nervous and uncomfortable. "I think, Lionel, that I must speak to Bubbles very seriously!" she said at last. "I haven't a doubt *now* that she really has got some uncanny power—a power of stirring the imagination—of making those about her think they see visions."

"But why should she have chosen that you should see such—such a vision as that?" he asked, almost in a whisper.

"Ah, there you have me! I can't imagine what should prompt her to do such a cruel, unseemly thing."

"You think it's quite impossible that Bubbles personated either of these—these"—he hesitated for a word, and Blanche answered his only half-asked question very decidedly.

"If there'd been only one figure there, I confess I should have thought that Bubbles had in some way dressed up, and 'worked it.' You know how fond she used to be of practical jokes? But there were two forms—absolutely distinct the one from the other."

Lionel Varick took a turn up and down the long room. Then he came and stood opposite to her, and she was shocked at the change in his face. He looked as if he had been through some terrible physical experience.

"I wish you'd arrange for her to go away, at once—I mean, to-morrow. Forgive me for saying such a thing, but I feel that nothing will go right while Bubbles is at Wyndfell Hall," he exclaimed.

Blanche looked what he had never seen her look before—offended. "I don't think I can get her away to-morrow, Lionel. She's nowhere to go to. After all, she gave up a delightful party to come here and help us out."

"Very well," he said hastily. "Perhaps I ought not to have suggested anything so inhospitable"—he tried to smile. "But I will ask you to do me *one* favour?"

"Yes," she said, still speaking coldly. "What is it?"

"I want you to ask Miss Brabazon and her aunt to keep what happened this afternoon absolutely to themselves."

"Of course I will!" She was relieved. "I don't think either of them is in the least likely to be even tempted to speak of it."

CHAPTER XIII

But even while Varick and Blanche Farrow were arranging together that this disturbing and mysterious occurrence should remain secret, Helen Brabazon was actually engaged in telling one who was still a stranger to her the story of her amazing experience.

Perhaps this was owing to the fact that the door of the hall had scarcely shut behind her when she met Sir Lyon Dilsford face to face.

Almost involuntarily he exclaimed, with a good deal of real concern in his voice: "Is anything the matter? I hope you haven't had bad news?"

She said, "Oh, no," and shook her head; but the tears welled up again into her eyes.

When an attractive girl who generally shows remarkable powers of quietude and self-control breaks down, and proves herself a very woman after all, the average man is generally touched, and more than a little moved. Sir Lyon felt oddly affected by Helen's evident distress, and an ardent desire to console and to help her rose instinctively in his mind.

"Come into the study!" he exclaimed in a low voice. "And tell me if there's anything I can do to help you?"

She obeyed him, and, as he followed her in, he shut the door.

She sat down, and for a while he stood before her, gazing sympathetically into her flushed, tear-stained face.

"I'm afraid you'll think it so absurd," she said falteringly. "Even I can hardly believe now that what happened *did* happen!"

"Don't tell me—if you'd rather not," he said suddenly; a very disagreeable suspicion entering his mind.

Was it within the bounds of possibility that James Tapster had tried to—to kiss her? Sir Lyon had a great prejudice against the poor millionaire, but he instantly rejected the idea. If such a thing had indeed happened to her, Helen Brabazon was the last girl ever to offer to tell anyone, least of all a man.

Helen all at once felt that it would be a comfort to confide her strange, terrifying experience to this kind new friend.

"I'd rather tell you, I think."

She waited a moment, and then came out with a bald statement of what had happened. "I was sitting knitting, when something seemed to force me to look up—and I saw, or I thought I saw, the spirit of a dear, dead friend."

Sir Lyon uttered an exclamation of extreme astonishment.

"Yes, I know it was only my imagination," Helen went on in a low, troubled voice. "But it gave me a most fearful shock, and I feel that, however long I live, I shall never forget it!"

"I wish you would tell me a little more about it," he said persuasively. "I don't ask out of idle curiosity. I was very much impressed by what happened on the first night of our visit here—I mean at the séance."

"So was I," she said reluctantly. "But, of course, this had nothing to do with—with anything of that sort. In fact, Bubbles (as she has asked me to call her) was sitting, asleep, I think, in that curious old carved confessional box. My aunt and Mr. Varick were reading—Mr. Varick had just come up from the village with this morning's London papers; Miss Farrow was doing her embroidery, and I'd just been counting some stitches in my knitting, when I looked up and saw—"

She stopped, as if not able to go on.

"Was what you saw, what you took to be an apparition, close to the confessional?" asked Sir Lyon abruptly.

"No, not so very close—still, not very far away. It—she—seemed to be standing behind Mr. Varick, a little to his left, on the door side."

"I suppose you would rather not tell me who it was you saw?"

Sir Lyon thought he knew, but he wished to feel sure.

"I don't see why I shouldn't tell you," yet she hesitated. "It was poor Milly, Sir Lyon—I mean Mrs. Lionel Varick. She and I became great friends during the weeks preceding her death. She even told me that, apart from her husband, she had never cared for anyone as she grew to care for me. And yet—oh, Sir Lyon, what was so very, very terrible just now, was that I felt her looking at me with a kind of hatred in her dead face," and, as she uttered these last words, an expression of deep pain came over Helen Brabazon's countenance.

Sir Lyon then asked a rather curious question: "How was the apparition clothed?"

"In her shroud. A woman in Redsands made it. I saw the woman about it—perhaps that impressed it on my mind," her mouth quivered. "The figure standing there was exactly like Milly dead, excepting that her eyes seemed alive, and that there was that dreadful look of anger on her face."

"How long did the vision last?"

"Oh, not a whole minute altogether! When I first saw it I got up, and without knowing what I was doing, I screamed; and then she, Milly, seemed to fade away—to melt into the air.

"Did anyone else see anything?" asked Sir Lyon eagerly.

"No, I don't think so. In fact, I'm quite sure not. My aunt was sitting with her back to Mr. Varick."

There was a pause. And then Helen asked: "You don't believe that the dead *can* appear to the living—do you, Sir Lyon?"

"I've never been able quite to make up my mind," he said slowly. "But I do believe, absolutely, in what is now called materialization. I must believe in it, because I've witnessed the phenomena a number of times myself. But, of course, always under a most carefully prepared set of conditions. I wish you'd tell me," he went on, "exactly how the figure struck you? Can you describe to me in greater detail the appearance of what seemed to be the spirit of your friend?"

Helen did not quite understand what he meant, but she answered obediently: "It's very difficult to describe more exactly what I did see. As I told you just now, the eyes alone seemed to be really alive in the pale, waxen-looking face, and I thought the mouth quivered."

"I know," he interjected quickly.

"But the rest of her poor, thin, emaciated looking body seemed to be so stiff and still, swathed in the long, white grave-clothes—and I can't express to you the sort of growing horror of it all! I *knew* it was only a few moments, yet it *seemed* like hours of time. I felt as if I *must* call out and indeed I did. But before I could go on to utter her name, Miss Farrow spoke to me, my aunt got up from her chair, and Mr. Varick rushed forward! Of course it all happened in much less time than it takes to tell."

She looked at him earnestly. What a kind, dependable face he had!

"Have you, Sir Lyon, any explanation to suggest?" she asked.

"I don't suppose," he said slowly, "that you would accept my explanation, Miss Brabazon."

"I think I would," she said simply. "After what happened that first night I feel that anything is possible. I am *sure* my dear father's spirit was there."

"I am inclined to think so too. But as to this instance I am not so sure that what you saw was your dead friend. Unless—"

"Unless?" repeated Helen questioningly.

"You told me that during her lifetime you were on the best terms of friendship with this poor lady, and yet that on her dead face there was a look of hatred? How do you account for that?"

He looked questioningly, penetratingly, into the girl's distressed face.

Sir Lyon had always prided himself on his self-command and perfect self-control, and yet he would have given almost anything for a really honest answer to this question.

And poor Helen did give him an honest answer—honest, that is, from her own simple-hearted point of view. "I can't account for it!" she exclaimed. "But I am sure it was there. I felt the hatred coming out from her towards me. And oh, Sir Lyon, it was horrible!"

"Try and think it was not Mrs. Varick's spirit," he said impressively. "Try and tell yourself that it was either a dream, a waking phantom of your brain, or—or—"

"Or what?" asked Helen eagerly.

But there are thoughts, questions, suspicions that no human being willingly puts into words.

During the last few days Sir Lyon had become convinced that Lionel Varick had resolved in his powerful, unscrupulous mind to make Helen Brabazon his wife. It was in vain that he argued with himself that the question of Miss Brabazon's future concerned him not at all. He found himself again and again, when watching those two, giving a great deal of uneasy thought to the matter. Now and again he would remind himself that Varick had been no greater an adventurer than many a man who, when utterly impecunious, has married an heiress amid the hearty approval and acclamation of most of the people about them. And Varick could not now be regarded as impecunious; he was a man of substance, though no doubt even his present income would seem as nothing compared with the Brabazon fortune.

Sir Lyon was ashamed of his growing distaste, even dislike, of his courteous host. It was as if in the last few days a pit had been dug between them. It was not pleasant to him to be accepting the hospitality of a man whom he was growing to dislike and suspect more and more every day.

And yet though he could have made a hundred excuses to leave Wyndfell Hall, he stayed on, refusing to inquire too closely into the reason.

At times he tried to persuade himself that he was keenly interested in the problem presented by Bubbles Dunster. The girl was beyond question a most rare and exceptional medium. At one time he had made a close study of psychic phenomena; and though he had come to certain conclusions which had led to his entirely giving up the practices which had once seemed to him the only thing worth living for, he was still sufficiently interested in the subject to feel that Bubbles' powers were well worth watching.

Sir Lyon would have given much to have been present at what, if Helen's account were correct, had been an extraordinary example of what is called materialization.

Had this terrible vision of Mrs. Varick been an emanation of Helen Brabazon's own brain—some subconscious knowledge that she, Helen, was now the object of Varick's pursuit? Or was this woman, whom they all called "poor Milly," an unquiet spirit, wandering about full of jealous, cruel thoughts, even with regard to the two who had evidently been so selflessly devoted to her—her girl friend and her husband?

And then, suddenly a queer feeling of intense relief swept over him. Whether a sentient being or not had appeared to Helen Brabazon, there could be no doubt that what had just happened would make the course of Varick's wooing more arduous. He was ashamed to find that this conviction made him suddenly feel oddly light-hearted—almost, so he told himself, a young man again!

CHAPTER XIV

As he walked into his bedroom, which was pleasantly warm—for there was a good fire, and the curtains across the three windows were closely drawn—Dr. Panton told himself that he was indeed beginning the New Year very well.

Half-an-hour ago the whole party, with the exception of Miss Burnaby, who had gone to bed at her usual time, had stood outside the front door under the starry sky while the many clocks of Wyndfell Hall rang out the twelve strokes which said farewell to the Old Year, and brought the New Year in. Then they had all crowded back again into the hall, and, hand in hand, sung "Auld Lang Syne."

As everyone had shaken hands and wished each other a Happy New Year, many and sincere had been the good wishes felt and expressed. Even James Tapster had looked genial and happy for once. He was beginning to feel as if he would, after all, throw the handkerchief to Bubbles (his own secret, graceful paraphrase for making an offer of marriage). But as yet Dr. Panton knew nothing of this little under-current in the broad stream which seemed to be flowing so pleasantly before him. Had he done so, he would have been startled and distressed, for he had already, with a shrewd medical man's judgment, "sized up" his fellow guest, and found him very much wanting.

Thus not knowing or divining anything of the various human under-currents, save, perhaps, that he guessed Donnington to be in love with Bubbles, Dr. Panton went off to bed in a very cheerful and contented state of mind. So contented was he that as, with leisurely fingers, he lit the candles on his dressing-table, he incidentally told himself that Wyndfell Hall was the only house in which he had ever stayed which, lacking any other luminant but lamps and candles, yet had amply enough of both!

Lighting a pipe—for he didn't feel in the least sleepy—he drew forward a deep, comfortable armchair close to the fire, and took up a book. But soon he put it down again, and, staring at the dancing flames, his mind dwelt with retrospective pleasure on the last few hours.

Seated between Helen Brabazon and Bubbles Dunster, he had thoroughly enjoyed the delicious New Year's Eve dinner composed by Varick's *chef*. Miss Brabazon had admitted to having a headache this evening, and she certainly looked very far from well—less well than he had thought her to be when they had first seen one another again, after so long an absence, this afternoon.

And yet, as is sometimes the case, a look of languor suited her; and he thought she had grown decidedly better-looking in the last year. At Redsands Miss Brabazon had been a little too buxom, a little too self-possessed, also, for his taste. And yet—and yet how wonderfully good she had been to poor Mrs. Varick! With what tender patience had she put up with the invalid's querulous bad temper, never even mentioning it to him, the doctor, who so often received painful confidences of the kind from those who were far nearer and dearer to a dying patient than Helen had been to querulous Milly Varick.

As for Miss Bubbles, he felt it would be easy to lose one's heart to that strange, queer young creature. They had made real friends over Span. And, apropos of Span, Dr. Panton frowned to himself. He feared that the dog was going to be the one blot on this delightful visit. Span had been very, very badly behaved—setting up that unearthly howl whenever his master brought him in contact with the rest of the party. Yet he was quite good in the servants' hall. "It is clear that, like so many cleverer people than himself, Span likes low company," Bubbles had whispered mischievously to Span's master. "I daresay they're all very much nicer than we are, if we only knew it!" she had gone on, but Dr. Panton had shaken his head. He had no great liking for the modern domestic servant. He was one of the many people who consider that the good old type of serving-man and waiting-woman has disappeared for ever. To-night, remembering Bubbles' words, he gave a careless, rueful thought to the question of how Varick, who was always generous about money, must be cheated—"rooked" was the expression the doctor used in his own mind—by these job servants who were here, so his host told him, just for the one month. Still, they were all fulfilling their part of their contract very well, especially the *chef*! Everything seemed to go on oiled wheels at Wyndfell Hall. But this might be owing to clever Miss Farrow, for Varick had told him that Miss Farrow was acting as hostess to the party.

Panton didn't much like that composed, clever-looking lady. She made him feel a little shy, a little *young*—a sensation he didn't very often experience nowadays! She treated him with a courtesy which, if elaborate, was also distant. It was odd to think that Miss Farrow was the unconventional, friendly Bubbles Dunster's aunt.

Sir Lyon Dilsford, on the other hand, he liked very much. He smiled a queer little smile as he thought of this new acquaintance. He had looked up in the middle of dinner, and caught a rather curious look on Sir Lyon's face. It was a thoughtful, considering, almost tender look. Was Sir Lyon attracted to Helen Brabazon? Well, Miss Brabazon, with her vast wealth, and Sir Lyon, with his fine old name, and agreeable, polished personality, would seem well matched, according to a worldly point of view. But Panton told himself that he would *far* prefer Lionel Varick were *he* a young woman. But he feared there was no hope of such a chance coming Miss Brabazon's way. Varick's heart—his big, sensitive heart—was buried in the grave of his wife....

How strange to think that "poor Milly"—for so had even her doctor come to call her in his own mind—had been born and brought up in this delightful old house! She had once spoken to him of her unhappy girlhood, coupling it with an expression of gratitude to her husband for having so changed her life.

"Poor Milly" was very present to Dr. Panton to-night. He, who had hardly given her a thought during the last twelve months, found himself dwelling on her to an almost uncanny extent. He even recalled some unusual features of her illness which had puzzled and worried him greatly. He dismissed the recollection of certain of her symptoms with an effort. There is no truer saying—at any rate from a doctor's point of view—than "Let the dead bury their dead." He had done his very best for Mrs. Varick, lavished on her everything that skill and kindness could do, and she had been extraordinarily blessed, not only in her devoted husband, but in that sudden, unexpected friendship with another woman—and with such a good, conscientious, sweet-tempered young woman as was Helen Brabazon....

Half-past one struck on the landing outside his room, and Dr. Panton got up from the comfortable easy chair; time to be going to bed, yet he still felt quite wide awake.

He walked over to the window nearest to the fire-place, and drew back the heavy, silk-brocaded curtain. It was a wonderful night, with a promise, he thought, of fine weather—though one of the men who had stood outside with him had predicted snow. What a curious, eerie place this old Suffolk house was! Probably the landscape had scarcely changed at all in the last five hundred years. Below he could see gleaming water....

He let fall the curtain, and, blowing out the candles, got slowly, luxuriously, into the vast, comfortable four-post bed.

As he composed himself to sleep, broken, disconnected images floated through his brain. Bill Donnington—what a nice boy! And yet not exactly, he felt, in sympathy with any of the people there. He wondered why Bill Donnington had come to spend Christmas at Wyndfell Hall. Then he remembered—and smiled in the fitful firelight. What a pity there wasn't some nice, simple, gentle girl for young Donnington! That was the sort of girl he, Panton, would have chosen for him. Miss Bubbles, so much was clear, rather despised the poor lad. She had implied as much in her clever, teasing, funny way, more than once.

And the thought of Bubbles unexpectedly brought up another image—that of James Tapster. Of the little party gathered together at Wyndfell Hall, Tapster was the one whom the doctor felt he really didn't like. He couldn't imagine why Varick had asked that disagreeable fellow here!

While the men were still in the dining-room, and Varick had gone out for a moment to look for some very special, new kind of cigarette which had come down from London a day or two before, Tapster had spoken very disagreeably of the richness of the French *chef's* cooking. He had seemed to think it an outrage that something of a special, very plain, nature had not been provided for him every day, and he had hinted that perhaps the doctor could suggest some antidote to all this richness! There was another reason, so Panton's sleepy mind told him, why he didn't like his sulky, plain fellow-guest. It became suddenly, unexpectedly, clear to him that Tapster was much taken with Miss Bubbles. The man had hardly taken his eyes off her during the whole of dinner, and it had been a disagreeable, appraising look—as if he couldn't quite make up his mind what she was worth! He told himself, while remembering that look, that Tapster was the kind of man who is always hesitating, always absorbed in some woman, and yet always afraid to try his luck—in the hope that if he waits, he may do better next time! Miss Bubbles was a hundred times too good for such a fellow, however rich the fellow might be....

Gradually Panton felt himself slipping off into that pleasant condition which immediately precedes a dreamless, healthful sleep.

And then, all at once, his senses became keenly alert, for a curious sound became audible in the darkening room. It was without doubt a sound created by some industrious mouse, or perhaps—though that idea was a less pleasant one—by a greedy rat. Swish, swish—swish—just like the rustling of a lady's silk dress!

Panton stretched out his right arm, and knocked the wall behind him sharply twice or thrice, and the sound stopped suddenly. But after a few minutes, just as he was dropping off, it began again. But it no longer startled him, as it had done the first time, and soon he was fast asleep.

It might have been a moment, it might have been an hour, later, when there came a sudden, urgent knocking at his door. He sat up in bed.

"Come in," he called out, now wide awake.

The door opened slowly—and there came through it a curious-looking figure. It was James Tapster, arrayed in a wonderful dressing-gown made of Persian shawls, and edged with fur. He held a candlestick in his hand, and the candle threw up a flickering light on his pallid, alarmed-looking face.

"Dr. Panton," he whispered, "I wish you'd come out here a moment."

And the doctor, cursing his bad luck, and feeling what he very seldom felt, thoroughly angry, said ungraciously: "What is the matter? Can't you tell me without my getting out of bed?"

Last night's excellent dinner, which couldn't have hurt any healthy man, had evidently upset the unhealthy millionaire.

"Can't you hear?" whispered Tapster. His teeth were, chattering; he certainly looked very ill.

"Hear! Hear what?"

Tapster held up his hand. And then, yes, the man sitting up in the big four-post bed did hear some very curious noises. It was as if furniture was being thrown violently about, and as if crockery was being smashed—but a very, very long way off.

This was certainly most extraordinary! He had done Tapster an injustice.

He jumped out of bed. "Wait a minute!" he exclaimed. "I'll get my dressing-gown, and we'll go and see what it's all about. What extraordinary sounds! Where on earth do they come from?"

"They come from the servants' quarters," said Tapster.

There came a sudden silence, and then an awful crash.

"How long have these noises gone on?" asked Panton.

He had put on his dressing-gown, and was now looking for his slippers.

"Oh, for a long time."

Tapster's hand was trembling, partly from excitement, partly from fear. "How d'you account for it?" he asked.

"One of the servants has gone mad drunk," replied Panton briefly. "That's what it is—without a doubt! We'd better go down and see what can be done."

And then, as there came the distant sounds of breaking glass, he exclaimed: "I wonder everyone hasn't woken up!"

"There is a heavy padded door between that part of the house and this. My room is on the other side, over what they call the school-room. I left the padded door open just now when I came through—in fact I fastened it back."

"That wasn't a very clever thing to do!"

The doctor did not speak pleasantly, but Tapster took no offence.

"I—I wanted someone to hear," he said humbly; "I felt so shut off through there."

"Still, there's no use in waking everybody else up," said Panton, in a businesslike tone.

He didn't look forward to the job which he thought lay before him; but, of course, it wasn't the first time he had been called in to help calm a man who had become violent under the influence of drink. "Go on," he said curtly. "Show me the way! I suppose there's a back staircase by which we can go down?"

He followed his guide along the broad corridor to a heavy green baize door. Stooping, he undid the hook which fastened the door back. It swung to, and, as it did so, there came a sudden, complete cessation of the noise.

"Hullo!" he said to himself, "that's odd."

The two men waited for what seemed to Panton a long time, but in reality it was less than five minutes.

"Would you like to come into my room for a few moments? I wish you would," said Mr. Tapster plaintively.

Unwillingly the doctor walked through into what was certainly a very pleasant, indeed a luxurious room. It was furnished in a more modern way than the other rooms at Wyndfell Hall. "There's a bath-room off this room. That's why Varick, who's a good-natured chap, gave it me. He knows I have a great fear of catching a chill," whispered Mr. Tapster.

"We'd better go down," said the doctor at last.

"D'you think so? But the noise has stopped, and, after all, it is no business of ours."

Dr. Panton did not tell the other what was really in his mind. This was that the man who had now become so curiously quiet might unwittingly have done a mischief to himself. All he said was: "I have a feeling that I ought to go down, at any rate."

The words had hardly left his lips before the noises began again, and, of course, from where the two men were now, they sounded far louder than they had done from the doctor's bed-room. Heavy furniture was undoubtedly being thrown about, and again there came those curious crashes, as if plates and dishes were being dashed against the wall and broken there in a thousand pieces.

"I say, this won't do!" Quickly he went towards the door, and as he reached the corridor he saw the swing door between the two parts of the house open, and Miss Farrow came through, looking her well-bred, composed self, and wearing, incidentally, a short, neat, becoming dressing-gown.

"I can't think what's happening!" she exclaimed. She looked from the one man to the other. "What *can* be happening downstairs?"

As Panton made no answer, Mr. Tapster replied for them both: "The doctor thinks one of the servants got drunk last night."

"Yes, that must be it, of course. I'll go down and see who it is," she said composedly.

But Dr. Panton broke in authoritatively: "No, indeed, Miss Farrow! If it's what I think it is, the fellow will probably be violent. You'd better let me go down alone and deal with him."

There had come again that extraordinary, sudden stillness.

"I think I'd rather come down with you," she said coolly.

All three started going down the narrow, steep wooden staircase which connected that portion of the upper floor with the many rambling offices of the old house.

Tapster and Blanche Farrow each held a candle, but Dr. Panton led the way; and soon they were treading the whitewashed passages, even their slippered feet making, in the now absolute stillness, what sounded like loud thuds on the stone floor.

"Listen!" said Blanche suddenly.

They all stood still, and there came a strange fluttering sound. It was as if a bird had got in through a window, and was trying to find a way out.

"D'you know the way to the kitchen? I think that the man must be in the kitchen, or probably the pantry," whispered the doctor to his hostess.

"I think it's this way."

Miss Farrow led them down a short passage to the right, and cautiously opened a door which led into the kitchen.

And then they all three uttered exclamations of amazement and of horror. Holding her candle high in her hand, their hostess was now lighting up a scene of extraordinary and of widespread disorder.

It was as if a tornado had whirled through the vast, low-ceilinged kitchen. Heavy tables lay on their sides and upside down, their legs in the air. Most of the crockery—fortunately, so Blanche said to herself, kitchen crockery—off the big dresser lay smashed in large and small pieces here, there, and everywhere. A large copper preserving-pan lay grotesquely sprawling on the well-scrubbed centre table, which was the one thing which had not been moved—probably because of its great weight. And yet—and yet it had been moved—for it was all askew! The man who did that, if, indeed, one man could alone have done all this mischief, must have been very, very strong—a Hercules!

The doctor took the candle from Miss Farrow's hand and walked in among the débris. "He must have gone through that door," he muttered.

Leaving her to be joined by the timorous James Tapster, he went boldly on across the big kitchen, and through a door which gave into what appeared to be a scullery. But here everything was in perfect order.

"Where can the man have gone?" he asked himself in astonishment.

Before him there rose a vision of the respectable old butler, and of the two tall, well-matched, but not physically strong-looking footmen. This must be the work of some man he had not yet seen? Of course there must be many men employed about such a place as was Wyndfell Hall.

He retraced his steps. "I think you and Mr. Tapster had better go upstairs again, and leave me to this," he said decidedly. "I'll have a thorough hunt through the place, and it'll probably take some time. Perhaps the man's taken refuge in the pantry. By the way, where do the servants sleep?"

"Oddly enough, they're none of them sleeping in the house," said Blanche quietly. "They're down at what are called 'the cottages.' You may have seen a row of pretty little buildings not very far from the gate giving on to the high road? Those cottages belong to Mr. Varick. They're quite comfortable, and we thought it best to put all the servants together there. When I say all the servants"—she corrected herself quickly—"the ladies' maids and Mr. Tapster's valet all sleep in the house. But Mr. Varick and I agreed that it would be better to put the whole of the temporary staff down together in the cottages."

"In that case I think it's very probable that the man, when he realized the mischief he'd done, bolted out of doors. However, I may as well have a look round."

"I'll come with you," said Blanche decidedly. She turned to Mr. Tapster: "I think you'd better go upstairs, and try and finish your night more comfortably."

She spoke quite graciously. Blanche was the one of the party who really tolerated Mr. Tapster—Blanche and Mr. Tapster's host.

"All right, I think I will. Though I feel rather a brute at leaving you to do the dirty work," he muttered.

He set off down the passage; and then, a few moments later, he had to call out and ask Miss Farrow to show him the way—he had lost himself!

It took a long time to search through the big commons of the ancient dwelling. There were innumerable little rooms now converted into store cupboards, larders, and so on. But everything was in perfect order—the kitchen alone being in that, as yet, inexplicable condition of wreckage.

But at last their barren quest was ended, and they came up the narrow staircase on much more cordial and kindly terms with one another than either would have thought possible some hours before. Then the doctor, with an "Allow me," pushed in front of Miss Farrow in order to open wide the heavy padded door. "I wonder that you heard anything through this!" he exclaimed.

She answered, "I was awakened by Mr. Tapster talking to you. Then, of course, I heard those appalling noises—for he had left the padded door open. I got up and, opening my own door, listened, after you had both gone through. When there came that final awful crash I felt I *must* go and see what had happened!"

CHAPTER XV

"Spirits? What absolute bosh! Miss Bubbles has been pulling your leg, Varick. And yet one would like to know who has been at the bottom of it all—whether, as you say the butler evidently believes, it is the *chef* himself, or, as the *chef* told you, one of the under-servants. In any case, I hope no one will suppose that that sort of thing can be owing to a supernatural agency."

"Yet John Wesley did so suppose when that sort of thing happened in the Wesley household," came in the quiet voice of Sir Lyon.

The three men—Dr. Panton, Sir Lyon, and Lionel Varick—were taking a walk along the high road. It was only eleven o'clock, but it seemed much later than that to two of them, for all the morning they had been busy. An hour of it had been taken up with a very close examination of the servants, especially of the respectable butler and of the French *chef*. They had both professed themselves, together and separately, as entirely unable to account for what had happened in the night. But still, it had been clear to the three who had taken part in the examination—Blanche Farrow, Varick, and the doctor—that the butler believed the *chef* to be responsible. "It's that Frenchman; they're tricky kind of fellows, ma'am," the man had said in a confidential aside. And, though the *chef* was less willing to speak, it was equally clear that he, on his side, put it down to one of the under-servants.

Then, quite at the end of the interrogation, they had all been startled by not only the *chef*, but the butler also, suddenly admitting that something very like what happened last night had happened twice before! But on the former occasions, though everything in the kitchen had been moved, including the heavy centre table, nothing had been broken. Still, it had taken the *chef* and his kitchen-maids two hours to put everything right. That had happened, so was now revealed, on the very morning after the party had just been gathered together. And then, again, four days ago.

Miss Burnaby, who had slept through everything, exclaimed, when the happenings of the night before were told her by Mr. Tapster, "The place seems bewitched! I shall never forget what happened yesterday afternoon to Helen." Turning to Dr. Panton, she continued: "My niece actually believes that she saw a ghost yesterday!"

Helen said sharply, "I thought nothing was to be said about that, Auntie."

Meanwhile the doctor stared at her, hardly believing the evidence of his own ears. "You thought you saw a ghost?" he said incredulously.

And Helen, turning away, answered: "I would so much rather not speak about it. I don't want even to think about it ever again!"

An hour later, as Panton and Sir Lyon stood outside the house waiting for Varick, the doctor said a word to the other man: "A most extraordinary thing happened here yesterday. Miss Brabazon apparently believes she saw a ghost."

"Did she tell you so herself?" asked Sir Lyon quietly.

"No, her aunt mentioned it, quite as if it was an ordinary incident. But I could see that it was true, for she was very much upset, and said she would rather not speak of it."

They had then been joined by their host, and when once through the gate, the doctor's first words had proved that his mind was still full of all that had happened in the night.

"Surely *you* don't put down what happened last night to a supernatural agency?"

He was addressing Sir Lyon, and though he spoke quite civilly, there was an under-current of sarcasm in his pleasant, confident voice.

"At one time I was very deeply interested in what I think one may call the whole range of psychic phenomena," replied Sir Lyon deliberately, "and I came to certain very definite conclusions—"

"And what," said Varick, with a touch of real eagerness, "were those conclusions?"

Till now he had not joined in the discussion.

"For one thing, I very soon made up my mind that a great deal of what occurs at every properly conducted séance can by no means be dismissed as 'all bosh,'" answered Sir Lyon.

"Do you consider that the séance which took place the first evening you were here was a properly conducted séance?" asked Varick slowly.

"Yes—as far as I was able to ascertain—it was. I felt convinced, for instance, that Laughing Water was a separate entity—that was why I asked her to pass me by. To me there is something indecent about an open séance. I have always felt that very strongly; and what happened that evening in the case of Mr. Burnaby of course confirmed my feeling."

Varick uttered under his breath an exclamation of incredulous amazement. "D'you mean that you believe there was a *spirit* present? It would take some time to do it, but I think I could *prove* that it was what I took it to be—thought-reading of quite an exceptional quality, joined to a clever piece of acting."

"You'd find it more difficult than you think to prove that," said Sir Lyon quietly. "I've been to too many séances to be able to accept that point of view. I feel sure that Miss Bubbles was what they call 'controlled' by a separate entity calling herself 'Laughing Water.' But if you ask me what sort of entity, then I cannot reply."

Panton turned on him: "Then you're a spiritualist?" he exclaimed. "Of course I was quite unaware of that fact when I spoke just now."

There was an underlying touch of scorn in his voice.

"No, I do not call myself a spiritualist. But still—yes, I accept the term, if by it you mean that I believe there is no natural explanation for certain of the phenomena we have seen, or heard of, in the last twenty-four hours."

He purposely did not allude to what had happened between tea and dinner in the hall last evening, but he felt certain that it was very present to Varick himself.

"I spoke just now of the curious occurrences in the Wesley household," he observed, turning to the young doctor. "That, of course, is the most famous case on record of the sort of thing which took place in the kitchen last night."

"But why," cried Varick, with a touch of excitement, "why should all these things happen just now at Wyndfell Hall? I know, of course, the story of the haunted room. But most old houses have one respectable ghost attached to them. I don't mind the ghost Pegler fancies she saw—but, good heavens, the place now seems full of tricksy spirits! Still, it's an odd fact that none of the servants, with the one exception of Miss Farrow's maid, have seen anything out of the way."

Here the doctor broke in: "That's easily accounted for!" he exclaimed. "I understand from Miss Farrow that her maid—a remarkable person without doubt—has held her tongue ever since she saw, or thought she saw, a ghost. But if the other servants knew everything we know, there'd be no holding them—there'd be no servants!"

"Of course, I admit that in the great majority of instances those who think they see what's commonly called a ghost probably see no ghost at all," said Sir Lyon thoughtfully. "They've heard that a ghost is there, and therefore they *think* they see it."

"Then," said Varick, turning on him, "you don't believe Pegler did see the ghost of Dame Grizel Fauncey?"

Sir Lyon smiled. "I daresay you'll think me very illogical, but in this one case I think Pegler *did* see what is commonly called a ghost. And I'll tell you why I think so."

Both men turned and looked at him fixedly, both in their several ways being much surprised by his words.

"I have discovered," said Sir Lyon in a rather singular tone, "that this woman Pegler saw nothing for the first few days she occupied the haunted room."

Panton stared at the speaker with an astonished expression. "What exactly do you mean to imply?" he asked.

Sir Lyon hesitated. He was, in some of his ways, very old-fashioned. It was not pleasant to him to bring a lady's name into a discussion. And yet he felt impelled to go on, for what had happened in the hall yesterday afternoon had moved and interested him as he had not thought to be interested and moved again.

"The woman saw nothing," he said, slowly and impressively, "till Miss Dunster arrived at Wyndfell Hall. I take that to mean that Miss Dunster is a very strong medium."

"A medium?" repeated the doctor scoffingly. "Who says medium surely says charlatan, Sir Lyon—not to say something worse than charlatan!"

Sir Lyon looked thoughtfully at the younger man. "I admit that often mediums are charlatans—or rather, they begin by being mediums pure and simple, and they end by being mediums *qua* charlatans. The temptations which lie in their way are terrible, especially if, as in the majority of cases, they make a living by their—their"—he hesitated—"their extraordinary, as yet misunderstood, and generally mishandled gift."

"Do you mean," asked Varick gravely, "that you believe Bubbles possesses the power of raising the dead?"

Sir Lyon did not answer at once, but at last he said firmly: "Either the dead, or some class of intermediate spirits who personate the human dead. Yes, Varick, that is exactly what I do mean."

All three men stopped in their now slow pacing. Dr. Panton felt too much surprised to speak.

Sir Lyon went on: "I think that Miss Bubbles' arrival at Wyndfell Hall made visible, and is still making visible, much that would otherwise remain unseen."

As he caught the look of incredulous amazement on the doctor's face, he repeated very deliberately: "That is my considered opinion. As I said just now, I have had a very considerable experience of psychic phenomena, and I realized, during that séance which was held the first evening I spent here, that this young lady possessed psychic gifts of a very extraordinary nature. There is no doubt at all, in my mind, that were she a professional medium, her fame would by now be world-wide."

Perhaps it was the derisive, incredulous look on the young medical man's face which stung him into adding: "If I understand rightly"—he turned to Varick—"something very like what I should call an impromptu materialization took place in the hall yesterday—is that not so?"

There was a pause. Twice Varick cleared his throat. Who had broken faith and told Sir Lyon what had happened? He supposed it to have been Miss Burnaby. "Though I was present," he said at last, "I, myself, saw absolutely nothing."

"I, too, have heard something of it!" exclaimed Dr. Panton, looking from one of his two now moved, embarrassed, and excited companions to the other. "And you were actually present when it happened, Varick?"

As the other remained silent, he turned to Sir Lyon. "What was it exactly Miss Brabazon thought she saw?"

Sir Lyon, after a glance at Varick's pale, set face, was sorry that he had mentioned the curious, painful occurrence; and, though he was a truthful man, he now told a deliberate lie. "I don't know what the apparition purported to be," he observed. And he saw, even as he was uttering the lying words, a look of intense relief come over Varick's face. "But to my mind Miss Brabazon evidently saw the rare phenomenon known as a materialization. Miss Bubbles was lying asleep in the confessional which is almost exactly opposite the door through which one enters the hall from the house side, thus the necessary conditions were present."

"I wish *I* had been present!" exclaimed the doctor. "Either I should have seen nothing, or, if I had seen anything, I should have managed to convince myself that what I saw was flesh and blood."

As neither of his two companions said anything in answer to that observation, Panton went on, speaking with more hesitation, but also with more seriousness than he had yet shown: "Do I understand you to mean, Sir

Lyon, that you credit our young fellow-guest with supernatural gifts denied to the common run of mortals?"

"I should not put it quite that way," answered Sir Lyon. "But yes, I suppose I must admit that I do credit Miss Bubbles with powers which no one as yet has been able to analyze or explain—though a great many more intelligent people than has ever been the case before, are trying to find a natural explanation."

"If that is so," asked the doctor, "why have you yourself given up such an extraordinarily important and valuable investigation?"

"Because," said Sir Lyon, "I consider my own personal investigations yielded a definite result."

"And that result—?"

"—was that what I prefer to call by the old term of occultism makes for evil rather than for good. Also, I became convinced that the practice of these arts has been, so to speak, put 'out of bounds'—I can think of no better expression—by whatever Power it be that rules our strange world."

He spoke earnestly and slowly, choosing his words with care.

"If your theory contains a true answer to the investigations which are now taking place," exclaimed the doctor, "there was a great deal to be said for those mediaeval folk who burnt sorcerers and witches! I suppose you would admit that they were right in their belief that by so doing they were getting rid of very dangerous, as well as unpleasant, elements from out of their midst?"

The speaker looked hard at Sir Lyon. Nothing, as he told himself, with some excitement, had ever astonished him, or taken him so aback, as was now doing this conversation with an intelligent, cultivated man who seemed to have broad and sane views on most things, but who was evidently as mad as a hatter on this one subject.

And then, before Sir Lyon had perchance made up his mind what to answer exactly, Varick's voice broke in: "Yes," he observed, smiling a little grimly, "that's the logical conclusion of your view, Dilsford. You can't get out of it! If a human being really possesses such dangerous powers, the sooner that human being is put out of the way the better."

"No, no! I don't agree!" Sir Lyon spoke with more energy than he had yet displayed. "Everything points to the fact that those unfortunate people—I mean the witches and sorcerers of the Middle Ages—could have been, and sometimes were, exorcised."

"Exorcised?" repeated Panton. He had never heard the word "exorcised" uttered aloud before, though he had, of course, come across it in books. "Do you mean driving out the devil by means of a religious ceremony?" he asked incredulously.

"Yes," said Sir Lyon, "I do exactly mean that. As you are probably aware, there is a form of exorcism still in common use. And if I were our host here, I should have Wyndfell Hall exorcised, preferably by a Roman Catholic priest, as soon as Miss Bubbles is safely off the premises."

The doctor again looked sharply at the speaker—but no, Sir Lyon evidently meant what he said; and even Varick seemed to be taking the suggestion seriously; for "That's not a bad idea," he muttered.

The three men walked on in silence for a few moments.

"It would be interesting to know," observed Sir Lyon suddenly, "what Miss Farrow conceives to be the truth as to her niece's peculiar gifts. I fancy, from something she told me the other day, that she hasn't the slightest belief in psychic phenomena, I wonder if she feels the same after what happened yesterday and last night?"

"I can tell you exactly what Miss Farrow thinks," interposed Varick. "I had a word or two with her about it all this morning, after we'd examined the servants in the white parlour."

"What *does* she think," asked Sir Lyon. He had always been interested in Blanche Farrow, and, in a way, he was fond of her.

"She thinks," said Varick, a little hesitatingly, "that Bubbles, in addition to her extraordinary thought-reading gift, has inherited from her Indian ancestress a power of collectively hypnotizing an audience—of making people see things that she wants them to see. That's rather awkwardly expressed, but it's the best I can do."

"I quite understand," broke in the doctor. "You mean the sort of power which certain Indian fakirs undoubtedly possess?"

"Yes," said Varick. "And, as I said just now Bubbles has got Indian blood in her veins. One of her ancestors actually did marry an Indian lady of high degree, and Bubbles is descended from one of the children of that marriage."

"I think that may account for the potency of her gift," said Sir Lyon thoughtfully, "though, of course, many Europeans have had, and now possess, these curious powers."

"But though, in a sense, spiritualism is no new thing, even those who believe in it admit that it has never led to anything," observed Varick musingly.

"Very rarely, I admit; but still, sometimes even a dream has contained a revelation of sorts. Thus it is on positive record that a dream revealed the truth as to what was called the Murder of the Red Barn."

"Can I take it that you do believe the dead return?" asked the doctor abruptly.

"I think," said Sir Lyon deliberately, "that certain of the dead desire ardently to return—not always from the best motives. As to whether they themselves are permitted to come back, or whether they are able to use other entities to carry out that purpose, I am still in doubt."

As he spoke he saw a curious change come over Lionel Varick's face. The rather set smile with which he had been listening to the discussion gave way to an odd expression of acute unease. But at this particular moment it was not Varick with whom Sir Lyon was concerned, but with the frank, eager, pleasant-faced, young doctor, in whose estimation, as he realized, he was falling further and further down with every word he uttered.

"To tell you the honest truth," he went on, "even in the days when I did little else than attend séances and have sittings with noted mediums, not only in this country but also on the Continent, I could never quite make up my mind whether the spirit with whom I was in communication was really the being he or she purported to be! There was a time," he spoke with some emotion, "when I would have given anything—certainly most willingly twenty years of my life—to be so absolutely convinced. But there it is," he sighed, and was himself surprised at the feeling of depression which came over him. "Even the most earnest investigation of the kind resolves itself always, after a while, into a kind of will-o'-the-wisp that leads no-whither."

"Not always," exclaimed Panton sharply. "Last year I had a patient who'd become insane owing to what I suppose you would call an investigation into psychic phenomena."

"And yet," said Sir Lyon rather sternly, "to your mind, Dr. Panton, a pursuit which you admit was capable of leading one unfortunate human being into insanity, is 'all bosh'!"

"Of course I could only go by what the poor lady's friends told me," Panton said uncomfortably. "She was not under my care long. But I need hardly tell you, Sir Lyon, that any obsession that takes hold of a human being may in time lead to insanity."

"I suppose that, according to your theory"—it was now Varick who was speaking, speaking rather lightly, twirling his stick about as he spoke—"I suppose," he repeated, "that, according to your theory, if Bubbles Dunster left Wyndfell Hall to-morrow, the spirits would cease from troubling, and we should be at rest?"

"No, that doesn't exactly follow. I once heard of a case which interested me very much. A house which had never been haunted before—as far as anyone knew—became so, following on the sojourn there of a professional medium, and it remained haunted for four years. Then, suddenly, all the psychic phenomena stopped."

"What a strange thing," said Panton, with an under-current of irony in his voice; "but doubtless the owner had had the house exorcised, as you call it?"

"No," said Sir Lyon thoughtfully. "No, the house had not been exorcised. As a matter of fact, the medium was killed in a railway accident."

They walked on, and fell to talking of indifferent things. But though Sir Lyon had at one time held many such conversations with sceptical or interested persons, this particular conversation will never be forgotten by him, owing to a strange occurrence which happened in the afternoon of that same day. But for two fortunate facts—the bravery of young Donnington, and the presence of a clever medical man—the pleasant comedy in which they were each and all playing an attractive part would have been transformed into a peculiarly painful tragedy.

CHAPTER XVI

While three members of the party had thus been walking and talking, the principal subject of their discussion, Bubbles Dunster, had gone through an exciting and unpleasant experience.

When starting out for a solitary walk to give Span a run, she saw, with annoyance, James Tapster following her, and to her acute discomfiture he managed to stammer out what was tantamount to an offer of marriage. Though, in a sense, she had certainly tried to attract him, she felt, all at once, miserably ashamed of her success. So much so, indeed, that she pretended at first not to understand what he meant. But at last she had to leave such pretence aside, and then it was she who surprised Mr. Tapster, for, "You must let me have time to think over the great honour you have done me," she said quietly. "If you want an answer now, it must be *no*."

He protested sulkily that of course he would give her as much time as she wanted, and then she observed, slyly, "I am sure that you yourself did not make up your mind to be married all in a minute, Mr. Tapster. You weighed the pros and cons very carefully, no doubt. So you must give me time to do so too."

Bubbles' measured words, the feeling that she was, so to speak, keeping him at arm's length, took the hapless Tapster aback, and frightened him a little. He had felt so sure that once he had made up his own mind she would eagerly say "Yes!" Often, during the last few days, he had told himself, with a kind of mirthless chuckle, that *he* was not going to be "caught"; but when, at last, he had made up his mind that Bubbles would make him, if not an ideal, then a very suitable, wife, it seemed strange indeed that she was not eager to "nail him." That she was not exactly eager to do so was apparent, even to him.

Calling Span sharply to her, the girl turned round, and began making her way towards the house again; finally she disappeared with Span in the direction of the servants' quarters.

James Tapster, walking on by himself, began to feel unaccountably frightened. He asked himself, uneasily, almost uttering the words aloud in his agitation, whether, after all, he had been "caught"; and whether Bubbles was only "making all this fuss" in order to "bring him to heel"? But two could play at that game. He toyed seriously, or so he believed, with the idea of ordering his motor and just "bolting"; but of course he did nothing of the kind. The more Bubbles hung back, the more he wanted her; her coldness stung him into something nearer ardour than he had ever felt.

And Bubbles? Bubbles felt annoyed, uneasy, even obscurely hurt. It often happens that an offer of marriage leaves a girl feeling lonely and oppressed. Deep in her heart she knew she would never, never, *never*, become Mrs. Tapster. On the other hand, she was aware that there were many people in the London set among whom she now lived and had her being, who would regard her as mad to refuse a man who, whatever his peculiarities, possessed enormous wealth. If only she could have had a tenth part of James Tapster's money without James Tapster, what a happy woman she would have been!

As it was, Bubbles told herself fretfully that she had no wish to be married. She was not yet tired of the kind of idle-busy life she led; it was an amusing and stimulating life; and though she had her dark hours, when nothing seemed worth while, up to the present time there had been much more sunshine than shadow. The girl was sufficiently clever and sensitive to realize her good fortune in the matter of Bill Donnington. Sometimes, deep in her heart, she told herself that when she had drunk her cup of pleasure, amusement, and excitement to the dregs—perhaps in ten years from now—she would at last reward Donnington's long faithful love and selfless devotion. And rather to her own surprise, during the half-hour which followed Tapster's uninspired proposal, Bubbles thought far more of Donnington than she did of the man who had just asked her to become his wife.

Sitting all alone in the hall, crouching down on a footstool close to the fire, for somehow she felt tired—tired, and exhausted—she made one definite resolution. She would give up, as far as she was able, the practice of those psychic arts which she knew those who loved her believed to involve a real danger to her general well-being. What had happened the afternoon before had frightened her. She had been entirely unconscious of the awful phenomena which had taken place, and she was becoming seriously alarmed at her own increasing power of piercing the veil which hangs between the seen and the unseen. What she had told Donnington during their talk in the old darkened church had been true: she often felt herself companioned by entities who boded ill, if not to herself, then to those about her. Since yesterday, also, there had hung heavily over her mind a premonition that she, personally, was in danger. Now she told herself that perhaps the peculiar, disturbing sensation had only been a forerunner of James Tapster's unexpected offer of marriage.

"What would you say to our all going out for a walk?" Luncheon was just over, and Varick was facing his guests. The only one missing was Dr. Panton, who had gone up to his room, saying he had some work to do.

"I'm afraid it must be very wet and slushy," said Blanche Farrow dubiously. It had snowed in the night, and now a thaw had set in.

She had an almost catlike dislike of wet or dirt; on the other hand, she was one of those people who are generally willing to put aside their own wishes in favour of what those about them wish to do; and she saw that for some reason or other Lionel Varick wanted this suggestion of his to be carried out.

"I can take you to a place," he exclaimed, "where I think we shall find it dry walking even to-day. It's a kind of causeway, or embankment"—he turned to Helen Brabazon—"which some people say was built by the Romans."

"I think a walk would be very nice," she agreed.

Helen did not look like her usual cheerful, composed self. The experience which had befallen her the day before still haunted her mind to the exclusion of everything else. Perhaps a good long walk would make her feel a different creature, and chase that awful image of Milly Varick in her grave-clothes from her brain.

And so in the end the whole party started off, with the exception of Miss Burnaby and Dr. Panton. Bubbles tried hard to get out of going on what she frankly said seemed to her "a stupid expedition," but Donnington had a theory that the open air would do her good, and as for Varick, he exclaimed in a good-humoured but very determined tone: "If *you* won't come, Bubbles, I give the whole thing up!" In a lower voice he added: "Naughty as you are, you're the life and soul of the party."

And thus it was to please Varick, rather than Donnington, that Bubbles started on what was to be to all those that took part in it a memorable walk.

Poor Donnington! The young man felt alarmed and perplexed concerning Bubbles' general condition. He knew something that had shocked and startled her had happened the day before, but when he had tried to find out what it was, she had snubbed him.

Like so many people wiser and cleverer than himself, Donnington found it impossible to make up his mind concerning psychic phenomena. When kneeling by Bubbles' side in the dimly-lit church he had accepted, almost without question, her own explanation of her strange and sinister gift, but by now he had argued himself out of the belief that such things could be in our work-a-day world.

There was someone else of the party who was also giving a great deal of anxious thought to Bubbles' uncanny powers. Blanche Farrow, like Helen Brabazon, could not banish from her mind the experience which had befallen her in the hall last evening. Every time she looked at Lionel Varick there rose before her that terrible vision of the two unquiet spirits who had stood, sentinel-wise, on either side of him....

Again and again in the long watches of a wakeful night, Blanche had assured herself that what she had seen was no more real than is a vivid dream. She had further told herself, taking comfort in the telling, that the power possessed by Bubbles was now understood, and accounted for, by those learned men who make a scientific study of hypnotism. Yet, try as she would, she could not banish from her mind and from her memory the unnerving experience.

They were crossing the moat bridge when there came a shout from the house. They all stopped, to be joined, a minute later, by Dr. Panton. "It's an extraordinary thing," he exclaimed, "I fully intended to give up this afternoon to writing, but somehow I suddenly felt as if I *must* look out of the window! You all looked so merry and bright that I have thrown my work to the winds, and here I am, coming with you."

"I was rather counting on you to keep Miss Burnaby company."

Varick's tone was not very pleasant, and Panton for a moment regretted he had come; but as he had passed through the hall he had seen the old lady nodding over a book, and he was well aware that had he stayed indoors, it would have been to work up in his own room.

Bill Donnington suddenly discovered that Bubbles was wearing absurd, high-heeled, London walking shoes. "Go back and put on something more sensible," he said shortly; "I'll wait for you—we'll soon pick up the others."

But Bubbles answered sullenly: "My heavy walking boots got wet this morning."

Even as she spoke, she stood irresolute. Why not make her unsuitable foot-gear an excuse for staying at home? She told herself discontentedly that she hated the thought of this walk. But Donnington would have none of it. "Never mind," he said firmly, "you can change your shoes and stockings the minute you come in."

Bubbles submitted with an ill grace, and after the whole party were clear of the islet on which stood Wyndfell Hall, she refused pettishly to walk anywhere near him. She hung behind, even rejecting the company of James Tapster, to whom, however, she was for the most part fitfully gracious; and when, at length, the whole party were sorting themselves into couples, she found herself walking last with Varick, the others being all in front of them.

Varick was disagreeably conscious that with his present companion his charm of manner—that something which drew to him all women and most men—availed him not at all. Still, to-day, he was determined to get on good terms with Bubbles. So well did he succeed that at last something impelled her to say rather penitently: "I want to tell you that what happened yesterday afternoon was not my fault, and that I'm very sorry it happened, Lionel."

Donnington, who was just in front, heard Varick answer, lightly: "You can hardly expect me to believe that, Bubbles! But I would give a good deal to know how you do it?" As she made no answer, he went on: "It's a remarkable thing to be able to will people into seeing something which is not there!"

Donnington strained his ears to hear the low, defiant answer: "I give you my word of honour that I knew nothing, *nothing*, till you came and woke me up!"

What was it that had happened yesterday? The young man felt almost unbearably anxious to know. All he knew was that it had greatly affected, surprised, and disturbed those who had been there.

Suddenly Varick's tones floated again towards the listener: "I'll take your word for it, my dear girl. After all, it's all in the picture. What with our ghosts, our practical jokes, and so on, we're having a regular old-fashioned Christmas! Still, when I heard Miss Brabazon give that dreadful cry, I did feel that one could have too much of a good thing."

Even Donnington detected the false *bonhomie* in Varick's voice.

Bubbles laughed back, not very pleasantly. "I did you a good turn when I got rid of Mr. Burnaby. I thoroughly scared him! Your nice young doctor's a very good exchange for that disagreeable old man."

"Yes, and Panton's a very clever fellow, as well as one of the best," said Varick heartily. "I am glad he managed to get out this afternoon."

"I thought you didn't want him to come," said Bubbles sharply.

"I knew he had some important work to finish."

Varick felt annoyed. Somehow Bubbles always seemed to be convicting him of insincerity.

They were now close to the embankment, of which their host had drawn an attractive picture. But Blanche looked up at it with some dismay. The scene under the wintry sky looked wild and singularly dreary. Many of the fields were under water, and stretches of the marshy land were still covered with wide streaks of snow. Across the now sullen-looking, cloudy sky there moved a long processional flight of cawing rooks.

The whole party closed up for a few moments. Then they walked up the steps which led to the high causeway along which Varick had promised his friends a dry walk. Sure enough, once they had reached the top, they found that the melting snow had already drained off the narrow brick path. Even so, it was slippery walking, and for her part Blanche Farrow felt sorry that they had left the muddy road.

The party soon separated into couples again, Miss Farrow and Dr. Panton leading, while Bubbles and Varick came last, behind all the others. "We must look just like the animals going into the ark," said the girl disagreeably.

Whatever the others might be feeling, Dr. Panton was thoroughly enjoying this muddy walk. He found it singularly pleasant to be with agreeable, well-bred people, who were all so fit that not one of them, with the exception of James Tapster, had even asked him a question bearing on health—or the lack of it. It had been pleasant, too, to meet Miss Brabazon again, for they had become friends, rather than acquaintances, over poor Mrs. Varick's deathbed.

Behind Dr. Panton and Miss Farrow—for the brick path which formed the crest of the embankment only held two walkers comfortably—were the least well-assorted couple of the party, Bill Donnington and James Tapster. They just plodded along side by side, now and again exchanging a laconic word or two. Tapster's half-formed hope had been that he would walk with Bubbles this afternoon; but, when it came to the point, he had made no real effort to secure her company.

The unfortunate man was feeling very nervous and uneasy—afraid lest he had been too precipitate in his wooing, for Bubbles frightened as well as fascinated him. Even he half realized that, as her husband, he would be tolerated rather than welcomed in a world of which he was anxious to form part, though in his heart he at once despised and feared its denizens.

At times he was even tempted to wish that she had said "No" at once— and that although he knew that he would have been very surprised and disappointed had she done so. On the whole he thought that after a period of maidenly hesitation she would say "Yes"; and, having inherited from an acquisitive father a positive, concrete kind of mind, as he trudged along he began ruminating over the question of Bubbles' marriage settlements. On one thing he was determined. Nothing should induce him so to arrange matters that in the event of his death Bubbles should be able to dower some worthless fortune-hunter with his, Tapster's, wealth! He felt certain that her father's solicitors would try and arrange that this might come to pass— "lawyers are such cunning devils"—and he grew purple with rage at the thought.

How surprised Donnington would have been could he have looked into his dull companion's mind!

In addition to Dr. Panton, two other people were really enjoying this uncomfortable walk, for Helen Brabazon and Sir Lyon Dilsford had plenty to say to one another. It was very seldom that Sir Lyon found a young woman interested in the subjects he himself had most at heart. He found it a curiously pleasant experience to answer her eager, ignorant questions on sociological and political subjects. It was clear that Miss Brabazon only regarded herself as the trustee of her vast wealth, and this touched her companion very much. Also, what had happened yesterday—that sudden, intimate confession of what had taken place in the hall—had made their relations to one another much closer. But neither of them had alluded to it again.

As for Lionel Varick and Bubbles Dunster, they were now lagging some way behind the others. More than once the girl suggested that she should slip away and go back to Wyndfell Hall alone, but her host would not hear of it. He declared good-humouredly that soon they would all be homeward bound; so, apathetically, Bubbles walked on, her feet and her head aching.

The old Roman embankment now formed part of the works connected with a big reservoir, and at last the walkers reached a kind of platform from whence they could see, stretching out to their right, a wide, triangular-shaped piece of water.

Blanche Farrow was for turning back; but Helen Brabazon, Sir Lyon, and Varick were all for going on, the more so that Varick declared that at a cottage which formed the apex of the reservoir they would be able to get some tea. So off they started again, in the same order as before, to find, however, that the narrow brick-way, instead of being drier—as one would have expected it to be above the water—was more slushy and slippery than had been the path running along the top of the older part of the embankment. Yet the steep bank leading down to the sullen, half-frozen surface of the reservoir had been cleared of the grass and bushes which covered the slopes of the rest of the causeway.

They had all been walking on again for some minutes when Donnington turned round. "Take care, Bubbles! It's very slippery just here."

"I'm all right," she called back pettishly. "Mind your own business, Bill. I wish you wouldn't keep looking round!"

Donnington saw Varick put out his right hand and grasp the girl's arm firmly; but even so it struck him that they were both walking too near the edge on the side to the water. Still, he didn't feel he could say any more, and so he turned away, and again began trudging along by the silent Tapster's side.

For a while nothing happened, and then all at once there occurred something which Donnington will never recall—and that however long he may live—without a sensation of unreasoning, retrospective horror welling up within him.

And yet it was only the sound—the almost stuffless sound—of a splash! It was as if a lump of earth, becoming detached from the wet bank, had rolled over into the deep water.

At the same moment, or a fraction of a moment later, Varick laughed aloud; it was a discordant laugh, evidently at something Bubbles had just said, for Donnington heard the words, "Really, Bubbles!" uttered in a loud, remonstrating, and yet jovial voice.

And then, all at once, some instinct caused the young man to wheel sharply round, to see, a long way back from the others, Varick standing solitary on the brick path.

His companion had vanished. It was as if the earth had swallowed her up.

"Where's Bubbles?" shouted Donnington.

But Varick, still standing in the middle of the path, did not look as if he heard Donnington's question. The young man set off running towards him.

"What's happened?" he cried fiercely. "Where's Bubbles, Varick?"

Varick was ashen; and he looked dazed—utterly unlike his usual collected self.

"She stumbled—and went over the side of the embankment. She's in the water, down there," he said at last, in a hoarse, stifled voice.

Donnington turned quickly, and stared down into the grey water. He could see nothing—nothing! He threw off his coat.

"Was it just here?"

He looked at Varick with a feeling of anguished exasperation; it was as if the horror and the shock had congealed the man's mental faculties.

Suddenly Varick roused himself.

"Can you swim?" He gripped Donnington strongly by the arm. "If not, it's—it's no good your going in—you'd only drown too."

Donnington wrenched himself free from the other's hold, and, rushing down the bank, threw himself into the icy cold water....

Suddenly he saw, a long way off, a small, shapeless, mass rising ... he swam towards it, and then he gave a sobbing gasp of relief. It was Bubbles ... Bubbles already unconscious; but of that he was vaguely glad, knowing that it would much simplify his task.

Very soon, although he was quite unaware of it, the affrighted, startled little crowd of people gathered together just above the place where he was painfully, slowly, swimming about, looking for a spot where he could try and effect a landing with his now heavy, inert burden.

Dr. Panton threw himself down flat across the path and held out a walking stick over the slippery mud bank, but the stick was hopelessly, grotesquely out of Donnington's reach.

All at once Blanche Farrow detached herself from the others and began running towards the cottage which formed the apex of the reservoir. "I'm going for a rope," she called out. "I'll be back in three or four minutes." But, thanks to Dr. Panton's ingenuity, the man in the water had not to wait even so short a time as that.

"Have any of you a good long scarf?" asked the doctor, and then, quite eagerly for him, James Tapster produced a wonderful scarf—the sort of scarf a millionaire would wear, so came the whimsical thought to Sir Lyon. It was wide and very long, made of the finest knitted silk. When firmly tied to the handle of the walking stick, the floating end of the scarf was within reach of Donnington. With its help he even managed to secure a foothold on the narrow one-brick ledge which terminated the deep underwater wall of the reservoir.

The doctor called down to him with some urgency: "I wish you could manage to hoist her up, Donnington. *Time* is of the utmost importance in these cases!"

But Donnington, try as he might, was too spent to obey; and it seemed an eternity to them all before Blanche Farrow reappeared, helping an old man to drag a short ladder along the muddy path.

And then, at last, after many weary, fruitless efforts, the inert, sodden mass which had so lately been poor little Bubbles Dunster was pushed and hoisted up the slippery bank, and stretched out on to the narrow brick way.

Mr. Tapster, who had shown much more agitation and feeling than any of those present would have credited him with, had taken off his big loose coat and laid it on the ground, and at once Varick had followed his example. But as Bubbles lay there, in the dreadful immobility of utter unconsciousness, both Blanche Farrow and Helen Brabazon believed her to be dead.

A tragic, fearfully anxious time of suspense followed. Blanche looked on, with steady, dry eyes, but Helen, after a very little while, turned away and hid her face in her hands, sobbing, while the doctor was engaged in the painful process of trying to bring the apparently drowned girl to life. More than once Blanche felt tempted to implore him to leave off those terribly arduous efforts of his. It seemed to her so—so horrible, almost degrading, that Bubbles' delicate little body should be used like that.

Everyone was too concerned over Bubbles to trouble about her rescuer. But all at once Varick exclaimed: "We don't want you down with rheumatic fever. I'll just march you back to the house, my boy!"

"Not as long as she's here," muttered Donnington, his teeth chattering. "I'm all right; it doesn't matter about me."

He alone of the people gathered there believed that Dr. Panton's perseverance would be rewarded, and that Bubbles would come back to life. It did not seem to him possible that that which he had saved, and which he so loved and cherished, could die. Though he was beginning to feel the reaction of all he had gone through, his mind was working clearly, and he was praying—praying consciously, in an agony of supplication.

And at last, with a sensation of relief which brought the tears starting to his eyes, Dr. Panton saw that his efforts were to be successful; Bubbles, after a little choking gasp, gave a long, fluttering sigh....

It was then that the doctor had to thank Sir Lyon and Helen Brabazon. One of them, or both of them together, had thought of going back to the house and of getting an invalid chair which Helen remembered having seen in a corner of one of the rooms when she had been shown over the house by her host.

Even so, it was a very melancholy little procession which followed the two men carrying the chair on which Bubbles now lay in apathetic silence.

But everything comes to an end at last, and, after having seen Bubbles put to bed, Dr. Panton turned his attention to Donnington, and he did not leave his second patient till the young man felt, if still shivery and queer, fairly comfortable in bed. Then the doctor went down to find the other three men in the dining-room, having hot drinks.

Of the three Varick and Sir Lyon showed on their faces traces of the emotion and anxiety which they had been through; but James Tapster looked his normal, phlegmatic self.

"I wonder what exactly happened?" exclaimed Panton at last. "I suppose the whole thing was owing to these high-heeled shoes which women *will* wear."

Varick nodded, and, as he saw that Panton expected him to say something, he muttered: "Yes, it must have been something of the kind that made her trip."

"It was a near thing," went on the doctor thoughtfully. "She was very far gone when we got her out at last. I don't mind admitting now that, when I began, I had hardly any hope of being able to bring her round."

He waited a moment and then added, as if to himself: "In fact, there came a time when I would have left off, discouraged, but for the look on that boy's face."

"What boy?" asked Tapster, surprised.

"Donnington, of course! I felt I must bring her back to life for his sake."

James Tapster opened his mouth. Then he shut it again. He told himself that it would, of course, have been very disappointing for Donnington to have plunged into that icy water all for nothing, as it were.

The four men remained silent for awhile, and then Varick said slowly: "She can't have been in the water more than a minute before Donnington was in after her—for of course I gave the alarm at once."

Sir Lyon looked at him quickly. "I thought Donnington turned round and missed her?"

"Donnington must have heard me call out." Varick was lighting a cigarette, and Sir Lyon saw that his hand shook; "and yet when I saw her roll down the bank I was so paralyzed with horror that my voice seemed to go."

He looked appealingly at his friend Panton.

"Yes, I can well understand that," said the doctor feelingly. "I have known shock close the throat absolutely." He added: "Did you see her sink and rise again twice before Donnington got at her, Varick? I have always wondered whether drowning people always come up three times—or if it's only an old wives' tale."

"Yes, no, I can't remember—"

Varick put his hand over his eyes, as if trying to shut out some dreadful sight. Then he groped his way to a chair, and sat down heavily.

"I say, Varick, I *am* sorry."

Dr. Panton looked really concerned. "We've been thinking so much of Miss Bubbles and of her rescuer that we have forgotten you!" he exclaimed.

Their host leant forward; he buried his face in his hands. "I shall never forget it—never," he muttered brokenly. "The horror that seized me—the awful feeling that I could do nothing—nothing! I felt so absolutely distraught that I seemed to see *myself*, not Bubbles, floating down there—on the surface of the water."

He looked up, and they were all, even Tapster, painfully impressed by his look of retrospective horror. Dr. Panton told himself that Lionel Varick was an even more sensitive man than he had hitherto known him to be.

CHAPTER XVII

Dinner was to be half an hour later than usual, and Dr. Panton, as he went off to his comfortable, warm room, felt pleasantly, healthily tired.

He had gone in to see his patients for a moment on his way upstairs, and they were both going on well. Bubbles was beginning to look her own queer, elfish little self again. She was curiously apathetic, as people so often are after any kind of shock, but it was clear that there were to be no bad after-effects of the accident. As for Donnington, the young man declared that he felt quite all right, and he was even anxious to get up for dinner. But that, of course, could not be allowed.

"All's well that ends well," muttered the doctor, as he threw himself for a moment into a chair drawn up invitingly before the fire.

He did go on to tell himself, however, that he now felt a little concerned over Lionel Varick. Varick now looked far more really ill than did either Bubbles or Bill Donnington.

The doctor recalled a certain terrible day, rather over a year ago, when Varick had broken down utterly! It was the afternoon that poor Milly was being put into her coffin; and, by sheer good luck he, Panton, happened to call in. He had found Varick sitting alone, looking very desolate, in the dining-room of the commonplace little villa, while from overhead there came the sounds of heavy feet moving this way and that.

All at once there had come a loud knock at the front door, and Varick, starting up, had uttered a fearful cry. Then, sitting down again, he had begun trembling, as if he had the ague. He, Panton, had been so concerned at the poor fellow's condition that he had insisted, there and then, on taking him along to his own house, and he had kept him there as his guest till the day of Mrs. Varick's funeral.

As these memories came crowding on him, the door of his room opened quietly, and the man who was filling his mind walked in.

Varick was already dressed for dinner, and, not for the first time, the doctor told himself what a distinguished-looking man his friend and host was.

"Panton," said Varick abruptly, "I have something on my mind."

The doctor looked up, surprised. "What is it, my dear fellow?" he asked kindly.

"I can't help thinking that in some inexplicable way I pushed Bubbles Dunster over the edge of that embankment. Has she said anything to you about it?"

Dr. Panton got up and came over to the speaker. He put his hand heavily on Varick's shoulder, and almost forced him down into the chair from which he had himself risen.

"Look here," he exclaimed, "this won't do at all! Pull yourself together, man—you mustn't get such fancies into your head. That way madness lies. Still, you may as well try and get it off your chest once for all. Tell me exactly what *did* happen? Begin at the beginning—"

As Varick remained silent, the doctor went on, encouragingly: "I will start you by reminding you that Miss Bubbles was wearing the most absurd high-heeled shoes. Young Donnington spoke to her about them, and that drew my attention to her feet as we came out of the gate. She even tripped when we were just past the bridge. Do you remember that?"

"No, I didn't notice her at all."

"Well, tell me exactly what happened just before she fell over the edge of the embankment?"

"I don't know that there's very much to tell." Varick was now staring into the fire, but at last he began in a strained, tired voice:

"Donnington had just shouted out that we were walking rather too near to the edge, and so I took hold of her arm. But you know what Bubbles is like? She's a queer kind of girl, and she tried to wrench herself free. Then I gripped a little harder and—well, I don't know exactly what did happen! I suppose her foot turned, for I suddenly felt her weight full on me, and then, and then—"

"Yes," said Dr. Panton soothingly, "I know exactly what happened. You instinctively straightened yourself to try to put her on her feet again, but she'd already lost her balance—"

"I suppose that's what did happen," said Varick in a low voice.

"—And her foot turning again, she rolled down the steep embankment," concluded the doctor firmly. "You did nothing, my dear chap, absolutely nothing, to bring the accident about! Put that idea, once and for all, out of your mind."

"I would," said Varick painfully, "I would, but that I'm afraid—in fact, I feel sure—that she thinks I pushed her in. She turned the most awful look on me, Panton, as she fell over the edge. I shall never forget it."

"That look had nothing to do with you," said the doctor decidedly. "It was simply the terrified look of a human being on the brink of a frightful death."

"You're a good friend," muttered Varick, getting up. "I'll leave you to dress now."

"Wait a moment!" exclaimed Panton; "there's one thing about Miss Bubbles' accident which does trouble me, I admit. It puzzled me at the time; and I can see it is puzzling young Donnington too."

Varick, who was already at the door, stayed his steps and turned round.

There had come back into his face the strained look which had softened away while he listened to his friend's sensible remarks. "Yes," he said impatiently, "yes, Panton? What is it that puzzles you?"

"I wish I knew exactly how long Miss Bubbles was in the water. She was very, very far gone when that boy managed to clutch hold of her. Did you see her go down again, and come up again twice? Forgive me, my dear fellow, I'm afraid I'm distressing you."

"You asked me that downstairs," said Varick, "and I told you then that—that I didn't know."

"I thought," said Dr. Panton, "that you remembered so clearly all that had happened—by what you said just now."

"Yes, up to the moment when she fell in, I remember everything. But once she was in the water everything became blurred. All I can say is that it seemed as if hours drifted by before I saw you all come running up towards me—"

"Come, come," said Panton, a trifle impatiently. "As a matter of fact it can't have been more than three minutes. Still, it was long enough for the girl to go as near the Great Divide, as a friend of mine calls it, as I've ever known a human being go."

"I suppose," said Varick slowly, "that if you hadn't been there Bubbles would now be dead?"

"Well, yes, I'm afraid that's true," said the doctor simply. "I should have expected that clever, intelligent Miss Farrow, to say nothing of Miss Brabazon, to know something about First Aid. But neither of them know anything! The only person who was of the slightest use was young Donnington; and I suspect—" he smiled broadly.

"What do you suspect?" asked Varick rather quickly.

"Well, I suspect that he's in love with Miss Bubbles."

"Of course he is." Varick's contemptuous tone jarred a little on Panton. "But Bubbles intends to become Mrs. Tapster."

"I should be sorry to think that!"

"Why sorry? The modern young woman—and Bubbles is a very modern young woman—knows the value of money," said Varick dryly.

He waited a moment. "I'll leave you now, Panton, and I'll see that the dinner-bell isn't rung till you're quite ready."

"All right. I won't be ten minutes—"

But Varick lingered by the door. "Panton," he exclaimed, "you've been a good friend to me! I want to tell you that I shall never forget it. As long as there's breath in my body I shall be grateful to you."

As the doctor dressed he told himself again that Varick had never really recovered from the strain of his wife's long illness. Under that rather exceptionally calm, steadfast-looking exterior, the man was extraordinarily sensitive. How upset, for instance, Varick had been about Miss Pigchalke's crazy advertisement. He, Panton, had felt quite sorry that he had said anything about it.

While putting on his tie, he told himself that what the dear fellow wanted now was a good, sensible second wife. And then, as he formulated that thought to himself, the young man—for he was still quite a young man—stopped what he was doing, and rubbed his hands joyfully. Why, of course! What a fool he had been never to think of it before—though to be sure it would really have been almost indecent to have thought of it before. Helen Brabazon? The very woman for Lionel Varick! Such a marriage would be the making of his highly-strung, fine-natured friend.

As he hurriedly finished dressing, Panton plumed himself on his cleverness. With all his heart he hoped the day would come when he would be able to say to Varick: "Ages before *you* thought of her, old chap, *I* selected Miss Brabazon as your future bride!" He hoped, uneasily, that Sir Lyon was not seriously in the running. But he had noticed that Sir Lyon and Miss Brabazon seemed to have a good deal to say to one another. Women, so he told himself ruefully, like to be "My lady." But she was certainly fond of Varick—she had been fond of him (of course, only as a woman may be of a friend's husband) during those sad weeks at Redsands.

As the doctor came out of his room he decided to go in for a moment and see Bubbles Dunster. Somehow he did not feel quite easy about her. He wondered, uncomfortably, if there could be anything in Varick's painful suspicion. After her aunt and Helen Brabazon between them had put her to bed, and he had come in, alone, to see how she was, she had said abruptly: "I wonder if it's true that doctors can keep a secret better than most men?" And when he had made some joking answer, she had asked, in a very serious tone: "You're a great friend of Lionel Varick, eh?" He had answered: "Men don't vow eternal friendships in the way I'm told young ladies do; but, yes, I hope I am a great friend of Lionel Varick's. I've a high opinion of him, Miss Bubbles, and I've seen him under circumstances that test a man."

She had looked at him fixedly while he said these words, and then she had opened and shut her eyes in a very odd way. He now asked himself if it was probable—possible—conceivable—that she blamed Varick for her accident? He, Varick, evidently thought so.

And then, as he walked along the darkened corridor, there came over Dr. Panton a most extraordinary feeling—*a feeling that he was not alone.*

He stayed his steps, and listened intently. But the only sound he heard was the ticking of a clock. He walked on, and all at once there came a word repeated twice, quite distinctly, almost as if in his ear. It was a disagreeable, an offensive word—a word, or rather an appellation, which the clever young doctor had not heard applied to himself for a good many years. For, twice over, was the word "Fool!" repeated in a mocking voice, a voice to whose owner he could not at the moment put a name, and yet which seemed vaguely familiar.

Then he remembered. Why, of course, it was the voice of that crazy, unpleasant old woman who had called on him last spring! But how had Miss Pigchalke found her way into Wyndfell Hall? And where on earth was she?

He looked round him, this way and that; and his eyes, by now accustomed to the dim light thrown by a hanging lamp, saw everything quite distinctly. He was certainly alone in the corridor now. But Miss Pigchalke had as certainly been there a moment ago. He wondered if she could have hidden herself in a huge oak chest which stood to his right? Nay, there she could not be, for he remembered having been shown that it was full of eighteenth-century gala gowns.

And while he was looking about him, feeling utterly perplexed and bewildered, through a door which was ajar there suddenly passed out Lionel Varick.

"Is anyone in there?" asked the doctor sharply.

Varick started violently. "You did startle me!" he exclaimed. "No, there's no one in there—I came up to look for a book. But as I told them to delay dinner yet a little longer, would you mind if we went in and saw Bubbles together on our way downstairs? I feel I should rather like to get my first interview with her over—and with you there."

"I don't see why you shouldn't." But there was a doubtful ring in Dr. Panton's voice. He would, as a matter of fact, have very much preferred that Varick should not see the girl to-night, especially if there was the slightest truth in the other's suspicion that Bubbles believed him to have been in any way instrumental, however accidentally, in making her fall into the water.

His mind worked quickly, as minds are apt to work when faced with that sort of problem, and he decided that on the whole he might as well let Varick do as he wished.

"You'd better not say very much to her. Just say you hope she's feeling all right by now—or something of that sort."

But when they came to the closed door of the girl's room he turned and said: "I'll just go in and prepare her for your visit—if you don't mind?"

Bubbles was lying straight down in bed, for, at her own request, the bolster had been taken away. Her head was only just raised up on the pillow. By the light of the one candle he could see her slender form outlined under the bed-clothes. Her eyes were closed, her features pinched and worn. There was something almost deathly in the look of her little face.

He wondered if she was asleep—if so, it would be rather a relief to him to go outside the door and tell Varick that she mustn't be disturbed. But all at once she opened her eyes widely, and there even came the quiver of a smile over her face.

"Doctor?" she said plaintively. "Doctor, come nearer, I want to ask you a question."

"Yes?" he said. "What is it, Miss Bubbles?"

"I want to ask you," she said dreamily, "why you brought me back? I was beginning to feel so much at home in the grey world. There were such kind people there, waiting to welcome me. Only one friend I felt sad to leave behind----"

"Tut-tut!" he said, a little startled. "You were never anywhere near leaving us, Miss Bubbles."

"I know I was, and you know it, too. But you called me back. Confess that you did!"

"I'll confess nothing of the sort," he answered a little shortly.

There was a little pause, and then he went on, "There's someone outside the door who wants to see you; someone who's feeling most awfully miserable about you."

A look of unease and of anxiety came over her face. "D'you mean Mr. Tapster?" she said hesitatingly.

"Good heavens, no!" He was surprised, and a little disgusted. "Can't you guess who it is?"

He saw the look in her face grow to shrinking fear. "I can't guess at all," she said weakly. "You won't allow Bill to get up—I know that because he sent me a message. Bill's the only person I want to see."

"He'll come soon enough," said Dr. Panton, smiling.

"It was really Bill who saved me," she went on, as if speaking to herself.

"Of course it was Bill!" he spoke now with hearty assent. "You've a splendid friend in that young man, Miss Bubbles, and I hope you're properly grateful to him?"

"I think I am," she said slowly. "I'm trying to be."

"And the other friend who wants to see you—may he come in for a minute?"

"The other friend? Do you mean Sir Lyon?"

"No, no—of course not!" He spoke with a touch of impatience now.

"Mr. Tapster," said Bubbles, nervously flying off at a tangent, "wants me to marry him, Dr. Panton. He asked me—was it yesterday morning, or this morning?" She knitted her brows. "Of course, I had to help him out. The moment he'd said it, he began to hope that I'd say 'No'—so I thought I'd punish him, by leaving him in suspense a bit."

"He was very distressed at your accident," said the doctor rather stiffly. Bubbles' queer confidence had startled him.

"Most men only really want what they feel is out of their reach," she whispered. "When he thought me gone, he wanted me back again. He's like that. He'll make a much nicer widower than he will a husband!"

She looked up and smiled, but he felt as if she was keeping him at arm's length.

"It's Mr. Varick who's outside the door and who wants to come in and see you," he said suddenly, in a matter-of-fact voice.

Bubbles turned her head away quickly. "Not to-night, doctor; I'm too tired." She spoke very decidedly, and in a stronger voice than she had yet used. "I'd rather wait till I get up before seeing Mr. Varick."

"He only wants to come in for a minute—do see him."

Dr. Panton spoke persuasively, but he told himself that Varick was right—Bubbles *had* got that extraordinary, horrible notion into her head. "He's very much upset," he went on, "he thinks that unconsciously he may have given you some kind of push over the edge of the embankment."

He saw her face change. It crimsoned darkly.

"Has he told you that?" she muttered.

"Yes, he has; and he's awfully upset about it, Miss Bubbles."

"I suppose I had better see him. I shall have to see him some time."

She said the words between her teeth, and, making an effort, she sat up in bed.

Dr. Panton went to the door, and opened it.

"Come in," he called out; "but don't stay long, Varick. Miss Bubbles is very tired to-night."

Varick came in slowly and advanced with curiously hesitating, nervous steps, towards the bed. "Well, Bubbles," he exclaimed, "I'm glad you're no worse for your ducking!"

She looked at him fixedly, but said nothing. Dr. Panton began to feel desperately uncomfortable.

"I hope you'll be quite all right to-morrow," went on Varick.

"I think I shall, thank you."

Bubbles seemed to be looking beyond her visitor—not at him. She seemed to be gazing at something at the other end of the room.

"You've brought someone in with you," she said suddenly. There was a curious tone—almost a tone of exultation—in her voice. "Who is it?" she asked imperiously. "Tell me who it is—Lionel."

She very rarely called Varick "Lionel."

He wheeled round with a startled look. "There's no one here," he answered, "but Dr. Panton and myself."

"Oh yes, there is." Bubbles spoke very positively. "There's a woman here. I can see her quite distinctly in the firelight. She's got a fat, angry face, and untidy grey hair. Hullo, she's gone now!"

Bubbles fell back on to her pillow and closed her eyes. It was as if she was dismissing them.

Varick turned uneasily to the doctor. "Is she delirious?" he whispered.

The doctor shook his head. He also was startled—startled more than surprised. For in just Bubbles' words would he have described the odious woman who had come to see him last spring, and whose voice he had heard within the last few minutes.

He now had no doubt that Miss Pigchalke had been in the corridor, or, more likely, in some room opening out of it, and that she had followed Varick into this darkened room and then, noiselessly, slipped out again.

Bubbles opened her eyes.

"I'll come up after dinner for a few minutes," said Dr. Panton. Bubbles made no answer; her eyes were now following Varick out of the door.

The doctor lingered for a moment. "You're *sure* there was someone there?" he asked.

"Of course I'm sure." Bubbles spoke quite positively. "I'm sure"—and then he saw a change come over her face—"and yet I don't know that I am quite sure," she murmured dreamily.

As Dr. Panton went down the shallow oak staircase he felt in a turmoil of doubt and discomfort. To his mind there was no reasonable doubt that Miss Pigchalke had somehow effected an entrance to Wyndfell Hall. She had lived there for long years; she must know every corner of the strange old house.

When he reached the hall where the whole party was gathered together, he went up to Blanche Farrow. "May I speak to you a moment?" he whispered.

"What is it?" she asked anxiously. "Isn't Bubbles so well?"

"Oh, yes; Miss Bubbles is going on all right. But, Miss Farrow? I want to tell you something that, if possible, I should like to keep from Varick."

"Yes—what is it?"

"Someone who has a grudge against him, a tiresome old woman who was companion to Mrs. Varick for many years, has somehow got into this house. She spoke to me just as I came out of my room. I didn't see her, but I heard her voice quite distinctly. And when Varick and I went into Miss

Bubbles' room for a moment, on our way downstairs, she followed us in— Miss Bubbles described her exactly. Then suddenly she disappeared. I am sure she's hiding in one of the bedrooms."

"What a horrid idea!" exclaimed Blanche.

"Now comes the question—can we manage to hunt her out, and get her away from the house, without Varick knowing?"

"But why shouldn't he know?" asked Blanche hesitatingly.

"Look at him," said the doctor impressively. And Blanche, glancing quickly across the room, was struck by Varick's look of illness.

"There's no reason for telling him anything about it," she admitted. "But hadn't we better wait till after dinner before doing anything?"

"Perhaps we had."

Dinner was a curious, uncomfortable meal; even Sir Lyon and Helen Brabazon felt the atmosphere charged with anxiety and depression.

Miss Burnaby alone was her usual placid, quietly greedy self. She had expressed suitable regret at all that had happened, but most of the party realized that she had not really cared at all.

When the ladies passed through into the white parlour, Blanche slipped away. She got hold of her firm ally, the butler, and explained in a very few words what she thought had better be done. Accompanied by Pegler, they went into every room, and into every nook and cranny of the house, upstairs and down—but they found no trace of any alien presence.

Miss Pigchalke, so much was clear, had vanished as quietly and silently as she had come.

CHAPTER XVIII

One—two—three—four—five—six—Bubbles heard the clock in the dark corridor outside her room ring out the harmonious chimes, and she turned restlessly round in her warm, comfortable bed.

It was very annoying to think she would have to wait two hours for a cup of tea, but there it was! She had herself told Pegler she didn't want to be disturbed till eight o'clock. She still felt too "done," too weak, to get up and try to find her way to the kitchen to make herself some tea.

She lay, with her eyes wide open, longing for the daylight, and looking back with shrinking fear to a night full of a misty horror.

Again and again she had lived through that awful moment when Varick had pushed her over the edge of the embankment, to roll quickly, softly, inexorably, into the icy-cold water.

She knew he had pushed her over. To herself it was a fact which did not admit of any doubt at all. She had seen the mingled hatred and relief which had convulsed his face. It was with that face she would always see Lionel Varick henceforth.

There had been a moment when she had thought she would tell Dr. Panton; then she had come to the conclusion that there was no good purpose to be served by telling the strange and dreadful truth.

Some noble lines of Swinburne's which had once been quoted to her by a friend she loved, floated into her mind—

> "But ye, keep ye on earth
> Your lips from over-speech,
> Loud words and longing are so little worth;
> And the end is hard to reach.
> For silence after grievous thing's is good,
> And reverence, and the fear that makes men whole
> And shame, and righteous governance of blood,
> And Lordship of the Soul.
> And from sharp words and wits men pluck no fruit,
> And gathering thorns they shake the tree at root;

For words divide and rend,
But silence is most noble till the end."

As she lay there, feeling physically so ill and weak, while yet her mind worked so clearly and quickly, she set herself to solve a painful puzzle. Why had Varick tried to do her to death? She admitted to herself that she had never liked him, but she had never done him any harm. And they had been on good terms—outwardly—always.

For hours, amid fitful, nightmarish snatches of sleep, and long, lucid intervals of thought, Bubbles had wrestled with the question.

And then, lying there in the early morning, Bubbles *suddenly knew*. Varick hated and feared her because she had unwittingly raised his wife from the dead. And, believing that if he killed her, he would lay that sinister, vengeful, unquiet ghost, he had deliberately planned yesterday's expedition in order to do that which he had so nearly succeeded in doing.

Bubbles gave an eerie little chuckle which startled herself. "I'd have haunted him!" she muttered aloud. "He'd have found it more difficult to get rid of me dead than alive."

Even as she murmured the words, the door opened, and she heard a voice say, hesitatingly, "Then you're awake, Bubbles? Somehow I felt you were awake, and I thought you might like a cup of tea."

It was Bill Donnington, with a lighted candle in one hand, and a cup of tea in the other.

How glad she was to see him! How very, very glad! Yet he only looked his usual sober, unromantic self, standing there at the bottom of her pretty old walnut-wood bed, looking at her with all his wistful, faithful soul in his eyes.

Bill was fully dressed, and Bubbles burst out laughing, feebly.

"You *are* an early bird!" she exclaimed. "And a very proper bird, too. I suppose you thought you mustn't come into my room in a dressing-gown?"

"I haven't slept all night," he said stiffly. "So I got up an hour ago. I came and looked in here, as a matter of fact, on my way to the bathroom. But you were asleep. And then, after I was dressed, I went down to the kitchen, and made myself a cup of tea. I thought I'd make one for you, too, just on chance."

He came up close to her, and Bubbles, shaking back her short curly hair, took the cup from him. "This *is* delicious! You *are* a good sort, Bill!"

He sat down on the end of her bed while she thirstily, greedily, drank the tea he had brought her. In all her gestures there was something bird-like and exquisite. Even when she was greedy Bubbles was dainty too.

"I do hope you're feeling none the worse"—he began.

And she mimicked him, gleefully, speaking in a low whisper. "None the worse, thank you! It's a comfort, sometimes, to be with a person who always says exactly what you might expect he would say! I'm always sure of that comfort with you—old thing."

"Are you?" He smiled his slow, doubtful smile, and Bubbles said suddenly: "You've gone and left the door open."

He stood up, irresolute. "I suppose I ought to go away," he said hesitatingly.

She exclaimed: "No, no, Bill! I won't have you go away! I don't want you to go away! I want you to stay with me. But you must shut the door, for it's very cold."

"D'you think I'd better shut the door?" he asked.

And then Bubbles seized his lean, strong hand. "Oh! I see what you mean!" she exclaimed. "You actually think your being in here is more proper if the door is open? But it isn't a bit—for everyone in the house but us two is fast asleep! Still, that won't go on long. So shut the door at once! I've something very important to say to you—something which I certainly don't want Pegler to hear me say to you. Pegler may come down any moment—she's such a good sort, under that stiff, cross manner. It's so queer she should disapprove of me, and approve of my Aunt Blanche, isn't it?"

He got up, and going to the door, shut it.

"Lock it!" she called out. "Lock it, Bill! I don't want to be disturbed;" she repeated in an odd voice, "I've something very important to say to you."

But this time he did not obey her, and as he came back towards the bed he said anxiously, "D'you still feel *very* bad, Bubbles?"

There was a tone of great tenderness and solicitude in his voice.

"Of course I do. So would you, if you'd died and come to life again."

"You didn't do that," he said in a low voice. "But you were very nearly drowned, Bubbles. However, we must try to forget it."

Again she mimicked him: "'We must try to forget it.' I was waiting for you to say that, too. As if we should ever forget it! But we won't think about it just now—because we've got to think of something else that's much more to the present purpose."

"Yes," he said soothingly. "Yes, Bubbles?"

Poor Bill felt very uncomfortable. He did not wish prim Miss Pegler to come in and find him sitting on Bubbles' bed, when no one was yet up in the house. These modern, unconventional ways were all very well, and he knew they often did not really mean anything, but still—but still ...

"Did you ever hear of the King's Serf?" asked Bubbles suddenly.

"The King's Serf?" he repeated, bewildered.

"When the rope which was hanging some poor devil of a highwayman broke—when the axe was too blunt to cut a robber rascal's head off—when a man being condemned to death survived by some extraordinary accident—well, such a man became thereafter the King's Serf. He belonged to the King, body, soul, and spirit, and no one but the King could touch him. He lost his identity. He was above the law!"

Bubbles said all this very, very fast—almost as if she had learnt it off by heart.

"What a curious thing," said Bill slowly.

Bubbles had so many queer, out-of-the-way bits of knowledge. She was always surprising him by the things she knew. It was the more curious that she never seemed to open a book.

"Come a little nearer," she ordered. "You're so far away, Bill!"

She spoke with a touch of imperious fretfulness, and he moved a little further up the bed.

"Nearer, nearer!" she cried; and then she suddenly sat up in bed, and flinging her arms round him, she laid her dark, curly head on his faithful heart. "I want to tell you," she whispered, "that from now onward I'm Bill Donnington's Serf—much more than that poor brute I've told you of was ever the King's Serf. For, after all, the King hadn't cut the rope, or blunted the edge of the hatchet----"

"Bubbles!" he exclaimed. "Oh, Bubbles, d'you really mean that?"

"Of course I mean it! What I gave I had, what I gained I lost, what I lost I gained."

"What do you mean, darling?" he whispered.

"I mean that the moment that stupid doctor allows me to get up—then you and I will skip off by ourselves, and we'll say, 'Hullo, here's a church! Let's go in and get married.'"

She waited a moment, but Bill Donnington said nothing. He only held her closer to him.

"In the night," went on Bubbles, "I was wondering if we'd be married in that strange old church near here, our church, the church with the animals. And then I thought no, we wouldn't do that, for I am not likely to want ever to come back here again. So we'll be married in London, in a City church, in the church where John Gilpin and his family went to what I suppose they called 'worship.' It's there you will have to say you worship me, Bill!"

She lifted her head, and looked into his face. "Oh, Bill," she said, her voice trembling a little, "you do look happy!"

"I am happy, but I—I can't quite believe it," he said slowly; "it's too good to be true."

"I hope you'll go on being happy," she said, again pressing closer to him. "But you know that sometimes, Bill—well, I *shall* dine at Edmonton while you do dine at Ware. It's no good my trying to conceal that from you."

"I—I don't understand," he stammered out. What did Bubbles mean by saying that?

"You'll know soon enough," she said, with that little wise look of hers—the little look he loved. "But whenever I'm naughty or unreasonable, or, or selfish, Bill—I'm afraid I shall often be *very* selfish—then you must just turn to me, and say: 'You know, Bubbles, when all's said and done, you're my Serf; but for me you wouldn't be here.'"

Bill Donnington looked at her, and then he said solemnly and very deliberately: "I don't feel that you ought to marry me out of gratitude, Bubbles."

She took her hands off his shoulders, and clapped them gleefully. "I was waiting for that, too!" she exclaimed. "I wonder you didn't say it at once—I quite thought you would."

He said seriously: "But I really mean it. I couldn't bear to think that you married me just because I dragged you out of the water."

"I'm really marrying you, if you want to know," she exclaimed, "because of Mr. Tapster! During the last few days—I wonder if you've noticed it, Bill?" (he had, indeed)—"that man has looked at me as if I was *his* serf—that's a polite way of putting it—and I don't like it. But I've got a friend—you know Phyllis Burley? I think she'd do for him exactly! It would be so nice, too, for she's devoted to me, and we should have the use of one of their motors whenever we felt like it."

Bill shook his head decidedly. "We never should feel like it," he said; "even if Phyllis did marry Mr. Tapster, which I greatly doubt she'd even think of doing."

"I'm going to tell him to-day," she went on, "that he's got to marry her. There's nothing indelicate about my saying that, because they've never met. But it'll work in his brain, you see if it doesn't, like yeast in new bread! Then I'll bring them together, and then, and then—"

"And then," said Bill deliberately, "you'll never, with my goodwill, see him again. So find him a wife whom you don't like, Bubbles."

She looked at him meditatively. "Very well," she said. "That will be my first sacrifice for you, Bill. I'll save him up for Violet Purton. She's a horrid girl—and won't she make his money fly!"

He was smiling at her rather oddly.

"Bill!" she exclaimed, startled. "Bill! I do believe you're going to be master—"

And then she flung her arms again round his neck. "Kiss me," she commanded, "kiss me, Bill. And then you must go away, for it isn't proper that you should be here, at this time of the morning, now that we're engaged!"

CHAPTER XIX

That same morning, but a good deal later, Blanche Farrow woke with a start to find Pegler standing at her bedside with just one letter in her hand.

Pegler was smiling. It was not a real smile, but just a general softening of her plain, severe face.

Pegler knew that her lady had been rather "put out" at not having received her usual Christmas letter from Mr. Mark Gifford. She had spoken of it twice to Pegler, once lightly, on December 27, and then again, in a rather upset way, on the 29th. After that she had pretended to forget all about it. But Pegler felt sure Miss Farrow did remember—often. And now here was the letter—a much fatter letter than usual, too.

Pegler, of course, said nothing. It was not her place to know the handwriting of any of the gentlemen who wrote to her mistress.

Miss Farrow took the letter, and there came a faint, a very faint, flush over her face. She said: "I hope Miss Bubbles has had a good night. Have you been in to her yet, Pegler?"

"Yes, ma'am. She looks rather excited-like. But as you know, ma'am, that's a good sign with her."

"Yes, I think it is, Pegler."

Pegler slipped noiselessly away, and then Blanche opened the envelope containing Mark Gifford's long-delayed Christmas letter.

"Home Office, "*December 23rd.*
"MY DEAR BLANCHE,
"'How use doth breed a habit in a man!' Well anyhow, as you know, it is my custom, which has now attained the dignity of a habit, always to write you a letter for Christmas. Hitherto I have always known where it would find you, but this year is an exception, for I really have no idea where you are.
"This year is an exception in another respect also. Hitherto, my dear Blanche, I have, with a tact which I hope you have silently appreciated, always managed to keep out of my

Christmas letter any reference to what you know I have never given up hoping for even against hope. But this time I can't keep it out because I have had a really good idea. Even a Civil Servant may have a good idea sometimes, and I assure you that this came to me out of office hours—as a matter of fact it came to me when I was sitting in that funny little old Westminster churchyard where we once spent what was, to me, the happiest of half-hours.

"I know you have thought me unsympathetic and disapproving about that which holds for you so great a fascination. Disapproving, yes; I can't help disapproving of gambling, especially in a woman; but unsympathetic, no—a thousand times no. Sympathy is understanding, and, believe me, I do understand, and therefore I propose this plan.

"If you will do me the honour of marrying me, I propose that once or even twice every year you should go off to Monte Carlo, or wherever else you like, and play to your heart's content. I promise never to reproach you, above all never to administer those silent reproaches which I think are always the hardest to bear. Yes, I will always play the game, I pledge myself to that most faithfully.

"Forgive me for referring to something which makes my plan easier to carry out. This year two accidents, the death of one colleague, and the premature retirement of another, have pushed me up the ladder of promotion, and, in addition, there has been a legacy. The English of that is that for our joint *ménage* we shouldn't want your income at all; we could quite well do without it, and you would be perfectly free to use it in whatever way you like.

"There! That is my plan. Now, dearest of women, say yes and make us both happy, for you would make me so happy that I couldn't help making you happy too. I wish I had any idea where you will be when you read this letter, on which hangs all my hopes. Perhaps you will read it at Monte, out on the Corniche Road. Don't let the fact that you have been lucky at play make *me* unlucky in—you know what!

"Yours ever (this is no figure of speech),
"Mark Gifford."

Blanche Farrow sighed and smiled, as she deliberately read the long letter through twice. Somehow it warmed her heart; and yet would she ever be able to give up the life which in many ways suited her so well? If she married Mark—dear, kind, generous-hearted Mark—various friendships which, even if they did not mean so much to her as they appeared to do, yet meant a good deal in her present lonely life, would certainly have to be given up. To take but one instance. It had almost been an instinct with her to keep Lionel Varick and Mark Gifford apart. In the old days she had been disagreeably aware of how absolutely Gifford had always disapproved of Varick, and of Varick's various ways of trying, often successfully, to raise the wind. Of course, everything was now different with regard to this particular friend. Varick had become—by what anyone not a hypocrite must admit had been a fortunate circumstance—a respectable member of society; but, even so, she knew, deep in her heart, that he and the man whose letter she held in her hand would never like one another.

And yet she was tired—so tired!--of the sort of life she led, year in and year out. Her nerves were no longer what they had once been. For instance, the strange series of happenings that had just taken place here, at Wyndfell Hall, had thoroughly upset her; and as for the horrible thing that had occurred yesterday, she hadn't been able to sleep all night for thinking of it. Nothing that had ever happened in her now long life had had quite the effect on Blanche Farrow that Bubbles' accident had had. She had realized, suddenly, how fond she was of the girl—how strong in all of us is the call of the blood! As she had stood watching Dr. Panton's untiring efforts to restore the circulation of the apparently drowned girl there had gone up from Blanche's heart a wild, instinctive prayer to the God in whom she did not believe, to spare the child.

Perhaps just because she had not broken down before, she felt the more now all that had happened in the way of the strange, the sinister, and the untoward during the last fortnight. And all at once, after reading yet again right through the quiet, measured letter of her old friend and constant lover, Blanche Farrow suddenly burst into a passion of tears.

And then it struck her as funny, as even absurd, that she should cry like this! She hadn't cried for years and years—in fact, she could hardly remember the day when she had last cried.

She jumped out of bed and put on her dressing-gown, for it was very cold, and then she went and gazed at her reflection in the one looking-glass in the room. It was a beautiful old Jacobean mirror fixed over the dressing-table.

Heavens! What a fright she looked! Do tears always have that disfiguring effect on a woman? This must be a lesson to her. She dabbed her eyes with a wet handkerchief, and then she went over to the writing-table and sat down.

For the first time in her life Blanche Farrow wrote Mark Gifford a really grateful, sincere letter. She said, truly, how touched she was by his long devotion and by all his goodness to her. She admitted, humbly, that she wished she were worthy of it all. But she finally added that she feared she could never find it in her heart and conscience to say that she would do what he wished. She had become too old, too set in her ways....

Yet it was with a heavy heart that she wrote her long letter in answer to his, and it took her a long time, for she often waited a few moments in between the sentences.

How strange was her relationship to this man of whom she saw so little, and yet with whom she felt on close, intangible terms of intimacy! His work tied him to London, and of late years she had not been much in London. He knew very little of her movements. Why, this very letter had been sent to her, care of her London club, the club which had its uses—principally—when she wanted to entertain Mark Gifford himself to lunch or dinner.

His letter had wandered to yet another address—an address she had left at the club weeks ago, the only address they had. From thence it had reached the last house where she had been staying before she had come to Wyndfell Hall. The wonderful thing was that the letter had reached her at all. But she was very glad it had come, if only at long last.

After her letter was finished, she suddenly felt that she must put in a word to account for the delay in her answer to what should have received an immediate reply. And so she added a postscript, which, unlike most women's postscripts, was of really very little importance—or so the writer thought.

This unimportant postscript ran:

> "Your letter had followed me round to about half-a-dozen places. Bubbles Dunster and I have been spending Christmas in this wonderful old house, Wyndfell Hall, our host being Lionel Varick. He struck oil in the shape of an heiress two years ago. She died last year; and he has become a most respectable member of society. I know you didn't much like him, though he's often spoken to me very gratefully of the good turn you did him years ago."

Blanche hesitated, pen in hand. Of course, it was not necessary that she should mention the name of her host. She might rewrite the last page of her letter, and leave the postscript out. It was unfortunately true that Mark had taken a violent prejudice against the man he had befriended to such good purpose years and years ago. She had been still young then—young and, as she was quite willing to admit now, very foolish. In fact, she looked back to the Blanche Farrow of those days, as we are sometimes apt to look back at our younger selves, with amazement and disapproval, rather than sympathy. But there was a streak of valiant honesty in her nature. She let what had been written stand, only adding the words:

> "The party is breaking up to-morrow; but Bubbles, who had a disagreeable accident yesterday, will stay on here for a few days with me. All the same, I expect we shall be in London by the ninth; and then, perhaps, you and I might meet."

It was by Bubbles' special wish—nay, command, that her engagement to Bill Donnington was publicly announced that very morning, at breakfast, by her aunt. Everyone was much interested, and said the usual good-natured, rather silly, civil things; hence Blanche was glad Bill Donnington had breakfasted early, and so was not there.

Helen Brabazon was extremely excited and delighted at the news. "I suppose it happened yesterday morning!" she exclaimed. "For, of course, they haven't seen one another alone since then. If they were already engaged, what awful agony poor Mr. Donnington must have gone through while you were trying to bring her to life again?"

She turned to Panton, and he answered thoughtfully, "I could see he was most terribly upset. Don't you remember how he refused to go up to the house and change his wet clothes?"

Blanche couldn't help glancing furtively from behind the teapot and high silver urn at James Tapster. His phlegmatic face had become very red. Almost at once he had got up and gone over to the dresser, and there, taking a long time about it, he had cut himself some slices of ham. She noticed, with relief, that he came back with a huge plateful, which he proceeded to eat with apparent appetite.

"And when is the wedding to take place?" asked Helen.

"Almost at once," replied Blanche smiling. "Bubbles never does anything like anybody else! She's set her heart on going to town the very moment Dr. Panton allows her to get up. Then they're to be married without any fuss at all in one of the old City churches."

"What a splendid idea!" cried Helen. "That's just how *I* should like to be married."

"I, too," said Sir Lyon, in his pleasant voice. "To me there's always been something barbaric in the ordinary grand wedding."

But Blanche Farrow shook her head. "Perhaps because I'm so much older than all of you," she said good-humouredly, "I think there's a great deal to be said for an old-fashioned wedding: white dress (white satin for choice), orange blossoms, St. George's, Hanover Square, and all! I even like the crowd of people saying kind and unkind things in whispers to one another. I don't think I should *feel* myself married unless I went through all that—"

And then, at last, James Tapster said something. "Marriage is all rot!" he said, speaking, as was his unpleasant custom, with his mouth full. "There are very few happy married couples about."

"That may be your experience," said Varick, speaking for the first time since Blanche had told the great news. "I'm glad to say it isn't mine. I think marriage far the happiest state—for either a man or a woman."

He spoke with a good deal of feeling, and both Panton and Helen Brabazon felt very much touched. He had certainly made *his* marriage a success.

Meanwhile, Blanche suspected that Dr. Panton had just had a letter containing disturbing news. She saw him read it twice over. Then he put it carefully in a note-book he took out of his pocket. "I shall have to go to-morrow, a day earlier than I thought," he observed. "I've got an appointment in town on Thursday morning."

Then Mr. Tapster announced that *he* was going to-day, and though Varick seemed genuinely sorry, everyone else was secretly glad.

There are days in life which pass by without being distinguished by any outstanding happenings, and which yet remain in the mind as milestones on the road of life.

Such a day, at any rate to Blanche Farrow, was the day which saw the first disruption of Lionel Varick's Christmas house party. Though Mr. Tapster was the only guest actually to leave Wyndfell Hall, all the arrangements concerning the departures of the morrow had to be made. Miss Burnaby, Helen Brabazon, and Sir Lyon Dilsford were to travel together. Dr. Panton was going by a later train, as was also Bill Donnington. Blanche herself, with of course Bubbles, was leaving on the Saturday.

As the day went on Blanche realized that Varick much desired that Helen Brabazon should also stay on till Saturday. But she, Blanche, thought this desire unreasonable. Though she had come to like her, she found the good, thoughtful, conscientious, and yet simple-minded Helen "heavy in hand"; she told herself that if Helen stayed on, the entertaining of the girl would fall on her, especially if, as Dr. Panton insisted, Bubbles must not get up till Friday at dinner-time.

Looking back, Blanche Farrow told herself that that day had been full of curious premonitions. Yet it had opened, in a sense happily for her, with the coming of Mark Gifford's quaint, characteristic letter. Then had come the shock, and it had been a shock, of Bubbles' engagement, and of the girl's insistence on its being announced to the rest of the house party at once—at breakfast.

The only outstanding thing which happened, and it was indeed a small thing compared to the other two, was the departure of James Tapster. Blanche felt sorry for him—genuinely sorry. But she philosophically told herself that no amount of money, even had Bill Donnington never existed, could have made Bubbles even tolerably happy tied to such a man.

After Mr. Tapster had gone they all breathed the more freely. Yet Blanche somehow did not feel comfortable. What was wrong, for instance, with Lionel Varick? He looked ill at ease, as well as ill physically. Something seemed also to be weighing on Dr. Panton's mind. Even Sir Lyon Dilsford was unlike his pleasant easy self. But Blanche thought she knew what ailed *him*.

Her only sheet anchor of comfort during that long, dull afternoon and evening was the thought that Bubbles' life was set on the right lines at last ... and that Mark Gifford had not changed.

CHAPTER XX

"HONBLE. BLANCHE FARROW—Wyndfell Hall—
Darnaston—Suffolk—Very private—Meet me outside
Darnaston Church at twelve o'clock, midday, to-morrow,
Wednesday—MARK GIFFORD."

Blanche sat up in bed and stared down at the telegraph form. What on earth did this mean? But for the fact that she knew it to be out of the question, she would have suspected a foolish and vulgar practical joke.

She noted that the telegram had been sent off at 9.30 the night before (just after Mark must have received her letter). She also saw that it had been inscribed for morning delivery. That was like Mark Gifford. He was nothing if not careful and precise with regard to everything of a business kind.

Then she began asking herself the sort of rather futile questions people do ask themselves, when puzzled, and made uneasy by what seems an inexplicable occurrence. How would Mark get to Darnaston by twelve o'clock to-day? Surely he could only do so by starting before it was light, and motoring the whole way from London?

She gazed at the words "very private." What did they portend? Quickly she examined her conscience. No, she had done nothing—nothing which could have brought her into contact, even slightly, with the law. Of course, she was well aware that Mark had never forgotten, even over all these years, the dreadful scrape into which she had got herself by going to those gambling parties in the pleasant, quiet, Jermyn Street flat where she and Varick had first become acquainted. But that had been a sharp lesson, and one by which she had profited.

She next took a rapid mental survey of her family, all so much more respectable and prosperous than herself. The only person among them capable of getting into any real scrape was poor little Bubbles.

Bubbles was now practically well again. She had written out the announcement which was to appear in the *Times* and the *Morning Post*, and had insisted on its being sent off.

Donnington had been somewhat perturbed by the thought of their engagement being thus at once made public. But Bubbles had observed cheerfully: "Once people know about it, I shan't be able to get out of it, even if I want to!" To that Bill had said, sorely, that if she wanted to give him the chuck she should of course do so, even on the altar steps. Bubbles had laughed at that and exclaimed: "I only said it to tease you, old thing! The real truth is that I want father to understand that I really mean it—that's all. He reads the *Times* right through every day, and he'll think it true if he sees it there. As for his tiresome widow, she'll see it in the *Morning Post*—and then she'll believe it, too!"

Blanche Farrow told herself that this mysterious and extraordinary message might have something to do with Bubbles; and as she got up, she went on thinking with increasing unease of the unexpected assignation which lay before her.

It was a comfort to feel that that disagreeable man, James Tapster, was gone, and that the rest of the party, with the exception of herself and Bubbles, were going to-day.

Something had again been said about Miss Burnaby and her niece staying on, and she had heard Varick pressing them earnestly to do so; but the old lady had been unwilling to break her plan, the more so that she had an appointment with her dentist. Then Varick had asked why Miss Brabazon shouldn't stay on till Saturday? There had been a considerable discussion about it; but Blanche secretly hoped they would all go away. She felt tired and unlike herself. The events of the last few days had shaken her badly.

What an extraordinary difference a few moments can make in one's outlook on life! Blanche Farrow was uncomfortably aware that she would never forget what had happened to her on New Year's Eve. That strange and fearful experience had obliterated some of her clearest mental landmarks. She wished to think, she tried very hard to think, that in some mysterious way the vision she had seen with such terrible distinctness had been a projection from Bubbles' brain—Bubbles' uncanny gift working, perchance, on Lionel Varick's mind and memory. She could not doubt that the two wraiths she had seen so clearly purported to be a survival of the human personalities of the two women who each had borne Varick's name, and had been, for a while, so closely linked with him....

Yet long ago, when quite a young woman, she had come to the deliberate conclusion that there was no such survival of human personality.

Taking up Mark Gifford's mysterious telegram, and one or two unimportant letters she had just received, she went downstairs, to see, as she came into the dining-room, that only Varick was already down.

He looked up, and she was shocked to see how ill and strained he looked. He had taken poor little Bubbles' accident terribly to heart; Blanche knew he had a feeling—which was rather absurd, after all,—that he in some way could have prevented it.

But as he saw her come in his face lightened, and she felt touched. Poor Lionel! He was certainly very, very fond of her.

"I do hope Helen Brabazon will stay on with you and Bubbles," he said eagerly. "I think I've nearly persuaded Miss Burnaby to let her do so. Do say a word to her, Blanche?"

"I will, if you like. But in that case, hadn't we better ask Sir Lyon to stay on, too?"

"Dilsford!" he exclaimed. "Why on earth should we think of doing that?"

Blanche smiled. "Where are your eyes?" she asked. "Sir Lyon's head over heels in love with Helen Brabazon; and I've been wondering these last few days whether that quiet, demure girl is quite as unconscious of his state as she pretends to be!"

And then, as she began pouring out a cup of tea for the man who was now looking at her with a dismayed, surprised expression on his face, she went on composedly: "It would be rather amusing if two engagements were to come out of your house-party, Lionel—wouldn't it?"

But he answered at once, in a harsh, decided tone, "I think you're quite mistaken, Blanche. Why, they've hardly exchanged two words together."

Blanche put down the tea-pot. She began to laugh—she really couldn't help it. "You must have been deaf as well as blind!" she exclaimed. "They've been together perpetually! I admit that that's been his doing—not hers. For days past I've seen right into his mind—seen, I mean, the struggle that has been taking place between his pride and—yes, the extraordinary attraction that girl seems to have for him. He's no fortune-hunter, you know; also, he wants so little, the lucky man, that I think her money would be a positive bother to him."

Lionel Varick stared at Blanche Farrow. She had a way of being right about worldly matters—the triumph of experience over hope, as she had once observed cynically. But this time he felt sure she was wrong.

The feminine interest in a possible, probable, or even improbable love-affair always surprises the average man—surprises, and sometimes annoys him very much.

"Do you go so far as to say she returns this—this feeling you attribute to him?" he asked abruptly. He was relieved to see Blanche shake her head.

"No; I can't say that I've detected any response on her part," she said lightly. "But she's very old-fashioned and reserved. She certainly enjoys Sir Lyon's rather dull conversation, and she likes cross-examining him about the life of the poor. She's a very good girl," went on Blanche musingly. "She's a tremendous sense of duty. One can never tell—but no, I don't think the idea that Sir Lyon's in love with her has yet crossed her mind! And I should say that she really prefers you to him. She has a tremendous opinion of you, Lionel. I wonder why?"

He laughed aloud, for the first time since Bubbles' accident. He knew that what Blanche said was true, and it was a very pleasant, reassuring bit of knowledge.

"Old Burnaby would not think of allowing her to marry a penniless baronet," he said smiling.

Blanche looked across at him quickly. "Good and obedient as she is to both those old things, I don't think they'd be able to influence Helen Brabazon in such a thing as marriage."

"Well, you may be right," said Varick, doubtfully.

He felt strongly tempted to take Blanche into his confidence; to tell her, frankly, that he wished to marry Helen. Yet some obscure instinct held him back. Women, even the most sensible women, are so damned sentimental! So he told himself. Lately he had had the unpleasant, disconcerting feeling that whenever Helen looked at him she thought of "poor Milly."

"Still, I don't envy Sir Lyon his wooing," went on Blanche. "Helen is a girl who'll take a long time to make up her mind, and who will weigh all the pros and cons."

"Then you don't think," said Varick in a low tone, "that she would ever be swept off her feet?"

At one time he had felt sure she would be.

"By a grand passion? My dear Lionel, what an absurd idea! But hush—"

The door opened, and the object of their discussion came in. Helen Brabazon always looked especially well as breakfast. It was her hour.

"How's Bubbles this morning?" she asked.

And Blanche felt rather guilty. She hadn't been into Bubbles' room; her mind had been too full of other things. "She's going on very well," she answered composedly. "I think she might get up to-morrow, in spite of Dr.

Panton." And then, for she felt Varick was "willing" her to say it: "I do hope that you are going to stay on till Saturday, even if your aunt has to go away this afternoon."

"Yes," said Helen, and the colour deepened a little in her cheeks. "Yes, I've persuaded Auntie to let me stay on till you and Bubbles come up to London. It's only two days, after all."

"I *am* glad." There was a genuine thrill of satisfaction in Varick's voice. This meant that he and the girl would be practically alone together all to-morrow and Friday.

"I think Sir Lyon could manage to stay on too, if you ask him." Helen smiled guilelessly at her host. "I saw him just now. He and Dr. Panton were taking Span round to the kitchen, and when I said I was staying on, Sir Lyon said he thought he could stay on too, just till Saturday morning."

Blanche could not forbear giving a covert glance of triumph at Varick's surprised and annoyed face. "Of course," she said quickly, "we shall be delighted to have Sir Lyon a little longer. I thought by what he said that he was absolutely obliged to go away to-day, by the same train as you and Miss Burnaby."

"He certainly said so," observed Varick coldly.

And then, for Blanche Farrow was above all things a woman of the world, when the other two men came in she made everything quite easy for Sir Lyon, pressing him to stay on, as if she had only just thought of it. But she noticed, with covert amusement, that he was very unlike his usual cool, collected self. He actually looked sheepish—yes, that was the only word for it! Also, he made rather a favour of staying. "I shall have to telegraph," he said; "for I'd made all my arrangements to go back this afternoon."

"As for me," said Dr. Panton, "I must leave this afternoon, worse luck! But there it is." He turned to Varick. "I've got an appointment in London to-morrow morning—one I can't put off."

Donnington came in at last. He looked radiant—indeed, his look of happiness was in curious contrast to the lowering expression which now clouded Varick's face.

"Bubbles is nearly well again!" he cried joyfully. "She says she'll get up to-morrow, doctor or no doctor!" He looked at Panton; then, turning to Blanche, in a lower tone: "Also, she's shown me the most wonderful letter from her father, written to her before Christmas. I always thought he disliked me: but he liked me from the very first time we met—isn't that strange?"

"Very strange," said Blanche, smiling.

They all scattered after breakfast, but Miss Farrow noticed that Varick made a determined and successful attempt to carry off Helen Brabazon from Sir Lyon, who had obviously been lying in wait for her.

"What dogs in the manger men are!" she said to herself. And then she remembered, with a little gasp of dismay, her mysterious appointment with Mark Gifford. She knew him well enough to be sure that he would be in good time; but, even so, there was more than an hour to be got through somehow before she could start for Darnaston.

She went up to Bubbles' room. Yes, the girl looked marvellously better—younger too, quite different!

There came a knock at the door while she was there, and Donnington came in.

"If you'd been wise," said Bubbles, looking up at him, "you'd have made up to Helen Brabazon, Bill. She's like an apple, just ready to fall off the tree."

"What *do* you mean?" asked Blanche.

"Just what I say. She's tremendously in love with love!"

"D'you really think so?"

(If so, Sir Lyon's task would be an easy one.)

"I know it," said Bubbles positively. "I've made a close study of that girl. I confess I didn't like her at first, and I will tell you why, though I know it will shock Bill."

"I've always liked Miss Brabazon," he said stoutly, "why didn't you like her, Bubbles?"

"Because when she arrived here I saw that she was in love with Lionel Varick."

"Don't talk nonsense," said her aunt reprovingly. "You know I don't like that sort of joking."

And as for Bill, he turned and walked towards the door. "I've got some letters to write," he said crossly.

"Don't go away, Bill. It isn't a joke, Blanche—and I'm going really to shock *you* now—unless, of course, you're only pretending to be shocked?"

"What d'you mean?" said Blanche.

"I think Helen fell in love with Lionel Varick before his wife died."

Bill said sharply: "I won't have you say such disgusting things, Bubbles!" And he did indeed look disgusted.

"What a queer mind you've got," said Bubbles reprovingly. "I mean, of course, in quite a proper way; that is, without the poor girl knowing anything about it. But I thing *he* knew it right enough."

Blanche remained silent. Bubbles' words were making her feel curiously uneasy. They threw a light on certain things which had puzzled her.

"Lionel Varick marked her down long ago," went on Bubbles slowly. "On the evening that she arrived I saw that he had quite made up his mind to marry her. But as the days went on I began to hope that he wouldn't succeed." She uttered these last words very, very seriously.

Her aunt looked at her, surprised at the feeling she threw into her voice. As for Donnington, he was staring at her dumbly and, yes, angrily. At last he said: "And why shouldn't Varick marry her, if they both like one another?"

"You wouldn't understand if I were to tell you. You're too stupid and too good to understand."

Donnington felt very much put out. He did not mind being called stupid, but what on earth did Bubbles mean by saying he was too good?

"I'm sure Lionel's dead wife has been haunting Helen," went on Bubbles rapidly, "quite, quite sure of it. And I'm glad she has! I should be sorry for any nice girl—for any woman, even a horrid woman—to marry Lionel Varick. There! I've said my say, and now I shall for ever hold my peace."

They both stared at her, astonished by the passion and energy with which she uttered the curious words.

Bill looked down at the girl, and, though he felt hurt and angry with her, his heart suddenly softened. Bubbles looked very frail and tired lying there.

"Bill," she said, "come here," and he came, though not very willingly, closer to her.

She pulled him down. "I only want to tell you that I love you," she whispered, and his anger, his irritation, vanished like snow in the sun.

Blanche was already at the door. She turned round. "Well, I must be off now to see the *chef*, and to make all sorts of arrangements. Sir Lyon is staying on—rather unlike him to change his mind, but he's done so—at the last moment."

"I wish *I* could get a few more days' holiday," said Bill ruefully. "My number's up this afternoon."

The letters he had to write could go to blazes—of course he meant to spend each of the precious minutes that remained in the next few hours with Bubbles!

"You'll be able to escort old Miss Burnaby to town, for Helen's staying on," went on Blanche.

"Helen staying on?" exclaimed Bubbles. "I'm glad of that! Oh, and Sir Lyon's staying on, too?"

She suddenly gave one of her funny, eerie little chuckles; but she made no other comment.

"Yes," called out Blanche. "And Dr. Panton's going—so I've a good many little things to see to."

Bill sprang to the door, and opened it for her.

As it shut she heard Bubbles' voice, and it was a voice Blanche Farrow hardly knew. "Are you really sorry you're going away from your little kid, Bill?"

Blanche sighed sharply. After all, so she told herself, there is something to be said for love's young dream.

CHAPTER XXI

It marked ten minutes to twelve on the tower of the ancient chantry church of Darnaston as Blanche Farrow walked across the village green and past the group of thatched cottages composing the pretty hamlet which looks so small compared with its noble house of God. But, though she was early, the man she was to meet was evidently already there, for a big, mud-stained motor-car was drawn up in the lane which runs to the left of the church.

Feeling more and more apprehensive, she knew not of what, she walked up the path between the graves, and then suddenly she saw Mark Gifford—his spare, still active-looking figure framed in the stone porch, his plain, but pleasant, intelligent-looking face full of a grave welcome.

He stepped out of the porch and gripped her hand in silence.

She felt that he was deeply stirred, stirred as she had never known him to be—excepting, perhaps, on that occasion, years and years ago, when he had first asked her to be his wife.

Still holding her hand in that strong grasp, he drew her within the porch. "I'm so grateful to you for having come," he said. "I hope you didn't think what I did very odd?"

"I did think it just a little odd."

She was trying to smile—to be her usual composed self.

"I couldn't come to Wyndfell Hall," he said abruptly, "for a reason which you will soon know. But I had to see you, and, by a bit of luck, I suddenly remembered this splendid old church. I passed by here once on a walking tour, years and years ago. It's the sort of place people come a long way to see; so, if we are found here together—well, we might have met by accident."

"As it is, we have met by appointment," she said quietly.

She was feeling more and more frightened. Mark now looked so set, so grim.

"Would you rather stay out here," he asked, "or shall we go into the church?"

"I'd rather stay out here. What is it, Mark? Don't keep me in suspense."

They were standing, facing one another; he had let go her hand at last.

"What I've come to tell you will give you, I fear, a great shock," he began slowly, "for it concerns someone to whom I believe you to be deeply attached."

He looked away from her for the first time.

"Then it *is* Bubbles!" she cried, dismayed. "What on earth has the child done?"

He turned and again looked into her face, now full of a deeply troubled, questioning anxiety. "Bubbles Dunster?" he exclaimed. "Good heavens, no! It's nothing to do with Bubbles."

A look of uncontrollable relief came over her eyes and mouth.

"Who is it, Mark? You credit me with a warmer heart than I possess—"

But he remained silent, and she said quickly: "Come! Who is it, Mark?"

"Can't you guess?" he asked harshly. And, as she shook her head, he added, in a slow, reluctant tone: "I've always supposed you to be really attached to Lionel Varick."

Lionel? That was the last name she expected to hear!

"I don't know exactly what you mean by 'attached,' Mark," she said coldly. "But yes, I've always been fond of him—in a way I suppose you might call it 'attached'—since that horrid affair, years ago, when you were so kind both to him and to me."

"Don't couple yourself with him," he said sternly, "if, as I gather, you don't really care for him, Blanche." And then, almost inaudibly, he added: "You don't know the tortures of jealousy I've suffered at the thought of you and that man."

"Tortures of jealousy?" she repeated, astonished, and rather touched. "Oh, Mark—poor Mark! Why didn't you ask me? I've never, never cared for him in—in that sort of way. How could you think I did?"

"Yet you're here, in his house," he said, "acting (so you said in your letter) as hostess to his guests? And surely you've always been on terms of what most people would call close friendship with him?"

"Yes, I suppose I have"—she hesitated—"in a way. I've always felt that, like me, he hadn't many real friends. And, of course, in old days, ages ago, he was very fond of me," she smiled. "That always pleases a woman, Mark."

"Does it?" he asked, probingly; and as only answer she reddened slightly.

There came a little pause, and then Blanche exclaimed:

"I'm sorry, very sorry, if he's got into a new scrape, Mark; and I'm surprised too. Some two years ago he married a rich woman; she died not long after their marriage, but she was devoted to him, and he's quite well off now."

"Did you know her?" asked Mark Gifford, in a singular tone.

"No, I never came across her. I was away—in Portugal, I think. He wrote and told me about his marriage, and then, later, when his wife fell ill, he wrote again. He was extremely good to her, Mark."

"D'you know much about Varick's early life?" he asked.

"I think I know all there is to know," she answered.

What was Mark getting at? What had Lionel Varick done? Her mind was already busily intent on the thought of how disagreeable it would be to have to warn him of impending unpleasantness.

It was good of Mark to have taken all this trouble! Of course, he had taken it for her sake, and she felt very grateful—and still a little frightened; he looked so unusually grave.

"What *do* you know of Varick's early life?" he persisted.

"I don't think there's very much to know," she answered uneasily. "His father had a place in Yorkshire, and got involved in some foolish, wild speculations. In the end the man went bankrupt, everything was sold up, and they were very poor for a while—horribly poor, I believe. Then the elder Varick died, and his widow and Lionel went and lived at Bedford. I gather Lionel's mother was clever, proud, and quarrelsome. At any rate, she quarrelled with her people, and he had a very lonely boyhood and youth."

"Then you know very little of how Varick lived before you yourself met him? How old would he have been then, Blanche?"

"I should think four or five-and-twenty," she said hesitatingly.

"I suppose," and then Mark Gifford looked at her with a troubled, hesitating look, "I suppose, Blanche—I fear I'm going to surprise you—that you were not aware that he'd been married before?"

"Yes," she said eagerly, "I did know that, Mark."

What on earth was he driving at? That woman, Lionel Varick's first wife, was surely dead? She, Blanche, had had, by a curious accident, someone else's word for that. And then—there rose before her the vision of a ghastly-looking, wild, handsome face; quickly she put it from her, and went on: "He married, when he was only nineteen, a girl out of his own class. They separated for a while; then they seem to have come together again, and, fortunately for Lionel, she died."

"She died murdered—poisoned."

Mark Gifford uttered the dread words very quietly. "Almost certainly poisoned by her husband, Lionel Varick."

A mist came over Blanche Farrow's eyes. She turned suddenly sick and faint.

She put out her hand blindly. Gifford took it, and made her sit down on a stone bench.

"I'm sorry," he said feelingly, "very, very sorry to have had to tell you this dreadful thing, Blanche."

"Never mind," she muttered. "Go on, Mark, if there's anything else to say—go on."

As he remained silent for a moment, she asked, in a dull, tired tone: "But if this awful thing is true, how was it found out, after so many years?"

"It's a peculiar story," he answered reluctantly. "The late—I might say the last—Mrs. Varick, whose name, as you of course know, was Millicent Fauncey, had first as governess, and then as companion, an elderly woman called by the extraordinary name of Pigchalke. This Julia Pigchalke seemed to have hated Varick from the first. She violently disapproved of the engagement, quarrelled with Miss Fauncey about it, and the two women never met after the marriage. But Miss Pigchalke evidently cared deeply for poor Mrs. Varick; I've seen her, and convinced myself of that."

"What is she like?" asked Blanche suddenly.

"Well, she's not attractive! A stout, stumpy, grey-haired woman, with a very red face."

Blanche covered her eyes with her hands. "Go on," she said again, "go on, Mark, with what you were saying."

"Where was I? Oh, I know now! When Mrs. Varick died, within less than a year of her marriage, Miss Pigchalke suspected foul play, and she deliberately set herself to track Lionel Varick down. She made it her business to find out everything about him, and but for her I think we may take it that he would have gone on to the end of the chapter a respectable, and in time highly respected, member of society."

There was a pause. Blanche was staring before her, listening.

"About five weeks ago," went on Mark Gifford quietly, "Miss Pigchalke got into touch with the head of our Criminal Investigation Department. She put before him certain—one can hardly call them facts—but certain discoveries she had made, which led to the body of the first Mrs. Varick being exhumed." Blanche Farrow uttered a stifled exclamation of surprise, and Gifford went on: "I may add that Miss Pigchalke behaved with remarkable cunning and intelligence. She found out that the doctor at Redsands—the place where her poor friend died—was a firm friend of Varick's. She thinks him an accomplice, but of course we regard that as nonsense, for we've found out all about the man, and he is coming to see our toxological expert to-morrow."

(Then that was Dr. Panton's urgent appointment in town.)

"And now, Blanche, comes the curious part of the story! The doctor who had attended the first Mrs. Varick years and years ago *had* suspected foul play. He's a very old man now, and he retired many years ago, but he happened to come across an advertisement which Miss Pigchalke put into one of the Sunday papers asking for information concerning Lionel Varick's past life. *He answered the advertisement*, with the result that his one-time patient was exhumed. It was then found beyond doubt that the woman had been poisoned; and a few days ago the second Mrs. Varick's body was exhumed."

Blanche looked up, and in answer to her haggard look, he said: "Though perhaps I oughtn't to tell you so, there isn't a shadow of doubt that she also was foully done to death, and rather more intelligently than the other poor soul, for in *her* case the process was allowed to take longer, and the doctor attending her was quite taken in."

"How horrible!" muttered Blanche. "How very, very horrible!"

"Yes, horrible indeed! But why I've come here to-day, Blanche, is to tell you that to-morrow Lionel Varick will be arrested on the charge of murder. I have come to say that you and Bubbles must leave Wyndfell Hall this afternoon."

Blanche hardly heard what he was saying. She was absorbed in the horror and in the amazement of the story he had just told her, and in what was going to happen to-morrow to the man who had been for so long her familiar friend.

"It is an immense relief to me to hear that you never even saw the late Mrs. Varick." Mark Gifford went on: "I was afraid that you might have been mixed up with this dreadful business; that he might have used you in some way."

Blanche shook her head, and he went on, musingly: "There were two ladies living next door to the house at Redsands where the poor woman was done to death. They, I expect, will have to give evidence, at least I know that one of them will, a certain Miss—Miss—?"

"Brabazon?" supplied Blanche quickly.

"Yes, that's the name! A certain Miss Brabazon was a great deal with Mrs. Varick. She seems to have been an intimate friend of both the husband and wife. She used to go out with Varick for motor drives. Has he ever spoken to you of her?"

"Miss Brabazon is here, now, at Wyndfell Hall," exclaimed Blanche. "You must have heard of her, Mark? She's the owner of some tremendously big city business."

"Oh, I don't think it can be that girl!"

Mark Gifford looked surprised and perturbed.

"But I know it's that girl. She's become quite a friend of mine, and of Bubbles. Oh, Mark, I do *hope* Helen Brabazon won't be brought into this dreadful business—d'you think that will be really necessary?"

"I don't know," he said slowly. "But some of our people think that Varick may put up a fight. British criminal law is much too kind to murderers. Even if there's evidence enough to hang a man ten times over, there's always a sporting chance he may get off! There is in this case."

Blanche turned suddenly very pale. The full realization of what those words meant rushed upon her. He feared she was going to faint.

"Forgive me," she muttered. "It's stupid, I know; but you must remember that—that I've known Lionel Varick a long time."

"I'm not a bit surprised that you are so distressed," he said soothingly.

And then something happened which did surprise Mark Gifford! He was supposed to be a clever, intelligent man, and there were many people who went in awe of him; but he knew very little about women. This, perhaps, was why he felt utterly astounded when Blanche suddenly burst into tears, and began rocking herself backwards and forwards. "Oh, Mark!" she sobbed. "Oh, Mark, I'm so unhappy,—I'm so miserable—I'm so frightened. Do—do help me!"

"That's just what I came to do," he said simply. But he was very much troubled. Her face was full of a kind of agonized appeal....

Greatly daring, he bent down over her, and gathered her into his arms.

She clung to him convulsively; and, all at once, there came insistently to Mark Gifford, George Herbert's beautiful saying: "There is an hour in which a man may be happy all his life, can he but find it." Perhaps that hour, that moment, had come to him now.

"Blanche," he whispered, "Blanche—darling! You didn't really mean what you wrote yesterday? Don't you think the time has come when two such old friends as you and I might—"

"—make fools of themselves?"

She looked up at him, and there came a quivering smile over her disfigured face. "Yes, if you really wish it, Mark. I'll do just as you like."

"D'you really mean that?" he asked.

And she said firmly: "Yes, Mark—I really do mean it." And he felt her yielding—yielding in spirit as well as in body—in body as well as in spirit.

"I suppose you couldn't come back with me to London, now?" he asked a little shyly. "We could get the woman at the post office down there to send up a letter to Bubbles, explaining that you had to go away unexpectedly, and telling her to follow you to town to-day."

It was rather a wild proposal, and he was not surprised when he saw her shake her head. "I can't do that," she said. "But oh, Mark, I wish I could! Bubbles is in bed. There was an accident—it's too long to tell you about it now. But, of course, I'll manage to get her away to-day."

And then the oppressive horror of it all suddenly came back to her. "When did you say they were going to arrest Lionel?"

She uttered the words slowly, and with difficulty.

"They're going to arrest him to-morrow, Friday, in the early afternoon," he said in a low voice. "By God's mercy," he spoke simply, reverently, "I got your letter in time, Blanche."

He looked at her anxiously. "I'm afraid even now you will have some difficult hours to live through," and, as he saw her face change, "I trust absolutely to your discretion," he said hesitatingly.

"Of course," she gave the assurance hurriedly. "Of course you can do that, Mark."

Without looking at her, he went on:

"As a matter of fact, the house has been watched for some days. If he tries to get away he will destroy the—the sporting chance I mentioned just now."

"I must be going back," she said, getting up. "Several of the party were, in any case, leaving this afternoon, and I must manage to get everybody else away as well."

Her mind was in a whirl of conflicting feelings and emotions. And then, all at once, she was moved, taken away from the dreadful problem of the moment, by what she saw in Mark Gifford's face. It was filled with a kind of sober gladness. "Mark," she exclaimed, "what a selfish brute I've always been to you—never giving—always taking! I'll try to be different now."

She held out her hand; he took it and held it closely. "When shall I see you again?" he asked. "May I come and meet you and Bubbles at Liverpool Street to-morrow?"

"Yes—do. That will be a great comfort!" And then, acting as she very seldom did, on impulse, Blanche rather shamefacedly held up her face to his….

CHAPTER XXII

Again and again, as Blanche Farrow walked slowly back to Wyndfell Hall, she went over the meagre details of the strange story she had just been told. Again and again she tried to fill in the bare outlines of the tale.

Lionel Varick a murderer? Her mind, her heart, refused to accept the possibility.

Suddenly there came back to her a recollection of the curious, now many years old, circumstances which had attended her knowledge of Varick's first marriage.

Someone, she could not now remember who, had taken her to one of the cheap foreign restaurants in Soho, which were not then so much frequented by English people as they are now. She had been surprised, and rather amused, to see Lionel Varick at a neighbouring table, apparently entertaining a middle-aged, rather prim-looking lady, whom he had introduced to her, Blanche, rather unwillingly, as "my friend, Miss Weatherfield."

Then had come the strange part of the story!

When on her way to stay with some friends in Sussex a few days later, she found herself in the same railway carriage as Miss Weatherfield; and, during the course of some desultory talk, the latter had mentioned that she was daughter to the Chichester doctor who had attended Lionel Varick's wife in her last illness.

Lionel Varick's wife? For a moment Blanche had thought that there must be some mistake, or that her ears had betrayed her. But she very soon realized that there was no mistake, and that she had heard aright.

Successfully concealing her ignorance of the fact that their mutual friend was a widower, she had ventured a few discreet questions, to which had come willing answers. These made it clear why Varick had chosen to remain silent concerning what had evidently been a sordid and melancholy episode of his past life.

Miss Weatherfield told her pleasant new acquaintance that the Varicks, when they had first come to Chichester, had been very poor, the wife of an obviously lower class than the husband. But that Varick, being the gentleman he was, had not minded what he did to earn an honest living, and that through Dr. Weatherfield he had obtained for a while employment with a chemist, his work being that of taking round the medicines, as he was not of course qualified to make up prescriptions.

While Miss Weatherfield had babbled on, Blanche had been able to piece together what had evidently been a singularly painful story. Mrs. Varick had been a violent, disagreeable woman, and the kindly spinster had felt deeply sorry for the husband, himself little more than a boy. But she admitted that her father, while attending Mrs. Varick, had acquired a prejudice against the husband of his patient, and she added, smilingly, that it was without her father's knowledge or consent that she had given the young man, after the death of his wife, a valuable business introduction.

Miss Weatherfield evidently flattered herself that this introduction had been a turning-point in Varick's life, and that what appeared to her his present prosperity was owing to what she had done. In any case, he had shown his gratitude by keeping in touch with her, and on the rare occasions when she came to London, they generally met.

Blanche Farrow, even in those early days, was too much a woman of the world to feel as surprised as some people would have been. All the same, she had felt disconcerted and a little pained, that the man who was fond of telling her that she was his only real friend in the world had concealed from her so important a fact as that of his marriage.

After some hesitation she had made up her mind to tell him of her new-found knowledge, and at once he had filled in and coloured the sketchy outlines of the picture drawn by the rather foolish if kindly natured Miss Weatherfield. Yes, it was true that he had been a fool, though a quixotic fool—so Blanche had felt on hearing his version of the story. At the time of the marriage Varick had been nineteen, his wife five years older. The two had soon parted, but they had made up their differences after a separation which lasted four years. Varick's fortunes had then been at their lowest ebb, and the two had drifted to Chichester, where Mrs. Varick had humble, respectable relations. After a while the woman had fallen ill, and finally died. Blanche had seen how it had pained and disturbed Varick to rake out the embers of the past, and neither had ever referred to the sad story again.

And now, from considering the past, Blanche Farrow turned shrinkingly to the present.

In common with the rest of the world, she had at times followed the course of some great murder trial; and she had been interested, as most intelligent people are occasionally interested, in the ins and outs of more than one so-called "poisoning mystery."

But such happenings had seemed utterly remote from herself; and to her imagination the word "murderer" had connoted an eccentric, cunning, mentally misshapen monster, lacking all resemblance to the vast bulk of human kind. She tried to realize that, if Mark Gifford's tale were true, a man with whom she herself had long been in close sympathy, and whose peculiar character she had rather prided herself on understanding, had been—nay, was—such a monster.

Blanche felt a touch of shuddering repulsion from herself, as well as from Varick, as she now remembered how sincerely she had rejoiced when, reading between the lines of his letter, she had guessed that he was marrying an unattractive woman for her money. It was now a comfort to feel that, even so, she had certainly felt a sensation of disgust when it had come to her knowledge that Varick had assumed, with regard to that same unattractive woman, an extravagant devotion she felt convinced he did not—could not—feel. It had shocked her, made her feel uncomfortable, to hear Helen Brabazon's artless allusions to the tenderness and devotion he had lavished on "poor Milly."

Helen Brabazon? A sensation of pain, almost of shame, swept over Blanche Farrow. Were Helen to appear as witness in a *cause célèbre* the girl's life would henceforth be shadowed and smirched by an awful memory. And then there rose before her mind another dread possibility. Was it not possible—nay, probable—that she, Blanche Farrow, would be sucked into the vortex?

She remembered a case in which the prisoner had been charged with the murder of a relation through whose death he had received considerable benefit, and how four or five men and women of repute had been called to testify to his high character, and to the kindness of his heart. But their evidence had availed him nothing, for he had been hanged.

Blanche quickened her footsteps as, in imagination, she saw herself in the witness-box speaking on behalf of Lionel Varick.

She argued with herself that, after all, it was just possible that he might be innocent! If so, she would fight for him to the death, and that, however much it distressed and angered Mark Gifford that she should do so.

Absorbed in the dread and terrible thing he had come to tell her, she had not given him, the man who loved her, and whose wife she was to be, one thought since their solemn, rather shamefaced, embrace. Yet now the knowledge that, however, much he disapproved, Mark would stand by her, gave her a wonderful feeling of security, of having left the open sea of life for a safe harbour—and that in spite of the terrible hours, perhaps the terrible weeks and months, which now lay before her.

Turning the sharp angle which led to the gate giving admittance to the gardens of Wyndfell Hall, she suddenly met Helen Brabazon face to face, and for one wild moment Blanche thought that Helen *knew*. The girl's usually placid, comely face was disfigured. It was plain that she had been crying bitterly.

"I'm going to the village," she exclaimed; "I've got to go home to-day, and I must telegraph to my uncle."

"I hope you haven't had bad news?" said Blanche mechanically.

She was telling herself that it was quite, quite impossible that Helen knew anything—but as Helen, who had begun crying again, shook her head, Blanche asked: "Does Lionel know that you want to leave to-day?"

"Yes; I have told Mr. Varick," and then all at once she exclaimed: "Oh, Miss Farrow, I feel so utterly miserable! Mr. Varick has just asked me to be his wife, and it has made me feel as if I had been so treacherous to Milly. Yet I don't think I did anything to make him like me? Do you think I did?"

She looked appealingly at Blanche.

It was plain that what had happened had given her an extraordinary shock. "I am sure, now," she went on falteringly, "that Milly—poor, poor Milly—haunts this house. I have felt, again and again, as if she were hovering about me. I believe that what I saw in the hall, on that awful afternoon, was really *her*. Yet Mr. Varick says that Milly would be very pleased if he and I were to marry each other. Surely he is mistaken?"

"Yes," said Blanche slowly, "I think he is."

"I feel so miserable," went on the girl, still speaking with a touch of excitement which in her was so very unusual. "What happened this morning has spoiled what I thought was such a beautiful friendship! And then I feel frightened—horribly frightened"—she went on in a low voice.

"What is it that frightens you, Helen?" asked Blanche.

These confidences seemed at once so futile, and yet also so sinister, knowing what she now knew.

"I'm afraid that Mr. Varick will 'will' me into thinking I care for him," the girl confessed in a low voice. "He says that he will never give up hope, and that, although he knows he isn't worthy of me, he thinks that in time I shall care for him. But I don't want to care for him, Miss Farrow—I'm sure that Milly is jealous of me; yet at Redsands, when she was dying, it made her happy that we were friends."

"I don't think you need be afraid that Lionel will ever ask you to marry him again," said Blanche firmly. "And, Helen? Let me give you a word of advice. Never, never, tell anyone of what happened to you this morning."

The girl blushed painfully. "I know I ought not to have told you," she whispered, "but I felt so wretched." She hesitated, and then added: "Ever since it happened I have been remembering that first evening, when my dear father warned me to leave this house. Oh, how I wish I had done what he told me to do!"

"I think you are wrong there," said Blanche. "I think a day will come, Helen, and in spite of anything that has happened, or that may happen, when you will be very glad that you stayed on at Wyndfell Hall."

"Do you?" she said wistfully and then she went on, with a note of diffidence and shyness which touched the older woman: "You and Bubbles have both been so kind to me—would you rather that I stayed on with you? I will if you like."

"As a matter of fact, Bubbles and I are going away to-day, after all," said Blanche, "so let me send one of the men down with your telegram."

"I would rather take it myself—really!" and a moment later she disappeared round the sharp turning which led on to the open road.

Blanche walked on, her eyes on the ground, until there fell on her ears the sound of quick footsteps. She looked up, to see Varick's tall figure hurrying towards her.

They met by the moat bridge, and as he came up to her he saw her pull forward the veil which, neatly arranged round the rim of her small felt hat, was not really meant to cover her face.

"Let's walk down here for a moment," he said abruptly. "I want to ask you a question, Blanche."

They stepped off the carriage road on to the grass, and, walking on a few paces, stood together at the exact spot from which Varick, on Christmas Eve, had looked at the house before him with such exultant eyes.

Three weeks ago Wyndfell Hall had appeared kindly and welcoming, as well as mysteriously beautiful, with its old diamond-paned windows all aglow. Now, in the wintry daylight, the ancient dwelling house still looked mysteriously beautiful; but there was something cold, menacing, forlorn in its appearance. The windows looked like blind eyes....

He turned on her suddenly, and held out the telegram she had received that morning.

"One of the servants picked this up on the breakfast table and brought it to me. What the devil does it mean? If Mark Gifford wanted to see you why couldn't he come here?"

Blanche looked at him dumbly. Had her life depended on her speaking she could not have spoken just then.

He went on: "Have you seen Gifford? Did he say anything about me?"

He uttered the words with a kind of breathless haste. She had the painful feeling that he wanted to put her in the wrong, to quarrel with her. Even as he spoke he was tearing the telegram into small pieces, and casting them down on to the neat, well-kept grass path.

"I suspect I know the business he came about—" He was speaking quietly, collectedly, now, and she felt that he was making a great effort to speak calmly and confidently.

"I don't think, Lionel, that you can know," she answered at last, in an almost inaudible voice.

"Well, let me tell you what it is that I suspect," he said.

There was a long pause. He was looking at her warily, wondering, evidently, as to how far he dared confide in her. And that look of his made her feel sick and faint.

"I suspect," he said at last, "that Gifford came to tell you a cock-and-bull story concocted by my wife's companion, a woman called Julia Pigchalke."

"Yes, Lionel, you have guessed right."

It was an unutterable relief that he thus made the way easy for her; a relief—but she now knew that what Gifford had told her was true.

"He wants me to get everyone away from here to-day," she went on, in a tone so low that he could scarcely hear her.

"Away from here? To-day?" he repeated, startled.

"Yes, away before to-morrow midday." She moistened her dry lips with her tongue.

"I am the victim of a foul conspiracy!" he exclaimed. "Panton warned me that I should have trouble with that woman." He waited a moment, then: "Did Gifford tell you that they have sent for Panton?" he asked suddenly. So that, she told herself, was what had really put him on the track. She nodded, and he added grimly: "They won't get much out of him."

Then he was going to fight it—fight it to the last?

"You will stand my friend, Blanche," he asked, and slowly she bent her head.

"Of course you know what this woman Pigchalke wishes to prove?"

He was now looking keenly, breathlessly, into her pale, set face. "Come," he said, "come, Blanche—don't be so upset! Tell me exactly what it was that Gifford told you."

But she shook her head. "I—I can't," she murmured.

"Then I will tell you what perhaps he felt ashamed to say to any friend of mine—that is that Julia Pigchalke suspects me of having done my poor Milly to death! She went and saw Panton; she did more, she actually advertised for particulars of my past life. Did he know that?"

He waited, for what seemed a very long time to Blanche, and then in a voice which, try as he might, was yet full of suppressed anxiety, he added: "She had got hold somehow of the fact that I once lived at Chichester."

Blanche looked down, and she counted over, twice, the thirty little bits of the torn telegram before she answered, in a low, muffled voice: "It's what happened at Chichester, Lionel, that made them listen to her."

There was a long moment of tense, of terrible, silence between them.

At last Varick broke the silence, and, speaking in an easy, if excited, conversational tone, he exclaimed: "That's a bit of bad luck for me! I have an enemy there—an old fool of a doctor—father of that woman you met me with years ago."

He walked on a few steps, leaving her standing, and then came back to her.

More seriously he asked the fateful question: "I take it I am to be arrested to-morrow?"

He saw by her face that he had guessed truly, and as if speaking to himself, he said musingly: "That means I have twenty-four hours."

She forced herself to say: "They think you have a good sporting chance if you stay where you are."

"It never occurred to me to go away!" he said angrily. "I want you always to remember, Blanche, that I told you, here, and now, that, even if appearances may come to seem damnably against me, I am an innocent man."

She answered: "I will always remember that, and always say so."

He said abruptly: "I want you to do me a kindness."

She asked uneasily: "What is it, Lionel?"

"I want you to get Gifford to prevent the meeting which has been arranged for to-morrow morning between Panton and the Home Office expert called Spiller."

He waited a moment, then went on: "It was the summons to Panton which put me on the track of—of this conspiracy." And Blanche felt that this time Varick was speaking the truth.

She said, deprecatingly: "Mark would do a great deal to please me, but I'm afraid he won't do that."

"I think he may," he answered, in a singular tone, "you may have a greater power of persuasion than you know."

She made no answer to that, knowing well that Mark would never interfere with regard to such a matter as this.

"Can you suggest any reason I can give, why we should be all going away to-day?" she asked falteringly.

Without a moment's hesitation he answered: "You can say there has been trouble among the servants, and that I should feel much obliged if I could have the house cleared of all my visitors by to-night."

Then Blanche Farrow came to a sudden determination. "I will get them all away to-day, Lionel, but I, myself, will stay till to-morrow morning."

For the first time during this strange, to her this unutterably painful conversation, Varick showed a touch of real, genuine feeling. It was as if a mask had fallen from his face.

He gripped her hand. "You're a brick!" he exclaimed. "I ought to tell you to go away, too, but I won't be proud, Blanche. I'll accept your kindness."

CHAPTER XXIII

There are hours in almost every life of which the memory is put away, hidden, as far as may be, in an unfathomable pit. Blanche Farrow never recalled to herself, and never discussed with any living being, the hours which followed her talk with Lionel Varick.

Of the five people to whom she told the untrue tale so quickly and so cleverly imagined by their host, only one suspected that she was not telling the truth. That one—oddly enough—was Sir Lyon Dilsford. He guessed that something was wrong, and in one sense he got near to the truth—but it was such a very small bit of the truth!

Sir Lyon suspected that Varick had made an offer to Helen Brabazon, and that she had refused him. But he was never to know if his suspicion had been correct, for he was one of those rare human being who are never tempted to ask indiscreet or unnecessary questions from even their nearest and dearest.

In answer to Miss Farrow's apologies and explanations, everyone, of course, expressed himself or herself as very willing to fall in with the suggestion that they should all travel up to town together that day. It also seemed quite natural to them all, even to Bubbles, that Blanche should stay behind for the one night.

She was not the sort of woman to leave a task half done. She had engaged the servants, and she would remain to settle up with them. The average man—and most of them thought Varick an average man—is helpless in dealing with so complicated a domestic problem as a number of job servants.

As the hours of the early afternoon went by, Blanche more and more marvelled at Varick's extraordinary powers of self-command. Excepting that he was, perhaps, a little more restless than usual, he was at his best as the courteous, kindly host, now parting with regret from a number of well-liked guests.

He even succeeded in putting Helen Brabazon once more at her ease, for, choosing his opportunity, he told her, in a few earnest words which touched her deeply, that he had come to see her point of view, and to acquiesce in her decision.

Blanche heard him making an appointment with Dr. Panton to lunch at the Ritz on one of the days of the following week. He asked Sir Lyon to join them there; and Blanche saw the look of real chagrin and annoyance which passed over his face when Sir Lyon declined the invitation.

But even what was obviously sincere and real, seemed utterly insincere and unreal to Blanche Farrow, during those tense hours. Thus, when she overheard Donnington and Bubbles talking over the arrangements for their wedding, their talk seemed to her all make-believe.

At last, however, there came the moment for which she had been longing for what seemed to her an eternity.

Miss Brabazon, Sir Lyon, and Dr. Panton were the first to go off; followed after a few minutes' interval, Donnington, Bubbles, and the luggage.

Blanche noticed that Lionel's parting with Bubbles was particularly suave and cordial. But the girl was not at her best. When her host touched her, accidentally, she shrank back, and his face clouded. And, as the motor drove off, he turned to Blanche and said discontentedly: "I wish Bubbles liked me better, Blanche!"

She hardly knew what to answer, for it was true that the girl did not like Varick, and had never liked him. Yet it seemed such a strange thing for him to trouble about that *now*. But Lionel, poor Lionel, had always had an almost morbid wish to be liked — to stand well with people, so she told herself with a strange feeling of pain at her heart.

They walked back together into the house, and Blanche, going over to the fire-place, poured herself out another cup of tea.

In a sense she still felt as if she was living through a terrible, unreal dream, and yet it was an unutterable relief to be no longer obliged to pretend.

She glanced furtively at Varick.

He looked calm, cheerful, collected. "Will you excuse me for a few moments? I have got several things to do," he said. "Then I think I will go out and tramp about for a bit. It's been a strain for you as well as for me, Blanche," he added sympathetically.

"Yes, it has," she answered almost inaudibly.

"Is there anything I can get you?" he asked. "Will you be quite comfortable?"

She repeated, mechanically: "Quite comfortable, thank you, Lionel," and then, as an after-thought: "I suppose we shall dine at the same time as usual?"

"Certainly—why not?" He looked puzzled at her question. "Let me see—it's not much after five now; I'll be back by seven."

He walked to the door, and from there turned round. "So long!" he cried out cheerily, and she was surprised, for Varick seldom made use of any slang or colloquialism.

Feeling all at once utterly exhausted and spent, she drew a deep chair forward to the fire and lay back in it. Her mind seemed completely to empty itself of thought. She neither remembered the past nor considered the future, and very soon she slipped off into a deep sleep—the sleep of exhaustion which so often follows a great mental strain.

It must have been over an hour later that Blanche seemed to awaken to a perception that the big oak door behind her, which gave access to the deep-eaved porch, had opened and closed.

She looked round; and, in the candle-light, for the fire had died down, she saw Varick, looking neither to the right nor to the left, walk quickly across the long room and slip noiselessly through the door leading to the interior of the house.

Then it was seven o'clock? Nearly three-quarters of an hour before she must go up and dress for dinner.

Almost at once she was asleep again, to be, however, thoroughly awakened a few moments later by the opening and the shutting of a door.

It was the old butler, a man Blanche had come to like and to respect.

He held a salver in his hand, and on the salver was a letter. "Mr. Varick asked me to give you this note at a quarter-past seven, ma'am. I understood him to say that he might be late for dinner to-night as he had to go up to the Reservoir Cottage."

Blanche sat up, all her senses suddenly on the alert.

"Mr. Varick came in some minutes ago," she said, "at least, I think he did."

She was beginning to wonder if Lionel had really come in, or if she had only dreamt that he had done so.

"I don't think he came in, ma'am, for I've been in the dining-room, with the door open, for a long time. I would have heard him if he had come through and gone upstairs."

"You might see if he is in," she said quietly.

She took the letter off the salver, but did not break the seal till the old man had come back with the words: "No, ma'am, Mr. Varick is not in the house."

He lingered on for a moment. "I hope you will forgive me, ma'am, for mentioning that Mr. Varick told us we could all go off early to-morrow morning if we liked, instead of next Monday. He paid us up after the visitors had gone away, and he also gave us the bonus he so kindly promised. I never wish to serve a more generous gentleman. But the chef and I decided that we would ask you, ma'am, if it is for your convenience that we leave early to-morrow?"

"Anything that Mr. Varick has arranged with you will suit me," she said quickly. "As a matter of fact, I think he would like you to leave by the train I shall be going by myself."

As the man turned away she looked down at Varick's letter. On the envelope was written in his good, clear handwriting: "The Hon. Blanche Farrow, Wyndfell Hall." But no premonition of its contents reached her still weary, excited brain.

Written on a large plain sheet of paper, the letter ran:

> "My dear Blanche,—I fear I am going to give you a shock—for, by the time this reaches you, there will have been another accident—one very similar to that which befell poor little Bubbles. But this time there will be no clever, skilful Panton to bring the drowned to life.
>
> "I suggest that you begin to feel uneasy about a quarter past eight. I leave to your good sense the details of the sad discovery. I have but one request to make to you, kindest and truest of friends; that is, that you remember what I asked you to do with reference to Panton's appointment to-morrow morning. If you can get a telegram or telephone message through to Gifford to-night, I think that appointment will be postponed indefinitely. You will perhaps think me a sentimental fool for wishing to keep Panton's good opinion, but such is my wish.

"I am distressed at the thought of the trouble and worry to which you must inevitably be exposed to-night. On the other hand, much more trouble and worry in the future will thus have been saved, even to you.

"Yours ever,

"Lionel Varick.

"I trust to your friendship to destroy this letter as soon as read."

Blanche read the letter once again, right through, then she held out the big sheet of paper, and dropped it into the heart of the fire.

For the second time that day she burst into tears, shaken to the depths by the extraordinarily complicated feelings which filled her heart and mind, feelings of horror and of pain—and yet of intense, immeasurable relief!

Then she pulled herself together, and prepared to act, for the second time that day, her part in a tragi-comedy in which where there had been two characters there was now but one.

CHAPTER XXIV

Dr. Panton's appointment at the Home Office had been for half-past ten, and, though there happened to be on this early January day an old-fashioned, black London fog, he had been punctual to the minute.

It was now eight minutes to eleven, and he began to feel rather cross and impatient.

There was nothing to do in the big, ugly, stately room into which he had been shown. There was a bookcase, but it was locked, and he had not brought a paper with him—but that, perhaps, was a good thing, for the one electric globe gave a very bad light.

He wondered what manner of man Dr. Spiller might be—in any case a remarkable and distinguished person, one of the great authorities on poisons in Europe.

At last the door opened, and Dr. Panton felt surprised—even a little disappointed. Not so had he imagined the famous Spiller.

"Forgive me for having kept you waiting, Dr.—er—Panton."

The tone of the quiet-looking, middle-aged man who stood before him was extremely courteous, if a trifle uncertain and nervous.

"If I hadn't been lodging close by I should have been late, too, Dr. Spiller."

"My name is not Spiller," said the other quickly. "I have come to explain to you that the matter concerning which you were to see Dr. Spiller this morning has been settled. We should have saved you the trouble of coming here had we known where you were staying in London."

Dr. Panton felt, not unreasonably, annoyed. "If only Dr. Spiller had sent me a wire yesterday," he exclaimed vexedly, "he had my address in the country, I should have been saved a useless visit to London!"

"He couldn't have let you know in time, for the matter was only settled this morning."

There was a pause, and then the speaker added: "You will send in a minute of your expenses, of course?"

Dr. Panton bowed stiffly. He felt that he had been badly treated.

"I'm sorry you have been put to this inconvenience," and the courteous Home Office official really did look distressed. He waited a moment. "I think you know a friend of mine, Miss Blanche Farrow, Dr. Panton?" he said a little awkwardly.

"Yes; we've both been staying in the same house for the New Year."

Panton's good-humour had come back; he was telling himself, with some amusement, how very small the world is, after all!

There was a pause, and then Panton asked: "Do you happen to know Lionel Varick, who owns the beautiful house where Miss Farrow and I have both been staying, Mr.—er—?"

"Gifford," supplied the other quickly. "Yes, I have been slightly acquainted with Mr. Varick for some years." A very uncomfortable, peculiar look came over the speaker's face. "I wonder if you have heard of the terrible thing which happened yesterday at Wyndfell Hall?" he asked abruptly.

"I only left the house at five o'clock," exclaimed Dr. Panton; and then, as he saw the look of gravity deepen on the other man's face, he asked: "Was there a fire there last night? I trust not!"

"No," said the other, slowly, "nothing has happened to the house, Dr. Panton. But your friend Mr. Varick is dead. He went out for a walk in the dark, and seems to have slipped over the side of an embankment into deep water. His body was not recovered for some hours—in fact, not till early this morning."

Dr. Panton got up from the chair on which he had been sitting. He was too shocked, too taken aback, to speak, and the other went on:

"I cannot give you many details, for when Miss Farrow telephoned to me she was very much upset, and the line was very bad. But I may add that there is no doubt about it, for the news was confirmed, through another source, half an hour later."

"What a terrible thing! What an awful—awful thing!"

The young doctor looked overwhelmed with horror and surprise. "You must forgive me," he went on, "if I seem unduly shocked; but I have lost in Lionel Varick one of the best friends man ever had, Mr. Gifford—I'd have sold the shirt off my back for him and I think I may say he'd have done the same for me."

Mark Gifford, cautious man though he was, took a sudden resolution. "If you can spare the time," he exclaimed, "I wonder, Dr. Panton, if you would go back to Wyndfell Hall to-day? It would be an act of true kindness to Miss Farrow. I had thought of going myself; but, as you seem to have been such a friend of Varick's—?"

"Of course I'll go down—by the very first train I can catch!" answered Panton eagerly.

"Perhaps you could persuade Miss Farrow to come up to London at once, and leave all the sad details connected with the inquest, and so on, to you?"

"I will indeed! Miss Farrow must be terribly distressed, for I know she was a very, very close friend of poor Varick's."

Mark Gifford winced—it was a very slight movement, quite unperceived by Dr. Panton.

To the surprise of his subordinates, who had never seen him do so much honour to any male visitor before, Mr. Gifford accompanied the young medical man along the corridor, down the stone staircase, and through to the great outer arch which gives on to the quiet street.

At the moment of their final parting Dr. Panton exclaimed: "Am I to understand that Dr. Spiller will not be sending for me again?"

"I thought I had made it clear," replied Mr. Gifford mildly, "that the matter about which he wished to see you is now closed."